MAJOR DEMONS
BY: RANDALL J. MORRIS

CHAPTER 1

Hunting nephilim with a pregnant Lilith was driving Leech insane. After their brief meeting with the three Archangels, they had split into three groups of two. Uriel had gone with Raphael, Shadow with Gabriel, and Leech with Lilith.

"Leech!"

Leech sighed and walked back to Lilith's tent.

"Lily?"

"Do you still think I'm beautiful?"

"Of course."

"Seriously? I'm really fat."

"You're pregnant. That doesn't mean you stopped being hot." Lilith grinned at him.

"Right answer. So I'm hot enough for you to do a favor for me?"

"Lily, we're hunting nephilim… I don't really have time to…"

"You lied to me! You don't think I'm hot anymore!"

Leech sighed.

"What's the favor? What are you craving this time?"

"I would like the soul of a human who was very good for most of their life and then turned evil in old age and went to Hell. That should deal with this craving."

"Raven is already getting you a new hairbrush because the old one wasn't good enough. So I guess I'll send Gangrene?"

"Yes. Oh and I want my pony."

"Keshi is in Hell. You can't ride her when you're pregnant."

"I just want her up here."

"Why?"

"Because you haven't been paying enough attention to me and Keshi won't leave me to hunt nephilim!"

Lilith started to cry. Leech approached to comfort her. When he was within range, she spun off her bed and kicked him hard in the stomach.

"Ow! Lily you need to stop being insane! I've stopped every time you said you wanted more time with me. I doubt we're even on that nephilim's trail anymore. I haven't seen any evidence that he went this way for days."

"Don't blame me. Blame your daughter."

Leech's grinned widely and he kneeled in front of Lilith and put his hand on her belly.

"So it's a girl?"

"Well I'm not sure. It could be your son. Either way, I'm not responsible for any of this."

Leech laughed.

"I'll send Gangrene. Anything else before I send him?"

"Nope. Send Gangrene and then don't come back in here until you have all of my stuff!"

"So I'm not spending enough time with you… but I can't come in here unless I have your stuff?"

"Exactly."

"And in Lily-land… that doesn't violate… oh… I dunno… logic and common sense."

Lilith shrieked like a harpy, picked up a small mirror from her bedside table, and threw it at Leech. Leech barely made it out of the tent in time. Gangrene was grinning at him.

"You're not gonna think it's so funny when I tell you what she wants now."

Gangrene's grin vanished from his face.

"If I ever decide to impregnate Raven, I want you to remind me of this. Deal?"

"We'll see if I let you live that long. Now get back down to Hell and bring back her horse and a human soul that was good for most of its life and then turned evil."

Gangrene sighed and turned to leave.

"Oh and Gangrene… one more thing."

"Yes?"

"If I catch you smirking at my discomfort again, I will demote you to be an errand boy permanently."

Gangrene turned and started back towards Hell, mumbling about how insane the daughters of Vixen were.

Leech cautiously made his way back into Lilith's tent.

"Do you have my stuff?"

"No, but I have a gift for you."

Lilith thought about throwing him out again but decided to hear him out. Leech pulled a soft, dark green blanket from behind his back. Lilith raised an eyebrow.

"What the hell is that?"

"Well it's just…"

"Just what?"

"Let me finish!"

Silence followed Leech's outburst.

"It's the blanket I was wrapped in as a baby. I was hoping that we could wrap our kid in it when it's born. Boy. Girl. I don't really care. I'm just glad we're having one."

Lilith's eyes started to tear up.

"Oh I'm sorry, Leech. That's a beautiful thought."

She wiped her eyes and then laughed.

"I'll bet you were a cute baby."

"The absolute cutest."

Leech tossed her the dark green blanket and Lilith ran it through her hands.

"It's so soft. Call Gangrene back, Leech. I don't need that other stuff. I just want you. That's all I need. Oh and the hairbrush. Don't call Raven back. Just Gangrene."

"Done. I'll call Gangrene back and then I'm coming back in here for you. You're still really hot and we're long overdue for some make out time."

Lilith giggled.

"Hurry back then."

Leech left the tent and saw Gangrene leaning on his spear.

"So it worked?"

"It did. Where did you find a dark green blanket anyways?"

"It was draped over my horse under the saddle. Nicely played, General Leech."

"You should be taking notes. It's gonna be this bad when Raven has a baby. You need to be on top of your game."

Gangrene grinned.

"Noted. Should I instruct the armies to keep searching for the nephilim?"

"No. We're done for the night. We'll start back up tomorrow."

When Leech entered Lilith's tent again, he saw that Raven had returned and was brushing her hair.

"I totally understand, Lily. That last hairbrush was unbearable. This one is much better."

"It really is. Now get out. Leech is back."

Raven looked slightly offended, slammed the brush down on the table next to Lilith's bed, and stormed out.

"Did they find any new traces of the nephilim?"

"Nope. We still don't even know who it is. There's no need to worry about that right now though."

Lilith grinned at him mischievously.

"You're right. Come here, leechy face."

Leech leaned in and kissed her. Lilith cried out.

"Ah!"

"What is it? Is the baby coming? Raven, get in here! The baby is coming!"

Lilith grabbed Leech's hand and shook her head.

"It's not that."

Raven entered the tent with an extra pillow and blankets, ready to play midwife.

"False alarm, Raven. You can leave."

Raven threw the blankets on the ground and flipped them off. She turned and left.

"What was that then?"

"It's one of the nephilim. I can sense it. I feel this sometimes when Shadow is around. There's a nephilim stalking us."

Lilith pointed outside her tent.

As Lilith was uncertain of the exact location, Leech teleported in the direction she had pointed. After a few minutes of running, he saw a creature kneeling in the sand on a beach as the waves crashed in around it. The creature wore a black, hooded robe. It stood and turned to face Leech.

"Leech of the underworld. Abandon the nephilim girl in your camp and I will spare the demon armies that travel with you."

"Who the fuck are you to talk to me like that?"

The nephilim grinned.

"My name is Thanatos. My brother and I once saved the nephilim Lilith from death. It was only after we did so that our father revealed to us that she is our half-sister. We thought we were sent to aid Shadow."

"There's no way in hell you're taking her with you."

"Ah… but we're not in Hell… are we?"

Leech pulled the guns from his belt and quickly fired off a shot from each. The bullets were swallowed by the sand where Thanatos had been standing.

"Where are you hiding, Thanatos? You're only delaying the inevitable. I will slay you and you will fade into nothing more than a memory."

Though Leech couldn't see him, he could hear Thanatos's response.

"Much talk. Talking will win you nothing. All the same, the woman goes with me to my father's house. I go to take her now and there's nothing you can do to stop me."

Leech immediately teleported to Lilith's tent and saw Thanatos standing over a sleeping Lilith. Leech grabbed his scythe and slashed it across the back of Thanatos. Thanatos did not bleed, but turned to face Leech and fell on his knees. His eyes started to glow white.

"My father has misled me once again. While I have brought thousands to their death, I could not see my own demise. I can see yours though, Leech. I was also sent here to deliver that message. If you continue to pursue the nephilim, one of them will strike you down. Your death is fast approaching. This is my final prediction."

The robe of Thanatos fell to the earth, now devoid of its former occupant.

CHAPTER 2

Shadow could sense they were closing in. He had hoped by now he would be close enough to read the mind of the demon he was pursuing but when he tried, he felt something else. Something was resisting and blocking his power. Something powerful didn't want to give up information so easily. Shadow grinned. He was headed in the right direction.

"We're getting closer. The demon went this way."

Gabriel looked frustrated.

"The earth groans under the weight of chaos now running loose on its surface and we're chasing a demon sorcerer? I thought you were taking us to a nephilim, Shadow."

"This is more important than that. My uncle planted false memories in my mind. My mother's memories are no different from mine. I need to know what he added… and what he took away. We have no information on how we're going to defeat Abaddon."

"We cut off his head, young demon. I've done it enough times to know. No demon continues to live on without a head."

Sarah looked annoyed but tried to restrain her impatience.

"We've explained this to you, Grandfather. Abaddon is not a demon. He's a nephilim. He's Michael's son."

"The Archangels still don't agree on that. When we asked for proof, Abaddon could not produce the ice powers of an Archangel's offspring. There is no evidence that…"

Shadow lost his patience. He teleported in front of Gabriel and struck at his chest with an open palm. Gabriel caught Shadow's hand by the wrist but Shadow's hand still touched the Archangel's breastplate. Shadow's eyes turned white and frost began to creep from his fingertips onto Gabriel's armor.

"Is that enough proof for you, old one?"

Gabriel's eyes began to glow a fiery white. He shoved Shadow back.

"Strike at me again unprovoked and I will remove your limb."

Shadow's eyes shifted back to their natural red.

"I'm growing tired of your distrust, Gabriel. If you won't believe me after I told you, after your granddaughter told you, and after I froze your armor then I will go after my father on my own. Don't be surprised though when I enter the heavens afterwards and begin killing off…"

"Enough!"

Sarah saw Gabriel's hand reach for his sword. He had pulled it a couple of inches out of its sheath. She also noticed Shadow tightening his grip on Damnation, his dual-bladed scythe. She turned first to her grandfather.

"Grandpa, you are a being of light and reason. Ignoring the method, Shadow did give you evidence that nephilim exist. What demon do you know that could have spread frost on your armor?"

Gabriel's expression softened.

"I guess you're right, Sarah. That doesn't excuse…"

"I'm getting to that."

Sarah turned to Shadow.

"I know it's difficult for us to trust each other. Angels and demons have never worked together before like this. I need you to keep your impulsiveness under control though. We're here to help you."

"I could have dealt with all of this on my own. I'm *allowing* the angels to play a role in…"

"That's bullshit."

Gabriel gave Sarah a stern look but she ignored it.

"What… you would have formed that Legion abomination with Lilith and Leech? One powerful being cannot stop the onslaught of all the nephilim and the Dragon's armies. You need more than one powerful ally. Also… what do you think Legion would be like if you have to share your mind with a pregnant Lilith? You really think that's your best move?"

Shadow smirked.

"Fine. I'll play nice. I need the help for now. One thing I don't need is attitude from the angel of ancient asshood over there. I'm sick of it. Like it or not, I'm Michael's grandson and the angels wouldn't treat *him* this way. Trust goes both ways. If I'm going to play nice, I need the two of you to trust me."

"I already do."

Sarah turned to her grandfather. Gabriel glared at Shadow.

"Angel of ancient asshood?"

Shadow met his gaze but couldn't stop a smile from spreading across his face. Gabriel eventually smirked as well.

"I trust you more now that I know with certainty that you are a descendant of one of the archangels. I don't know for sure that it's Michael, but you definitely have the ice powers of one of the Seven. So there must be some good in you. We're wasting time. Let's find this demon. Lead on, Shadow."

Shadow nodded, turned, and continued up the winding path they had been following up the mountain. He whistled loudly to signal to their armies to continue following at a distance.

As they walked the winding path up the mountains, woodcarvers crafted eagles, caribous, lions, and other small trinkets for their livelihood. They were oblivious to the nephilim and angels that moved quickly up the mountain path and the armies that followed. As they made it to the next switchback, a five-year-old made his way into his father's workshop to see if he could help him. Sarah watched the encounter and smiled. She blessed the family as they continued up the mountain and then turned to Gabriel.

"Where are we anyways?"

"The mountains of Baguio. We're in the Philippines. There are powerful demons in this country as well as powerful angels."

"How do you know he's here, Shadow?"

"It was a story my uncle told me a long time ago. There's a demon named Bumalin that lives here. My uncle told me about how he would walk around this country erasing small memories when he was a minor demon. He made humans forget things… just small things. They couldn't remember where they had left their money or what they were sent to the market to buy. It generally led to small fights. It wasn't a very impressive amount of power but he kept practicing.

"Bumalin eventually became a middle demon. I don't know which of the Six he reported to and I honestly don't know that he cares to report to any of them anymore. No one from Hell knows much about him. Any time one of the Six would send a demon or two to bring Bumalin back with his horde of souls, the demons would return having forgotten why they were sent to earth in the first place."

Gabriel gave the story some thought.

"Why would your uncle tell you these things if he had Bumalin take your memory?"

"He never thought I would figure out what he did. I imagine if he knew how powerful I would become he would have killed me when I was a child."

Sarah put her hand on Shadow's shoulder. He brushed it off and quickened his pace. Once they passed the woodcarvers, they started to see children playing outside in the dirt and mud. Their parents were inside, generally watching gameshows on tube TVs. An old man stepped outside to burn his garbage in a pit. There was no sign of a demon.

"He's somewhere around here. I can feel it."

Shadow used one of his powers and split off into several copies of himself. All of them explored the area. All he found was more humans. A teenage boy roasting a goat. A mother doing her laundry in a nearby stream. An old man in a tattered cloak holding out a tin cup. Several small children playing with a monkey.

Sarah cried out. Shadow merged the copies of himself back into one and ran to her. She was lying on her back with her eyes closed. Shadow lifted her head. She looked at his face and became horrified.

"Get away from me, demon!"

Sarah crawled backwards several paces until she ran into Gabriel's legs. She tilted her head back and recognized her grandfather.

"Grandpa, it's a demon! He must have attacked me! Kill him!"

Shadow grinned and gripped Damnation.

"You have permission now, ancient one. Do we fight to the death?"

"Stop messing around, Shadow. You know that Bumalin stole part of her memory. You're right. He's around here somewhere…"

Gabriel closed his eyes and focused. Without warning, he grabbed the old man in the tattered cloak and lifted him into the air. His tin cup fell to the ground. The hood of his cloak fell to his shoulders and exposed the demon's face. The demon squirmed and placed its hand on Gabriel's head.

"Unfortunately for you, that isn't going to work on me, Bumalin. I am the Archangel Gabriel. Now let's have a chat about what you did to my granddaughter…"

CHAPTER 3

Murmur entered Dagon's tavern and was greeted by the demon cook. He was wiping his hands on a rag that was just as dirty as his hands were.

"It's been a while, Murmur. Here for a beer?"

"I don't have time for that right now, Dagon. I'm supposed to be meeting Nightmare and Astaroth. Can you point me in the right direction?"

"VIP room upstairs. Let me know if you change your mind on the beer."

Murmur thought for a moment.

"You know what? I do have time for a beer. Those assholes can wait another five minutes."

When Murmur finished his drink, he tossed a coin next to his mug and made his way upstairs to the VIP room. As he trudged up the stairs, he adjusted his shield Dragonscale on his back and made sure that his scythe could be quickly drawn from his belt. He didn't trust either of the major demons that he was meeting with. Murmur entered the room and took a seat across from Nightmare and Astaroth. Astaroth slid a drink to Murmur from across the table. It looked like the beer from downstairs but slightly darker in color.

"Have a drink."

Murmur slid the drink back.

"I already had one downstairs."

Astaroth feigned insult.

"What's wrong? You don't trust me?"

"The snake queen who gets her way by poisoning anyone in her way? No. I don't imagine I'll ever accept a drink from you."

Murmur turned to Nightmare.

"Why are we meeting? We have nothing to discuss."

"The three of us are running Hell without the Dragon present and we have nothing to discuss?"

"No. You two run your departments and I'll run mine. Three of the Six aren't even here so there's no reason for the three of us to meet."

"You've hit on exactly what we need to discuss. Shadow, Leech, and Lilith aren't here. They went to Earth to deal with something that isn't our problem. I think the three of us should take power while we have the opportunity."

Murmur laughed.

"So you want to start that stupid fucking war all over again? The descendants of the Dragon against the other three? Wow. You really don't learn lessons, do you?"

"I could ask you the same question. Remember what happened the last time you fought me? The trials?"

Murmur stood and grabbed Dragonscale and his scythe.

"I'm ready for Round 2 whenever you are."

Nightmare gripped his scythe, Rage, and grinned back at Murmur. Astaroth stood and held up both hands.

"Boys, that's enough. We're not here to fight."

Murmur responded without looking in her direction.

"No. You're just here to poison me, right?"

"If I drink it myself, will you sit back down and talk to us?"

Murmur nodded. Astaroth drained the mug in one gulp and slammed it down on the table. Murmur sat back down.

"Do you need to be excused to go to the ladies' room and vomit up the poison you just drank?"

"I'm fine."

Nightmare stood and started pacing the room.

"Let's just think about the opportunity we have here. Shadow, Leech, and Lilith are going to return to Hell with severely weakened armies from fighting nephilim topside. That's if they return at all. It's natural self-interest to consider the possibilities. We could each become the ruler of an entire additional department. My proposal is this… I kill Shadow and take control of the department of murder. Astaroth kills Lilith and takes the department of lust. Murmur, you kill Leech and take control of idolatry. If any of those three don't return, we divide the demons in their army equally."

Nightmare and Astaroth expected resistance, but Murmur asked an unexpected question.

"And what about the Dragon?"

"What about him? He doesn't really care much what we do anymore. He's up there with the other three trying to kill that horrid abomination, Abaddon. The entire Six have been killed and replaced in the past few months and the Dragon hasn't given a damn. I doubt he cares if the Six become the Three. Even if he does, I've proven that he doesn't always get his way. I marched into a camp of one of his armies and stole the berserker staff to fuse it with my scythe. He didn't have the power to stop me."

Murmur scratched his chin, considering the possibilities. Astaroth seemed uneasy.

"Not gonna lie, Murmur. I expected more resistance from you. I thought you were Shadow's friend."

Murmur pointed at Nightmare.

"Shadow had the opportunity to save me from being a pawn in that asshole's army and he didn't do anything. He just let me suffer. I had to take the major demon spot for myself and it would have taken a lot less time if I could have dedicated my time and energy to that end instead of wasting time in the department of lies. A shitty friend can be the same thing as an enemy when circumstances shift. Shadow has been a shitty friend and the circumstances have definitely shifted."

Nightmare was not convinced.

"You expect us to believe you won't run to Earth after this meeting and warn them? What reason do we have to believe that?"

"I honestly don't give a shit whether you believe it or not. My past actions evidence that I put my own self-interest above everything else and I only maintain friendships as long as they are mutually beneficial. Remember Tannin? He humiliated me in a fight. I put my revenge on hold because I needed him to climb the ranks. When he was no longer useful to me, I let him fight Belial and then I cleaned up the remains of that duel to take Dragonscale and my scythe. A few months ago, you might have accused me of being Tannin's friend as well. Friends with power aren't as useful as having power yourself. What reason do *I* have to think that you will be true to your word? You're the head of the department of lies, after all. I'm sure you'll attempt to kill us when the opportunity presents itself… or you'll attempt to take whatever armies we take for yourself… or…"

Nightmare laughed.

"Making counteraccusations to deflect suspicion. Amusing. I'm not on trial here. You have to convince *me*. You're the odd man out here, Murmur. Astaroth and I want the same things. You're the one we don't trust yet."

Astaroth nodded.

"Actually, we have a way for you to prove that you're dedicated to this. I'll be right back."

Astaroth got up and left the room. Murmur shifted in his seat so he would have easy access to his shield and scythe. Astaroth returned to the room with a small demon that was bound and gagged. Murmur recognized the little demon. It was Muan, the commander of Shadow's armies.

"You want me to get him to talk?"

Nightmare and Astaroth looked at each other and both laughed at the suggestion. Astaroth threw Muan on the table.

"Nothing like that, Murmur. We just want you to kill him."

Surprise registered briefly on Murmur's face but he quickly changed it back to a neutral expression and then the corners of his mouth arced up into a grin.

"I see the game you're playing. I'm supposed to kill Leech, but you want me to kill Muan before that which ensures Shadow comes after me. I'll have to deal with two major demons and if they kill me, the two of you will kill a weakened Shadow and Leech. I just explained how I played a similar role in the deaths of Belial and Tannin. Were you not listening?"

Nightmare shook his head.

"Nope. You're not talking your way out of this. We're the only three that know that this little guy is here. You kill him to prove that we can trust you. I'll spread the rumor that I did it. Shadow's death is my responsibility."

Murmur considered accusing Nightmare of lying again, but didn't see what good it would do. If he didn't kill Muan, Nightmare and Astaroth were going to attack him. He didn't have anything against Muan, but one of their lives was going to be forfeit. Murmur knew it had to be Muan's. Murmur nodded and removed the scythe from his belt.

"One condition. You need to bring a messenger demon in here and start spreading the word that you killed Muan *now*. I'll kill him after that."

"Not a problem."

Nightmare stomped his foot and the ground shook. A messenger demon from the department of lies ran into the room and bowed.

"You summoned me, General Nightmare?"

"Yes. You're to spread the word to all of Hell that I've killed Muan and I've issued an open challenge to Shadow. Make sure it reaches everyone."

The messenger nodded and exited the room. Nightmare turned back to Murmur.

"Well?"

Murmur swung his scythe and buried it in Muan's chest, pinning him to the table. The little demon screamed through his gag and finally settled into death.

CHAPTER 4

Raven asked what they were all thinking.

"What do we do now?"

Leech didn't have an answer.

"We can't really move much with Lilith in the condition she's in. The baby is going to come any day now. Since I killed Thanatos, we don't really have any leads on any nephilim in the area either. I'm thinking we should stay here until after Lilith has the baby."

Gangrene kicked his feet up and placed them on a tree stump.

"I'm fine with relaxing in the Caribbean. No argument here."

Raven rolled her eyes.

"What about after she has the baby? Is it really our job to kill off the Dragon's personal army *and* go after the nephilim? Why don't we just go back to Hell?"

"It's pretty simple. We need human souls. We can't keep receiving human souls if the nephilim kill the humans off. Earthquakes. Tornadoes. Hurricanes. The nephilim are messing with the elements. Deaths are only in the tens of thousands now but we can't let them stay up here and do whatever they want."

"Shouldn't this be the angels' job? They're the protectors of humanity."

"So you would put our food source in the hands of the angels?"

Gangrene closed his eyes.

"You guys need to relax. There's no point in discussing this. I know what we're going to do after Lilith has the baby."

Leech didn't look optimistic.

"And what's that, Gangrene?"

"Whatever the hell Lilith wants to do. It's what we've been doing up here for weeks. Why mess with the plan? Just take the opportunity to relax now while she's asleep."

Raven knocked his feet off the tree stump and sat in his lap. She stroked his cheek slowly and then slapped him across the face.

"Ow!"

"You don't do what Lilith tells you to… you do what *I* tell you to."

"Right. I forgot. We have two psychos in our group. I follow one and Leech follows the other. I also have to follow Leech. Come to think of it… I'm starting to think I got the shit end of this deal."

Lilith cried out in her tent. Raven and Leech were there in seconds. Leech stuck his head back out briefly.

"She's going to be making a lot of noise. The baby is coming. I think it's real this time… not like the other couple of times she just wanted attention and pretended the baby was coming."

"I'm not going in there."

"No… you're going to make sure *nothing* comes in here while this is happening. Get our armies to form a circle around the tent but give us plenty of room. Don't let anything within the circle. Understood?"

Gangrene nodded and ran off to organize the armies.

With Leech and Liliths' armies surrounding the soon-to-be parents in their tent, Gangrene paced nervously inside the circle. The birth of their child was taking a long time and Lilith was being very loud. Gangrene had a gut feeling that they were being watched and couldn't shake it, even from the center of two large armies of demons.

"Lord Gangrene."

One of the messenger demons ran to Gangrene's feet and bowed, gasping for air. Gangrene pulled the demon to his feet.

"Catch your breath."

"There's a nephilim outside our armies. He approached and demanded to speak with General Leech."

"His name?"

"He wouldn't say. He just demanded to speak to the General."

Gangrene opened a small sack on his belt. He removed some demon power rings and swapped them for rings on his fingers. Finally, he pulled his spear from its place on his back.

"Take me to him."

The nephilim looked confused as the army parted and Gangrene approached.

"I came here to speak with Leech."

"He's busy with something. I'm in charge here. Who are you and what do you want?"

"I'm here to speak with Leech and only Leech."

"Well you can tell me or I can have you killed. Your choice."

Gangrene raised his hand and a dozen archer demons trained their bows on the nephilim. He lowered his head slightly and grinned back at Gangrene.

"My name is Scapegoat. I serve Azazel, the ruler of this world and commander of the nephilim. I've received word that Lilith's nephilim baby is coming. I was sent to kill Leech and bring Lilith and her offspring to Azazel."

"My name is Gangrene. Lilith is having a baby right now. That's why Leech can't come out to see you. He's with her. As for the rest of your story, this is as far as you go. If you attempt to go after Leech, I will kill you. After your heart stops beating, I'll attach your limbs to four horses and have them run in opposite directions. Then I'll remove your head and bring it as a gift to General Leech."

Scapegoat laughed.

"It's funny that you think you can do all of those things. You obviously don't know who I am or the power of the nephilim commander that I serve…"

Scapegoat drew his two swords.

"…but I'd be happy to instruct you in such matters…"

The demon archers looked at Gangrene but he waved them off. This was his fight. Scapegoat looked amused.

"You're going to fight me yourself? Big mistake. These blades were forged by Azazel, one in the forges of Hell and one in the forges of Heaven. There's no way you can defeat me. You should command your armies to all attack me at once. At least that would be an interesting fight."

"Thanks for the narrative. I look forward to prying your swords from your cold, dead hands and adding them to my weapon collection."

Scapegoat swung at Gangrene with both blades. Gangrene attempted to block with his spear but the swords cut clean through, leaving him holding two small pieces of what had once been his favorite weapon. Scapegoat spun and came down with another strike. Gangrene caught one of his arms by the wrist and met the other blade with his spear point. It shattered. Scapegoat brought that hand up again to strike but Gangrene rolled backwards and backed up several paces. Scapegoat grinned at him.

"I told you it was pointless to fight me alone. Either attack with the full force you command or take me to Leech."

Gangrene put up his fists. The ten demon rings of power glistened in the sunlight.

"So be it. Every creature deserves to choose how they die."

Scapegoat swung his swords down at Gangrene's head. Gangrene caught both of his arms this time and focused his energy into his hands. Slowly, Scapegoat's arms began to sizzle and he let out a scream. He tried to pull his arms away but Gangrene held on. Finally, Scapegoat dropped one of the swords and Gangrene delivered a head-butt to the suffering creature's nose. Scapegoat stumbled back and pinched his nose to stop the bleeding. Gangrene looked at the sword that had fallen in the sand of the beach.

"The one forged in Hell. Fitting. It's mine now. It's what you get for breaking my spear."

Scapegoat spun his sword and adopted a defensive stance. Gangrene charged.

"What is it?"

Lilith sat up and waited for the answer. Raven wrapped the baby in the dark green blanket and then met Lilith's gaze.

"It's a nephilim, stupid."

Leech took Lilith's hand.

"Stop being a bitch, Raven. It's a girl."

Raven put a finger in front of the baby's face. The baby clamped down with both hands and tried to pull Raven's finger towards its mouth.

"Oh she's adorable! You know what the best name ever is for a baby girl? Raven. You guys should name her Raven."

"Not happening. You know… I think we should name her Gangrene."

Raven huffed.

"That's not funny, Leech. You can't name a girl Gangrene."

"Gangrene's parents did."

Leech grinned.

"Very funny. Well obviously the two of you want to be alone."

"You caught on. I thought I was going to have to tell you to get the fuck out again."

Raven handed the baby to Leech, flipped off the new parents, and left the tent.

"You don't really want to name her Gangrene, do you?"

"No. I was messing with Raven. What do you want to name her?"

"Well we are in the Caribbean… in St. Lucia…"

"You want to name her after a saint?"

"Lucia means light in Italian. It's a fitting name for a nephilim."

"You are such a nerd."

"Well Shadow will hate it. It's pretty much the opposite of his name. So that's bonus points…"

"I like it. It sounds pretty… plus I like pissing Shadow off."

"Lucia it is then."

CHAPTER 5

"Start talking. What did you do to her?"

Gabriel tightened his grip on Bumalin's throat.

"It was just a defensive move. She's confused. She'll be fine in…"

Bumalin struggled to breathe and Gabriel dropped him. He gasped for several seconds and then tried to run. Shadow cut him off.

"Oh I see. Cain's nephew. Well I can't say this is unexpected."

Shadow pulled Damnation from his belt.

"How long until Sarah regains her memory?"

"I'm fine, Shadow."

Sarah rubbed her head and then attempted to stand. She stumbled and fell back down. Remiel ran to her side and helped her get to her feet. Sarah looked angry.

"We told you guys to keep the armies a safe distance away. This demon is dangerous."

"Well it's also my job to watch over you so…"

Remiel quickly pulled an arrow from his quiver and fired a shot at Bumalin. Bumalin ducked under the approaching arrow and rolled towards the angel. He struck him in the head and Remiel fell backwards, unconscious.

"You guys really need to stop attacking me."

Gabriel drew his sword and pointed it at Bumalin.

"Give Shadow his memories back or I'll end you're pathetic existence here and now."

Bumalin grinned.

"Aren't angels supposed to ask nicely for things? That wasn't very nice."

Gabriel placed the point of his sword on Bumalin's throat.

"Can we stop playing this game? If you wanted to kill me, you would have done it already. It sounds like you need Shadow's memories pretty badly. I'm willing to trade them."

Gabriel withdrew his sword.

"What do you mean?"

"Normally, I can just take the memories I want. It doesn't seem like I can today. I don't favor my odds against Gabriel and Shadow. What I have is important enough that you won't kill me though. I'm willing to give Shadow's memories back in exchange for a memory or memories of equal value. We make a trade and I run the fuck away. You don't pursue me. I continue to feed off of the people, demons, and angels here in the Philippines. Do we have a deal?"

Shadow crossed his arms.

"How do we know that the memory we give you is of equal value?"

"Because I'll take it from the Archangel."

Gabriel shook his head.

"No you won't."

"I've read the minds of the two other angels. There's nothing that I want in either of their heads. I've already taken from Shadow when he was much younger. Your mind is the one I can't reach. One memory. One secret. For that I'll give you all the original memories of Shadow."

Sarah kicked Remiel to see if he would respond. He didn't move.

"I don't really think we have a choice, Grandpa. We need Shadow's memories back."

Gabriel sighed and thought for a few minutes.

"Can we find a way to extract the memories if I cut off his head?"

Bumalin raised one eyebrow.

"I'm right here. That's really not cool to say in front of the demon you're talking about."

Gabriel ignored him and looked at Shadow and Sarah.

"Well?"

Shadow shook his head.

"I talked to Jess about it before we left Hell. She couldn't think of a way to extract the memories. No demon has advanced the power as far as Bumalin has."

Bumalin started backing away.

"I'm not feeling really safe about our deal anymore. You guys are kind of being assholes…"

Shadow raised his hand and closed his eyes. Bumalin floated into the air, moved forward several paces, and then was dropped back on his feet. Sarah laughed.

"When did you pick up that power?"

"A few months ago. Haven't had a reason to use it. Most demons I interact with don't get enough time to think about running away."

"That's pretty hot."

Shadow grinned and Sarah blushed. Gabriel frowned.

"I mean… uh… that's a cool power, Shadow."

Bumalin shifted nervously.

"I really want to leave here. Do we have a deal?"

"I guess we do, memory thief, with one modification. I have one memory that is off limits. I will continue to lock it down. I will be killed if it falls into the hands of another. It's the day I was made an Archangel. Skip past it because I will not let you view it or have it."

"Killed? That's pretty dark for the angels. Fine. I imagine you're powerful enough to put that particular memory on lockdown. Unlock your mind with all the other memories and I'll pick what I want."

"I also don't want you sharing the memory you take. If it leaves your lips, I will remove your lips from your face with my blade."

"Not sure why you hang out with this guy, Shadow. He seems to like to slice stuff and threaten to slice stuff. No worries though, old timer. I'm a discreet memory thief."

Bumalin put his hand on Gabriel's forehead before the Archangel could add any more conditions. There was silence for a few moments and then Bumalin grinned. He removed his hand and a white mist swirled around his hand and wrist. He put his hand up to his ear and let the memory enter his own head.

"Interesting stuff. Does she know?"

Gabriel drew his sword.

"What did I say, stupid creature?"

"I didn't reveal anything. Just a general question."

Bumalin put his hand back to his ear and withdrew the memory. He put it in a jar and a small demon ran to his side to collect it. The demon grabbed the jar and ran off into the jungle.

"That's my insurance. If I'm killed, that gets sold to the highest bidder."

Shadow stepped forward.

"We aren't going to kill you this time. Hand over my memories and I'll give you time to run away. We have no interest in interfering with your business here."

Bumalin put his other hand to his other ear and withdrew a red mist. He walked up to Shadow and placed the mist on Shadow's forehead.

"Give it time. They'll eat away at the fake memories. It'll take a minute or two."

Bumalin turned to run and Sarah cut him off.

"You'll wait until Shadow remembers. You don't get to run off just yet."

Shadow pressed two fingers to his temples like he had a severe migraine.

"Oh God."

Sarah looked over at Shadow and Bumalin took the opportunity to run. Sarah started to run after him but Shadow caught her arm and stopped her.

"It's ok. I remember. Let him go."

Later that night, Sarah, Shadow, Gabriel, and Remiel sat around a fire. A crow flew towards them and landed on Shadow's shoulder. It looked like it was speaking to Shadow before it took off again. Remiel looked confused.

"Is it normal for birds to speak to demons on Earth?"

"That wasn't a bird. That was a demon that has a vested interest in pretending to be dead right now. He was checking in and letting me know where Bumalin is. I may need to use Bumalin's power again at some point."

Sarah scooted next to Shadow.

"So are you going to tell us what was in your memories?"

"It's pretty lame, actually. All of my memories of my father were fake. I never knew the guy. He came up from the lowest circle for a day because Persephone pleaded with the Dragon. He impregnated my mother. My uncle fed me lies and then trained me to be a weapon, hell-bent on freeing my father. Cain never expected me to find any of this out and he definitely didn't expect me to live after I freed my father."

Sarah intertwined her fingers with Shadow's and rested her head on his shoulder.

"I'm sorry, Shadow."

"I think I may have *something* that's helpful though. I now have a memory of sneaking into my uncle's armory. There were two swords on the wall. One of them was Michael's short blade."

Shadow reached into his cloak and produced the sword.

"I have that one. Cain gave it to me. The other was a short blade that was as dark as this one is light. I remember asking Cain about the two swords. He told me it was the Dragon's short blade. Apparently Abaddon had both at some point and Cain took them when Abaddon was dragged down to the lowest circle. All of those memories were pulled from me by Bumalin. Now that I have my memories back, I know that the Dragon's short blade is no longer in Cain's armory because I've been there since his death. It would make sense that Abaddon has it again."

Gabriel thought a moment and then asked a question.

"Can I see that sword?"

Shadow was taken aback by the request but Sarah nodded at him that it was alright. He handed it over to Gabriel. Gabriel looked it over with interest.

"I haven't seen this weapon in a long time. It is Michael's and I had heard it was given to Abaddon."

Gabriel tossed it back to Shadow.

"I know it will be safe in your hands. Thank you for letting me see it."

"No problem. Any comment on the memories?"

"Well it makes sense that Abaddon would have Satan's short blade. He would have access to lots of weapons with Azazel at his side, but that would be the most powerful. Abaddon likely reclaimed it shortly after he was freed. There's not much alive that could have stopped him or even slowed him down. I think he may eventually come after you to reclaim his other short blade. I imagine if he plans to kill Michael, he'll want to do it with one of Michael's swords."

"Where the hell *is* Michael, by the way? Does he not feel responsible for any of this mess? Abaddon is his son… or does he still not believe that?"

"It's… complicated, Shadow. I think he believes Abaddon to be his son but seeing him is too painful. It reminds him of the night he lost Persephone."

"He needs to get the fuck over it. I don't want to be cleaning up this mess any more than he does. I don't want to be up here hunting my own father."

"It's not that…"

"It's that simple. And you know what? If Abaddon picks a fight with Michael, I will not intervene. Abaddon can kill Michael for all I care. One less Archangel to worry about."

Shadow stood and started walking down the mountain. Gabriel sighed and shook his head.

CHAPTER 6

Jess threw a bottle of beer at Murmur's head. He narrowly avoided it and it shattered on the wall behind him.

"How could you kill Muan? He never did anything to you! Of all the stupid shit I've seen you pull…"

"Calm down."

"I will NOT calm down!"

Jess waved her staff and Murmur saw his armor start to glow. As he looked down, he saw the word "DUMBASS" appear in red, dripping letters on his armor. He laughed and defensively held up both hands.

"Jess, it wasn't Muan. I'm positive."

"How can you be sure of that?"

"First of all, I don't think Nightmare and Astaroth capable of catching the little bastard. He's quick and he's currently with Shadow. He's in command of several armies. The Archangel Gabriel is there with them. How in fuck's name would they have pulled that off?"

Aim walked into the room.

"He makes a good point, sis."

Jess waved her staff without looking at her brother. Two pieces of duct tape in the shape of a letter "X" floated towards his face and attached to his mouth.

"Second, the demon wasn't wearing that necklace Muan has. The one that lets him change into animals."

"The necklace of Iktomi?"

"Right. That thing."

"And it didn't occur to you that they could have simply taken it away from Muan after they captured him?"

Aim made a bunch of unintelligible sounds and then struggled to remove the duct tape from his mouth. Jess's spell kept it in place.

"Third, I have spies watching Astaroth. She's been experimenting with black magic that allows her to briefly make a demon look like another demon."

"That's some advanced spellcasting."

"She's a generally a poison-brewing bitch but I know she's experimented with magic before to aid her poison making. I trust the reports I've received."

"I'm not convinced."

"Fine. Fourth, Shadow told me Muan is still alive. He's currently taking the form of a crow and following a memory stealing demon named Bumalin in the Philippines."

"Oh. Well why didn't you tell me that to begin with?"

"Watching you be angry is amusing and I needed a good laugh."

Jess waved her staff again and stomped out of the room. Murmur looked down and saw the lettering on his armor change to the word "ASSHOLE." He laughed. Aim finally removed the duct tape from his mouth.

"Look, I know you're friends with Shadow but we really need to consider accepting Nightmare's offer. We're outnumbered down here and Shadow won't be coming back to help us any time soon. Have you thought about what we're going to do if Nightmare and Astaroth combine forces and attack us?"

"I know you like giving strategic advice and you're worried they'll figure out where my loyalties lie, but they still think I'm on their side. I told you there plan. They don't plan on doing anything until Shadow, Leech, and Lilith return. They might be prompted into action sooner if they receive word that one of them has died. All things considered, we're doing alright for right now though."

"So no backup plan? What if they figure out that you played them? What if they go back on the deal they offered you? What if they just wake up one morning and decide they want you dead? What then?"

"Then we need to be ready. Thoughts?"

Aim nodded.

"I've been thinking about what we can do to even the odds. While the Dragon is on Earth hunting down Abaddon, his legendary weapons are left basically unguarded. I mean… I'm sure they're guarded, but nowhere near the point that they usually are. Nightmare took the berserker staff and fused it with his scythe. We need to make sure we start collecting similar items that would turn a battle in our favor."

"I have Dragonscale and Cain's armor."

"Yes… *you* have those things. What if Nightmare kills you? We're kind of screwed at that point."

"I honestly don't care what happens to you dumbasses if I'm killed. I'll be dead. Kind of pointless to try to care about things when you're dead, right?"

"That wasn't my point. My point was to fortify the rest of your army with gear that will keep them alive longer than the other armies.

Jess and I still pretty much have shit for gear. No offense… but your entire army pretty much has shit for gear."

"What can we do about that? I don't know where the Dragon hides his gear."

Aim grinned and handed Murmur a scroll.

"I found this in that massive treasure heap Leviathan kept under his throne. It's a list of weapons he wanted but didn't have the power to acquire. Think about it. This is the department of jealousy. Leviathan will have had this list looked over hundreds of times. These are the valuable shit he couldn't get. We have a chance to go get them."

Murmur finally took an interest in Aim's ramblings.

"Alright then, what should we go after first?"

"Probably the weapon at the bottom of the list. That weapon will be the least protected."

Murmur scanned the list and then arrived at the bottom. Murmur grinned when he saw what it was.

"White Death, the legendary sniper rifle. How convenient for you, Aim. Any idea who I should give it to if we get it?"

"Obviously the best sniper in the army. Last I checked… that would be…"

"You?"

"We don't have to go after White Death first. Let's pick a weapon from the list at random."

Aim grabbed the scroll from Murmur and placed it on the ground. He closed his eyes and pointed at the bottom of the list.

"Well… it looks like I've randomly selected the White Death sniper rifle. Looks like that should be our first acquisition."

"I'm not agreeing to that yet. Have you scouted out the location on the scroll?"

"Yup. The scroll said at any given time the Dragon had 5,000 demons guarding it. We might have been able to take it but with severely heavy losses. I scouted the area with my sniper team. Less than 500 demons. They all carry guns. I'm sensing a theme."

"Do they have armor?"

"Generally no."

"So we're literally just killing them to get their guns and a sniper rifle you want? Aim this is the definition of being a selfish asshole."

"Well I could point out how hypocritical that sounds coming from you, with your Dragonscale shield and the ever-bleeding armor of Cain, but I imagine you'd kill me. Come on, boss. We need to get this army better equipped. I can pass my rifle down to one of the other snipers and then teach a group of demons how to shoot with the guns we take from the corpses of the cowboy demons."

"Cowboy demons?"

"That's kind of what the demons guarding White Death looked like. Cowboy demons."

"And we can pull this off without Nightmare and Astaroth figuring out that we took one of the Dragon's weapons? Explain that part to me."

Aim was silent for several seconds.

"I hadn't thought of that. Um… we make sure no one is watching us and leave no survivors?"

"You pointed out that Nightmare fused the berserker staff with his scythe. What if Nightmare goes after White Death and finds no weapon and nothing guarding where it's supposed to be?"

Aim was silent for several seconds.

"Murmur… I really, really want this sniper rifle. I want to break the record for most confirmed kills in a major war in Hell. This thing…"

Aim held up his sniper rifle.

"…is a piece of shit. I always have to aim three feet to the left. The bullets don't always put down my target so I consistently have to double tap with head shots. It's ridiculous and frustrating."

"Maybe you're aim is just three feet off."

"Fine! You want to joke around and be a jerk when I'm trying to strengthen our army then I won't help you anymore!"

Aim stomped towards the door and then stopped. He waited there for nearly a full minute before turning around.

"You were supposed to stop me."

"From throwing a tantrum? I'd rather just let you stomp out of the room."

"Please. I need this sniper rifle. It will pay off for you. I promise."

"*If* I agree to get it for you, I want it to pay off immediately."

"It will. I'll train the demons in your army with the guns that we…"

"Nope. Not what I had in mind. You'll owe me a death debt. For every demon that we lose getting your stupid gun, you have to kill one in Nightmare's army and another in Astaroth's army. Neither of them can find out that it was you. Agreed?"

"That's insane."

"My bad, Aim. I thought I was talking to the best sniper in Hell."

"I can definitely do it, but how can I stop Nightmare and Astaroth from figuring it out?"

"Not my problem. Do we have a deal?"

Murmur held out his hand. Aim reluctantly shook it.

CHAPTER 7

"You're going to have to give her to someone else at some point."

Lilith's eyes flared white briefly.

"Yeah? Try and take her from me."

"Hey now. I'm her dad… and you still haven't let me hold her."

"You can hold her for thirty seconds. Then I want her back."

"That's arbitrary. I want to carry her for the rest of the day."

"Aren't you supposed to be tracking down another nephilim? Stop making Gangrene do everything."

Leech briefly thought about reminding Lilith that she had made Gangrene and Raven run ridiculous errands for her and wait on her hand and foot for nine months but thought better of it.

"You're better at tracking the nephilim. I'll hold Lucia while you sense where the next one is. Then I'll give her back."

"You promise?"

"Um… sure."

"I don't believe you."

"Good call. I wouldn't believe me either."

Lilith laughed and handed over the baby. Leech smiled down at his new daughter.

"Alright but as soon as we know where we're going, I want her back."

"You can have her back when she craps herself."

"So you're saying you're cool with my thirty second time limit then?"

"Just find us a nephilim… or continue to banter with me. I'll take the delay."

Lilith stomped back into her tent and tried to sense a nearby nephilim. As she was trying to focus, Raven entered the tent.

"I want to hold the baby and so does Gangrene."

Gangrene yelled from outside.

"No he doesn't. Gangrene really doesn't care."

Raven yelled back out at him.

"Yes you do. Shut up."

"I don't have Lucia right now. Leech does. Go bother him. I'm trying to find a nephilim to hunt."

"Can I help?"

"I'm not sure. I really don't know how it works. I just know that I've been able to sometimes sense other nephilim around me. I'm not getting anything right now though."

Raven and Lilith turned to the front of the tent where a crow hopped through the opening and dropped a scroll in front of Lilith. Lilith leaned down and patted the crow on the head.

"Muan, I know that's you. You're safe here. Go ahead and change back."

Muan changed back into his demon form.

"Hello ladies. How are things?"

Raven stared wide-eyed at Muan.

"I had no idea that Muan could be such an adorable little bird. Change back."

"That's not why I'm here."

"Come on, Muan. Change back into a crow."

Muan flipped Raven off.

"I'm here to deliver a message from Shadow. He wants you and Leech to meet him with your armies. They have a lead on taking down Abaddon."

"Thanks, Muan. Are the other Archangels joining up as well?"

"Who the fuck knows? I haven't seen or heard from them for a while now. Shadow asked me to track them but I've lost their trail. For now it'll just be the three major demons and Gabriel."

"Has Shadow banged that Sarah angel chick yet?"

Muan looked at Lilith like she was crazy.

"How the hell would I know? I've been a bird for the past several weeks."

"Don't you think they would have super cute babies, though?"

"K. You're straying into crazy land. The details are in the scroll there. I'm going to go say hey to Leech and Gangrene and then leave."

Muan started to walk out of the tent but Raven cut him off and blocked his exit.

"Turn into a crow."

Muan sighed, changed into a crow, and hopped past Raven. Raven giggled.

Muan made his way outside and spotted Leech holding a newborn in the distance. He started to walk towards him when a flaming sword flew down from the sky, narrowly missing his face. It landed in the sand behind him. Muan looked around for the source.

"Death has made your reflexes slow, little imp."

Muan grinned.

"I see your aim still sucks, Gangrene."

Gangrene emerged from the trees, smiling.

"That would have decapitated a normal sized demon. I forgot to factor in what a tiny little thing you are."

Gangrene retrieved his sword and placed it back in its sheath.

"I'm glad you're still alive. We've heard rumors that Murmur killed you and other rumors that Nightmare killed you. I imagine both of them tried but you're still too small to hit."

"Did someone take your spear away? Is that why you switched over to swords? It can't be because you're more skilled with swords unless you were aiming for the sand behind me."

"Picked a fight with a nephilim. Some guy named Scapegoat. He came here to kill Leech and I decided that I liked the weapon I took from him better."

"Bullshit. He broke your spear. Why else wouldn't you still have it with you? You can have both a spear and a sword."

Gangrene grinned sheepishly.

"Yeah he kind of… broke my spear. I really like the sword though. There's supposedly a second one that goes with it. I'm going to take it after I kill Scapegoat."

"I'm amazed Scapegoat fought you at all. He's basically Azazel's little serving bitch."

"I guess Azazel is spread a little thin right now. He's doing Abaddon's dirty work. Scapegoat said he wanted Leech dead and to take Lilith and the baby with him back to Azazel. I am really getting tired of guarding Leech and Lilith's kid though. That little girl came from the two most annoying demons I know. Why would anyone want a hybrid of asshole and insanity?"

"I know what you mean. I just delivered Shadow's message to Lilith and Raven. I'd forgotten how annoying they are. Kind of makes me wish I was *actually* dead instead of pretending."

"What message?"

"Shadow wants Leech and Lilith to take their armies and to meet up with him and Gabriel. I have no idea where the other two Archangels are. Shadow found out some things that should give us a chance at taking down Abaddon."

"I'll tell Leech if you want to get back to Shadow."

Muan nodded then changed into a crow. He hesitated for a moment and then changed back into a grinning demon.

"Forgot to ask. You still dating that Raven chick?"

Gangrene rolled his eyes.

"Yes. At this point I'm not sure I have a say in the matter."

"I guess it still sucks to be you."

Muan changed back into a crow and flew away.

CHAPTER 8

"Apparently Azazel and Scapegoat are working for your dad, Shadow."

Shadow considered this for a moment.

"Gathering the nephilim, I'll bet. Are Leech and Lilith on their way?"

"I think so. It's kind of hard to tell what Lilith plans to do."

"So how did you find out about Azazel and Scapegoat?"

"Gangrene told me. Apparently Scapegoat showed up and wanted to kill Leech. Gangrene fought him and he ran away."

"That's our way to Abaddon then. We start catching nephilim alive until Azazel and Scapegoat show up to try to recruit them. Then we capture Azazel and Scapegoat."

"I see a few problems with that, Shadow. First, promise you won't hit me for speaking frankly."

"Nope. Continue."

"The last time we ran into Azazel, he took your scythes away. I'm not sure how you capture something that powerful."

"I have a solution for that. Next."

Muan looked like he wanted to press the issue but decided against it.

"How do we get them to tell us where Abaddon is? They might not respond to torture."

"We use Bumalin on them. Steal their memories. I told you he'd be useful."

Muan hesitated again.

"You're… *sure* that Azazel can't take Damnation away from you?"

"I already told you I've solved that problem. Don't ask me again."

"Fair enough."

"You still know where Bumalin is?"

"Yup. Jess taught me a little spell that lets me track demons. It takes me forever to get it right, but I followed him as a crow and then cast it on him when he was asleep so I would have plenty of time. I know where he is."

"Good. I want you to take off and try to find the other Archangels one more time. It bothers me that Uriel and Raphael have been missing for this long."

"You're worried about them?"

"I'm worried that they might betray us. If you don't find them over the next few days, come back. Right now getting to Bumalin is more important than finding the Archangels."

"Fine. Just one more quick thing before I take off."

"Yeah?"

"That dorky angel named Remiel keeps going over to your armies and telling them he's in charge when I'm not here. I know that normally you'd put him in his place, but you went ahead with Sarah and Gabriel looking for Bumalin. I'd either like you to put him in his place now or let me go kick his ass really quick before I take off."

Shadow laughed.

"I didn't think he had the guts to try something like that. Thanks for letting me know. I'll deal with it."

Muan nodded and flew away.

Shadow walked into the angels' camp and spotted Sarah and Remiel. As he made his way towards Sarah, Remiel cut him off and aimed an arrow at his head.

"What are you doing in our camp, demon?"

"I'm actually here to talk to you."

Remiel looked surprised.

"Muan tells me you've been trying to give commands to my armies. Do you have a death wish, Robin Hood?"

Remiel lowered his bow and frowned.

"Angels command demons. It's the natural order of things. We're beings of light and so they have to do whatever I say."

"Interesting. So by your reasoning, you can command me."

Remiel brought his bow back up and aimed his arrow at Shadow.

"Yes. I command you to leave this camp."

"Go fuck yourself."

The angels that had been watching this exchange collectively gasped. Sarah started making her way over.

"What did you say to me, Shadow?"

"Go… fuck… yourself."

Several angels grabbed their weapons and started advancing towards Shadow. Remiel held out his hands and stopped them. He saw that Sarah was nearly there and decided to act before she could stop them.

"I challenge you to a duel. To the death."

Shadow burst out laughing. Sarah shook her head in annoyance.

"Not gonna happen. The two of you will not be fighting."

"I'm sorry, my lady, but we will. Shadow has been disrespectful the entire time we've worked with him and it's time he learned his place."

"In about five minutes, my place will be impaling your lifeless corpse on a large stick, you idiot. You don't command me. You don't command my armies. Gabriel doesn't try to do either of those things. Are you better than Gabriel?"

"Do not speak the holy Archangel's name, filth. I will tolerate your words no longer. It is time you learned some manners."

Shadow pulled Damnation from his belt and dropped it on the ground. He did the same with Michael's short blade. Remiel pointed at the short blade with his bow.

"After I defeat you, I will return that to Michael the High Archangel."

Remiel fired three arrows in rapid succession at Shadow. Shadow raised his hand and all three burst into flames. The ashes fell to the ground long before they reached Shadow. Remiel drew a knife and charged. Shadow sidestepped the attack and tripped the angel. He fell hard on his face. Other angels were starting to look angry and some even started moving towards Damnation to block Shadow from retrieving it. Shadow held out his hands and both of his weapons rose from the ground and flew to him.

"It doesn't just have to be Remiel. I imagine a lot of you assholes have a problem with me. Go ahead and take a shot."

Several angels started to attack but Gabriel appeared and stopped them.

"Shadow is our guest. He is helping us track down and kill nephilim."

Remiel hopped back on his feet and bowed.

"Archangel Gabriel, he started it."

"You started it, you idiot, and the next time you try to command my armies I will put you down instead of just kicking your ass."

Gabriel looked like he wanted to say something but Sarah grabbed Shadow by the arm and walked him away from the angel's camp.

"I'm not interested in a lecture. I seriously can't take this anymore. Angels are the absolute worst fucking creatures in existence. I can see where the Dragon got his pride issues from. All of you think you're better than everyone else. Leech and Lilith are on their way here and I'm taking off with them. We don't need the Archangels anymore. I'll kill Abaddon myself. I don't want to see you, Gabriel, or your loyal dog, Remiel, again. The reason the nephilim are an abomination is that angels and demons should never mix."

Sarah said nothing but allowed a tear to roll down from each eye. She quickly wiped them away. Initially, Shadow was too angry to care. He looked at her with indifference until his breathing evened out. Finally, it occurred to him that maybe he had gone overboard. Sarah didn't treat him like the other angels did.

"I'm sorry. I didn't mean to lose control like that. I've taken in too many powers and they're starting to blend together and I'm just…"

Sarah leaned in, put her arms around Shadow's neck and pulled him down until their lips met. When Shadow got over the shock, he started to enjoy himself until she pushed him away and punched him hard across the face.

"What the hell was that for? I said I was sorry."

"When I first met you, I thought you were cute. You were different. You didn't treat Leech and Lilith like minions. They were your friends and I wanted to be a part of that, too. I don't know why, but I'm really attracted to your powers and the things you say and just… you in general. The problem with all of this is that I don't want to like you anymore. You keep blaming me for things that the other angels do. I don't get on your case and yell at you about demons or nephilim… so stop blaming me for the angels."

Shadow held up his hands in surrender.

"Alright. I said I was sorry."

Sarah looked at the ground.

"I don't want you to go away."

"Well I'm not working with the angels anymore. This whole experience has been a clusterfuck of a nightmare."

Sarah didn't look up and Shadow knew she was crying again. He realized that there actually was an angel that he could put up with.

"You can come with me, though. I trust you."

Sarah looked up and smiled.

"That's what I was hoping you'd say."

CHAPTER 9

"So what's the plan?"

Murmur shook his head.

"That's not how this is going to work. Your mission means your plan. I don't want you partially blaming me for any losses we take."

"No problem, boss. I was planning on listening to whatever you said and then suggesting a better plan anyways."

"Fine then. Let's hear what you've got."

"Currently, your army has five snipers. I use that term very loosely. One of them still sometimes points his gun the wrong way and looks down the barrel to clean it. It's enough for what I have in mind though. I'm going to position them in the following spots."

Aim pointed at five different spots around the cliff that led down to the demons guarding White Death.

"We start shooting. They'll start looking up and taking shots around the cliff edges. You teleport in and start butchering them while they're looking up."

"You want me to go down in there and take out 500 demons? On my own? This is about your death debt, isn't it?"

"Well yeah. If you die, I just have to kill one demon in Nightmare's army and one from Astaroth's. I believe in you, boss. 500 kills is nothing for the major demon of…"

Aim realized Murmur was looking at him like he wanted to kill him.

"It was a joke. You go in first and start butchering them. Then Jess teleports small groups of our armies in to surround them and close in. We'll take some losses but it'll be worth it. I'd like to remind you once again that you currently have five snipers. That's pitiful and we should all be ashamed of ourselves."

"And Jess is on board with this?"

"Do I think it's a good plan? No. Do I think it's a decent plan considering the fact that my idiot brother came up with it? Kind of. Am I willing to transport demons in to back you up? Absolutely. We can't let anything happen to our fearless leader, Murmur, the overly large teddy bear."

"I'd kind of like to kill both of you right now."

Aim smiled and started running towards his position on the cliff.

"Perfect, boss. Now take that attitude into the canyon and kill all the cowboy demons."

Aim signaled to the other snipers to take their places. The ragged band of demons ran to the spots he had pointed out to them earlier. None of them found adequate cover. Aim tried to signal to them that they needed to find better cover. None of them understood his signals. Jess, who was still standing next to Aim, shook her head.

"This is a really bad idea. You're going to get Murmur hurt down there."

"I think everything will be fine. He's a tough demon. Plus he knows that I want this sniper rifle really, really badly."

"And you think that affects his ability to kill 500 demons?"

"Shouldn't it?"

"I'm holding you responsible if he gets hurt."

Aim put his right eye up to the scope on his rifle.

"Yeah, yeah… Murmur said the same thing. Don't worry so much. Also… go get in position. It's kind of obvious where I am when you're standing right next to me. Not great for a sniper."

Jess waved her staff and a large sign appeared next to Aim's position. It pointed directly at Aim and said "I'm with stupid." Aim's read it and his eyes nearly popped out of his head.

"Not funny, Jess. Get that sign out of here."

Jess grinned and waved her staff again. The sign disappeared.

"Please go get in position. Murmur's life is actually in *your* hands. You need to be consistently transporting demons into the canyon to back him up."

"Fine. Just make sure the um… what are we calling them again?"

"Cowboy demons."

"They don't look like cowboys."

"It's because they're gunslingers and we're robbing them and… just call them cowboy demons. That's what they're called in my plan."

"Make sure the cowboy demons keep their focus on you and your 'snipers.'"

Jess made air quotes when she said the word snipers. Aim frowned and Jess jogged off to get into position. Aim gave the signal to get ready and his snipers started firing. Aim smacked his forehead and then joined in. After a few shots, he realized that he was the only one hitting any of the cowboy demons. Murmur teleported in and started attacking. He heard five loud bangs and saw all of Aim's snipers fall off the cliff.

"Shit."

Murmur cleared a path backwards with wide swings of his scythe. His armor and Dragonscale had deflected the shots fired on him but he was beginning to worry. The cowboy demons realized what was going on and closed in around Murmur. He was surrounded with hundreds of guns trained on him. He had barely made a dent in their ranks.

"Well, well, well… General Murmur. I thought you worked for the Dragon, but as soon as you realize he's gone to Earth you try to steal from him. So… you didn't think he would leave anyone competent in charge? And you try to distract us with… what was that? Six idiots with guns? I guess only one of them had any skill and he's stopped firing now. I guess he doesn't want to give away his position. In other words, you're screwed and I'll be taking your place when the Dragon finds out that Murmur, Jess, and Aim are all traitors."

Murmur held up his scythe.

"I have enough in me to at least take you down before I die. Go ahead and give the command. You won't become a major demon but maybe one of your demons will."

"I really don't believe that. Either way, you're about to die. You can't talk your way out of this. Jealousy will be the downfall of the major demon of jealousy. That's hilarious."

The commander raised his hand and dropped it. The demons started firing on Murmur but Murmur didn't hear hundreds of clinks as bullets hit his armor and shield. Murmur looked around and saw Jess standing next to him, holding her arms in the air. A dark, semi-circle covered both of them and was deflecting the incoming bullets.

"Hey, Murmur. So… my brother is a dumbass. All of his 'snipers' are dead. I would use air quotes for snipers, but my hands are kind of busy right now."

"How long can you hold that for?"

"Long enough to implement Aim's modified plan. In other words, Aim is a dumbass and it's my turn to put a better plan in play."

"What do you have in mind?"

"Don't stress the details; just be ready to kill in swarms."

A few seconds later and Jess was beginning to sweat. Murmur could tell that holding the dark shield up was taking its toll.

"Come on… you can do it."

Murmur grinned.

"I didn't know you liked to give yourself pep talks."

"Not me."

A dozen demons from Jess's army transported in outside the circle of cowboy demons and started attacking. They caught the cowboy demons by surprise and quickly killed off dozens. A few seconds later, another wave transported in and started attacking. By the time the third wave transported in, Jess was about to lose control of her spell.

"How did you…?"

"I had a backup plan for Aim's plan. I trained two other demons to cast transportation spells in case I needed to get in here and help. They're the ones who transported me in here. I can't cast it on myself… unless you want to hand over your scythe."

Murmur laughed.

"I think you're doing fine without it. I'm ready to resume killing. Let me know when…"

"3… 2… 1…"

Jess dropped the shield spell and waved her staff. Dark, shadowy hands started to appear from the ground, pulling the cowboy demons under the sand. Murmur resumed killing several demons with each swing of his scythe. When the cowboy demons fell to under 100 in number, their commander surrendered.

Aim walked down into the canyon, grinning at Murmur and Jess.

"See? My plan worked great!"

"What the fuck are you talking about? Your plan was idiotic. I'm going to refer to it from now on as the 'Aim Clusterfuck Campaign.' Murmur, I think my brother needs a performance review after this shit. This was embarrassing."

Murmur nodded.

"Jess is right. This was fucking terrible. I'm tempted to give the sniper rifle to her. She's the one who pulled this off tonight."

Aim's jaw dropped.

"But she doesn't even *need* a sniper rifle."

"That's enough. I don't want to hear from you for the next few days."

"But…"

"Days, Aim. Shut the fuck up."

Aim bowed his head and finally looked defeated. Murmur leaned over to Jess and whispered in her ear.

"Go get Aim his damn gun. Kill the prisoners and have your demons take inventory… what weapons we gained and how many we lost."

Jess nodded and ran off.

CHAPTER 10

"So Shadow really told the angels to get lost?"

"That's what our scouts report, Lily. They're returning to Heaven. Fine by me. I don't think the angels were really all that helpful or committed to dealing with this problem anyways."

Lilith pouted.

"I don't like it. I wanted Shadow to hook up with Sarah."

"Maybe he did. We won't know until we meet up with him. It shouldn't be…"

Leech was cut off as Azazel transported in front of them. Scapegoat appeared by his side and an army of nephilim appeared behind them.

"Allow me to introduce myself. I'm Azazel."

"We know who you are. You're the asshole Shadow warned us about."

Leech stepped in front of Lilith and Gangrene moved forward to stand next to him. Azazel smiled. He snapped his fingers and Leech's scythe appeared in his hands. His smile slowly arched down and he dropped the scythe before backing up several paces. Leech laughed and retrieved his weapon.

"Shadow warned me you might try to pull something like that. My name is Leech and my scythe slowly sucks the powers and strength of anyone who takes it from me. I'm the only exception. I promise you it's a powerful, unbreakable spell. If you want a fight, you'll fight fair."

"Turn over Lilith and the child and I'll let the rest of you go."

Leech's eyes started glowing red.

"There's no fucking way in Heaven, Hell, or Earth that I'll let you take either of them. We'll fight you to the death."

Leech turned and saw that all of their armies had abandoned them. Their fear of the nephilim was too great. He realized that he would have to take on Azazel, Scapegoat, and their entire army with Lilith, Gangrene, and Raven. Leech didn't need long to do the math. There was only one play to make.

"Gangrene, get Lilith and my daughter out of here."

Lilith shook her head.

"We're not leaving you."

"I'm sorry, but you are."

Leech held his scythe out for Gangrene to take. Gangrene refused to take it.

"Leech, you just got done explaining how it drains the life out of whoever touches it other than you. Even if it didn't do that, I won't take it. We're not abandoning you."

"Gangrene, the spell only targets anyone who takes the scythe from me. I'm *giving* it to you. Please just do as I say. Get them out of here."

Gangrene reluctantly took the scythe. He started pushing Lilith in the opposite direction but she refused to move.

"I'm sorry, Lilith."

Gangrene hit Lilith hard across the face with the butt of the scythe. He caught her before she fell. Gangrene handed baby Lucia over to Raven and hoisted Lilith over his shoulder.

"Leech, are you sure you want to do this?"

"I'm sure. Go."

Raven and Gangrene turned and ran. Azazel nodded as if he respected the way Leech had handled the situation. He grinned and started clapping slowly.

"Well done, Leech. You had your scythe ready for me, because you knew I'd try to take it. You didn't teleport out of here and lead me to Shadow. You were even able to get your friends to safety. That last part won't matter though. I can find them again after I kill you and this time there will be nothing to stop me from killing them. We were going to give Lilith and your child a pass for being nephilim and give them the option of joining Abaddon's forces. You've ruined that for them though."

"No worries, asshole. I don't plan on letting your army leave this place. You see, there's only one thing that I value more than ambition. Family. I won't let you harm my daughter. I won't let you harm Lilith. Shadow never needs my protection, but I'd step between you and him to kick your ass, too. Just like everyone else in fucking existence, you've underestimated me. I'm just a small little demon. The outcast offspring of Baal. Well fuck you and fuck your army. If I don't kill you all, I'll come back from the grave to finish you off. That's a promise."

Leech grabbed his axe and dragged it in the sand. He ran circles around Azazel's army. The nephilim all laughed at him. Azazel grinned but looked slightly curious.

"So we're wondering what the hell you're doing. Care to explain? Has your impending death driven you mad?"

"I'll show you what I'm doing."

Leech held out his hand and a large green circle formed around the nephilim conforming to the circle he had drawn in the sand with his axe. Azazel applauded once again.

"Oh cool. I had no idea you were a sorcerer, little guy. Thanks for the lights show."

"I'm not a sorcerer. This is the final evolution of a ring of power I received a long time ago. Your army is trapped in there and they won't be leaving. There's one way out, conversion into energy that I'll absorb."

"You're not that powerful."

"I'm the best friend of Shadow, the most powerful nephilim in existence. Command your army to step outside the circle if you're so sure."

Azazel nodded and one of the nephilim attempted to step outside the green dome surrounding Azazel's armies. He was converted into a green mist that flew through the air to Leech's outstretched hand. Leech breathed in the power and his eyes started to glow green. Azazel's jaw dropped.

"What do you think now, blacksmith? Are you worried that maybe you underestimated me?"

Leech held up his other hand and the green dome started to slowly shrink, causing the nephilim inside to panic. Several of them tried to teleport out but found that they couldn't. One by one, they were all converted into a green mist and flew through the air to Leech's outstretched hands. When Azazel looked back in Leech's direction, he saw nothing but a glowing green light. His army was gone. Azazel tried to teleport away but Leech teleported behind him and put him in a headlock.

"Shadow warned me that I couldn't kill you. You're simply too powerful. I don't believe that he was right. Regardless, I can slow you down and keep you away from my family. You see, I can't hold all the power I just took in from your army. That's why I'm glowing green. I'm about to go nuclear. You can try to teleport away, but I'll go with you and in a few more seconds…"

Azazel clawed at Leech's arm around his neck but Leech wouldn't let go. He looked up to the heavens as he felt his final seconds slip away.

"I love you, Lilith."

Leech exploded.

CHAPTER 11

"Where's Muan?"

"I sent him ahead to see what's taking Leech and Lilith so long to get here. We should have met up with them earlier today."

"Do you think they're alright?"

"Leech and I did our best before this nephilim hunting quest to make sure that he was a lot more powerful than anyone would suspect. I'm sure he's fine."

A crow dropped from the sky and arched slightly back up before landing on its feet. It turned into Muan and stood up.

"I… don't really have an easy way to say this."

Sarah looked concerned. Shadow looked angry.

"Just tell me."

"There are signs of a struggle. A large circle in the sand. Blood. Weapons everywhere… and…"

"Bodies? Are Leech and Lilith dead?"

"I don't really have the words. I'll take you there."

"What direction?"

Muan pointed and Shadow teleported away. Muan turned back into a crow and started flying towards the site. He kept his speed down so Sarah could follow. When they arrived, Shadow had fallen to his knees and had his back to them. He was staring at something obscured by sunlight. Sarah changed her angle and gasped. At the top of a sharpened stick that formed part of a cross was Leech's head, his mouth stretched wide open and his eyes still glowing a faint green. At the bottom of the cross were Leech's guns and axe. Sarah covered her open mouth with both hands and then ran to Shadow.

"Muan."

Muan ran to Shadow's side and kneeled.

"Take my armies back to Hell and reinforce Murmur. He's been worried about an attack from Nightmare and Astaroth. You can lead them if you want. I'm not a major demon anymore."

"General Shadow, you're the most capable of leading us into… they don't respect me like they…"

Shadow erupted in a ball of mixed white and black flames.

"Do what I fucking say. Get out of here. Take my armies with you. NOW!"

Muan nodded, changed back into a crow and flew off. Sarah looked frightened by Shadow's transformation but she walked up to him and hugged him.

"It's ok to cry if you need to."

Shadow laughed.

"I don't need to cry. I'm ANGRY! Do you know how disrespectful it is to impale a demon's head on a CROSS?"

Shadow erupted into flames again and Sarah jumped back. She decided to try a different approach.

"Do you know who did this?"

Shadow kneeled down in the sand and tasted the blood. He spit it out.

"It's nephilim blood. It was Azazel. He has to be badly wounded. I don't need my armies anymore. I'm going to find Azazel and I'm going to choke the life out of him. If I could, I would resurrect him just so I could kill him twice. He will pay for what he did to my friend."

"You just made a spur of the moment decision based solely on your grief, Shadow. Don't you want to take some time and think about whether you want to continue to be a major demon or not?"

"I don't need any more time. Do you know why? I don't belong there. I don't belong in Heaven and I don't belong in Hell. I'm an outcast from both places because I'm an abomination. So I'll run around here on Earth and kill angels and demons. That's what I *want* to do now. Fuck both sides. Neither of them is worth anything."

"You don't think that. You cared about Leech and he was a demon. You care about Lilith and she's a nephilim… and you care about me and I'm an angel. If you want to hunt Azazel and Abaddon, that's fine. Just don't let revenge be the motivation."

"What should my motivation be? Justice? Righteous indignation? Is that what the angels would prefer? They're all just words. Abaddon is destroying this whole world. Angels and demons won't admit it, but I'm the only one who can stop him. Michael could possibly stop him but he's a weak coward. Azazel killed my friend. So what he deserves is death. I'm going to kill him. I don't care what we call it, it's going to happen."

"We should go find Lilith, Gangrene, and Raven. Maybe they're hurt. Maybe they need our help. We should check."

"No. I'm going after Azazel."

"Fine. *We're* going after Azazel."

"I could leave right now and never see you again."

Sarah put her arm on Shadow's shoulder.

"Teleport away then. I'll go with you."

Shadow went to remove her hand but Sarah got behind him and jumped on his back, locking her arms around his neck.

"I'm not leaving you. You said I could go with you."

"I don't think you want to watch what I'm going to do to Azazel. It'll disturb your delicate sensibilities."

"Oh shut the fuck up, Shadow."

Shadow's face clearly showed his surprise before he smiled. Sarah climbed down from his back and moved in front of him.

"What did you just say to me?"

"You heard what I said."

"Yes, I did. I imagine Grandpa Gabriel and God did too. You're ok with that?"

"I'm going with you. You don't just get to dismiss me because I'm an angel. I'll watch whatever you do to Azazel. I think he needs to die. Not just for what he did to Leech, but for what he's done to thousands of angels, demons, and humans. He promotes war. I sent him to you a long time ago so he would either help you or you would kill him. Either way, I was fine with the result."

"That's really dark for you."

Sarah frowned at him.

"I like it."

Shadow leaned down and kissed Sarah. She shoved him away.

"No. Being evil is not hot."

"Agree to disagree. I think it was pretty hot."

"So I can go with you to find Azazel?"

"Sure."

"And then Abaddon?"

"Why do you need to be there for that? It's going to be terrible and I…"

"What?"

"I don't want you caught in the crossfire! I can't watch you die! I already lost Leech and I can't lose you because…"

"Because?"

"Leech was like a brother to me. He always had my back."

"You didn't answer my question."

"Because I have feelings for you. I don't know for sure but I think they might even be…"

"What?"

"The beginning of love."

Sarah leaned in and kissed Shadow. He pushed her away.

"No. Being good is not hot."

"Agree to disagree, Shadow. You used a word I never thought I'd hear you say."

"So did you."

Shadow grinned and Sarah laughed. Shadow decided then that he didn't want her with him when he faced off against his father.

CHAPTER 12

"Alright so what do we need to plan for this week?"

Jess stood and put her hands on the table.

"First, I'd like to thank Murmur for allowing Aim to stay a middle demon even though he's a dumbass."

Aim crossed his arms and frowned. Then he removed White Death from its holster on its back.

"I still don't give a fuck. I got my gun. I'll pay Murmur back for the demons we lost."

Jess ignored him and continued.

"Second, we need to figure out what cool thing I want and how we're going to waste hundreds of demon lives to get it. In other words, Round 2 of the Aim Clusterfuck Campaign."

Murmur held up a hand and listened.

"Do you guys hear that?"

Jess and Aim listened and nodded. Dagon entered the room.

"Murmur, there's thousands of demons outside. They sent in someone named Vine to talk to you."

"Thanks, Dagon. Send him in and we'd like another round of ale. Looking at Aim the Demon Sacrificer is pissing me off again and I'd like to get wasted."

Jess giggled and Aim frowned while continuing to clean his rifle. Vine entered the room and bowed.

"My name is Vine. I was a minor demon working for Leech. He was killed and now I command the armies of Leech and Lilith."

Murmur, Jess, and Aim all looked deeply disturbed.

"Sit down. Tell us what happened."

"We were in the desert hunting nephilim and we were ambushed by Azazel, Scapegoat, and their nephilim army. We fought as hard as we could but eventually had to turn and run. Leech was killed by Azazel. Lilith abandoned us and took Gangrene and Raven with her. I decided we should return to Hell and offer our armies to General Murmur. Specifically, my armies would like to work for Lord Aim and Lilith's former armies want to join Lady Jess's forces. Is this acceptable to you, General Murmur?"

"Lilith *abandoned* you guys? Leech took on Azazel alone?"

"As horrible as it sounds, yes to both. We were shocked. We would gladly continue to serve General Leech if he was still alive but

Lilith has abandoned her post as a major demon and her armies refuse to follow her any longer."

"Jess? Aim? Thoughts?"

Aim stopped cleaning his gun and looked up.

"Sounds like Vine made the best of a bad situation. I'll let his demons fall in with my army."

Jess rolled her eyes.

"You just need more demons to pay for the Clusterfuck Sniper Rifle of Asshood. I don't really buy that Lilith abandoned her armies."

Vine had a ready response.

"It may not be that simple, Lady Jess. She had just given birth not long before and may have fled to protect her child. Regardless, her armies no longer believe her fit to lead. You should have seen how crazy she was right before the kid was born. She's insane. They can't work for an insane demoness who ran at the first sign of trouble. Had she commanded her armies more efficiently, General Leech might still be alive."

"Murmur, I don't like the way this guy speaks. I think his story is a little... *off*. What do you think, Murmur?"

Murmur thought for a moment before giving his answer.

"Well regardless of how it happened, it sounds like Leech and Lilith are gone for now. We could definitely use the power down here. That effectively turns the odds back in our favor in a war with Nightmare and Astaroth. I think you should each take the armies and proclaim yourself major demons. What happened to the scythes of Leech and Lilith?"

Vine shrugged.

"No idea. I imagine Lilith has both of them."

"Right. So Jess takes Lilith's spot and Aim takes Leech's. It's the smart play to make right now. I don't see another way around it. Oh and we could use the reinforcements to go get Jess her new magic wand or whatever she's going to ask me for now that Aim got a new gun."

Jess's eyebrows shot up.

"Oh so it's ok for Aim to waste our demons getting a new gun but Jess can just keep limping along with a splintering staff that she's had for years."

Aim grinned.

"Sounds good to me."

"If that's how we're going to play it, I want White Death. I earned it more than Aim did."

"Guys, we're getting off topic. Do you both agree to take command of the armies?"

Aim nodded eagerly. Jess sighed and then nodded.

"Good. I seriously think it's our only option. It'll bring an uneasy stalemate between us and them. They won't want to make a move if we have superior forces."

Jess shifted uncomfortably.

"That's fine for now but it'll still cause some problems. What about when Shadow finds out? An angry Shadow scares the hell out of me. No offense, but I'm pretty sure he could kill everyone in this room… possibly at the same time."

"I'll explain it to Shadow. We go way back. It won't be a problem. If anyone ever finds Lilith, we can talk to her too. This doesn't have to be permanent if circumstances change."

"Should we send someone up to Earth and confirm Vine's story?"

"Jess… I think Shadow or Lilith will contact us soon enough. I'm not sending anyone up there to be killed by nephilim. Shadow knew my position when he went up there. Contrary to what Aim believes, I don't have demons to waste on pointless missions."

"You guys aren't going to let it go… like ever. Are you?"

"Maybe at some point… but not today, Aim."

Aim stood and started walking towards the door.

"If that's the case, I'm going to start putting a sniper team together. I have a lot of demons to go kill to pay for my new gun."

Jess stood as well.

"I'm going to start looking in to the legendary sorceress staff I want us to go take from the Dragon's collection. Don't worry. My plan won't lose us half of what Aim's did. I'll get back to you once I have everything ready to go and you can review it."

Murmur nodded and Jess left the room. Vine turned to leave as well.

"Wait. Where was Shadow when all of this went down?"

"We were on our way to meet him. I imagine he was close but he didn't get there in time to help us. Would you like me to track him down?"

"No. No point. Like I said, he'll contact me when he's ready. Go down to Aim and help him get his sniper team organized."

Vine bowed and left the room. Murmur sighed and shook his head.

"Just come back down here, Shadow. Saving the humans was never our responsibility."

CHAPTER 13

Lilith could see Gangrene and Raven's faces hovering over her. She saw their mouths moving but couldn't understand what they were saying. She closed her eyes and tried to focus.

"I think she's waking up."

"Finally. Why did you have to hit her so hard?"

"Leech told me to get her out of there. You know how stubborn she is. This was the only way."

Lilith opened her eyes again. She sat up in a panic.

"The baby?"

Raven held up baby Lucia, who was napping.

"Ok. Then what happened? Where's Leech?"

Gangrene and Raven looked at each other with concern and sadness.

"How much do you remember?"

Lilith frowned.

"I remember you clocking me in the head with a scythe."

"And right before that?"

"Before that… Azazel appeared and…"

An intense migraine overcame Lilith. She closed her eyes and rested her head in her hands.

"Leech um…"

She opened her eyes and tried to shake out the cobwebs in her head. It finally dawned on her.

"Leech took on Azazel and his army alone. What happened to him?"

Gangrene slowly exhaled.

"I'm sorry, Lilith. Leech is dead. A day after we left, I circled back. Leech took out the nephilim army and injured Azazel but there's some pretty clear evidence that…"

"We have to go back. I want to see."

Raven shook her head.

"It's terrible, sis. You don't want to see it."

"I need to. Everyone touch my shoulders and we'll teleport back."

Gangrene and Raven did as requested. When they reached the spot, Lilith fell on her knees and started to cry. Raven nudged Gangrene and he ran towards the cross to retrieve Leech's head. Raven put her free arm around Lilith.

Gangrene grabbed a sack from his belt, knocked down the cross, and placed Leech's head in the sack. The sack started to glow a light green. He also retrieved Leech's guns and axe and returned everything to Lilith. Lilith opened the sack.

"Why are his eyes still glowing?"

"He drained an entire nephilim army before he exploded. I imagine there's some residual power in there. I mean I know he had already given me my scythe, but I imagine he could have taken on Shadow or Abaddon shortly before he went nuclear."

Raven removed her arm from Lilith and elbowed Gangrene hard in the ribs.

"Ow."

"Be sensitive. I don't want to hear you say nuclear again."

Lilith attached Leech's guns around her waist and his axe to her back. She took Lucia back from Raven.

"We're done. I'm not doing this anymore. We're going back to Hell. Jess can help me see him again."

"The armies abandoned us, sis. We don't have much say in Hell anymore."

Lilith held up her scythe.

"I'll trade this for one more chance to see Leech. After that… I want to go somewhere and die."

Raven started to cry and Gangrene shook his head.

"It'll pass, Lilith. Don't say things like that."

"It hurts too much, Gangrene. I can't do this anymore."

"Think of the baby. She needs you… and Leech gave his life to save the two of you."

"And what do I tell her when she grows up? That her father was killed and I know who did it but I'm too weak to avenge him? She'd be better off without me."

"Shadow will kill Azazel. Trust me. As soon as he finds out what happened to Leech, he'll be all over it. He'll cut Azazel into little, bite-sized pieces. I agree that we're done up here though. Let's get back to Hell."

Lilith reacted angrily to hearing Shadow's name.

"Where the hell *was* Shadow? Why didn't he show up and save us? Why didn't he try to warn Leech that he shouldn't take on Azazel alone?"

Gangrene shifted uncomfortably.

"Lilith, I've known both Shadow and Leech for a while. I imagine they talked about what to do in case Azazel attacked. That's why Leech knew to rig his scythe so Azazel couldn't take it away from him. I don't think Shadow intended that to be anything more than a way for Leech to keep his scythe though. Shadow wouldn't have told Leech to take him on. Shadow would have told Leech to run away. Now that being the case, I also think I know how Leech would have *taken* that advice. He would have ignored it if he didn't see a way out. He saw our armies turn and run and knew that eventually, no matter how fast all of us got away, Azazel would find us again and kill all of us. So he did what he could. He killed Azazel's armies and injured him to the point that he can't teleport all over looking for us. Honestly, I'd be surprised if that motherfucker Azazel isn't dead. Leech was an absolute beast in the end. Every bit the powerful major demon I respected."

Lilith and Raven both started to cry. Gangrene started to regret his speech.

"I'm sorry. I didn't mean to upset either of you. I just… needed to say it for myself. I'll never regret leaving Shadow to follow Leech. Leech was a badass to the very end. He had to fight for everything he was ever given and he deserved to be a major demon. I just wish he was still around to…"

Gangrene trailed off. He fought hard to not let the tears flow. He needed to be strong for Raven and Lilith. Leech had entrusted their safety to him and he couldn't break down. Raven put her head on his shoulder and gave him a hug.

"Once we're back in Hell, we need to contact Shadow and let him know what happened. If there's someone on this Earth who can kill Azazel, it's Shadow. We need to get to Hell first before any of that though. I promised Leech I would keep everyone safe and that's what I'm going to do."

Lilith stood.

"Alright. I'll teleport all of us back to Hell. Grab my shoulders and we'll get out of here."

Right as they were about to go, they saw a crow land at Lilith's feet and change into Muan.

"That actually saves us a lot of time. Muan, you need to let Shadow know that Leech is dead. He took on Azazel and…"

"Oh… he knows. He's furious."

Gangrene saw Shadow's armies following Muan.

"Shadow doesn't want to be a major demon anymore. He turned his forces over to me. I'm taking them back to Hell to give command of his armies to Murmur. Then I'm coming back to help him. He's going after Azazel and Abaddon. Actually, I saw you guys and I'm hoping you can do me a favor. I want to get back to Shadow. Only Sarah is with him right now. I'm afraid his anger is going to drive him to do something stupid and I need to make sure he has adequate backup. I don't want his armies and I don't want to be a major demon either."

Muan saw the scythe in Gangrene's hand.

"Leech named you as his successor?"

"He did. Right before he…"

Gangrene trailed off.

"Then take command of Shadow's armies. They know you and they respect you from back when you and I led them. Return to Hell as a major demon."

Gangrene nodded. He turned to Shadow's former armies.

"Muan needs to get back to Shadow. I will take command from this point on. Does anyone have a problem with that?"

No one objected. They remembered Gangrene and were willing to fight for him.

CHAPTER 14

"So you never told me. How did Gabriel take it when you told him and the rest of the angels to take off and go back to Heaven?"

"Not very well considering I was the one who convinced them to come down here in the first place."

"And we still have no idea where the other two Archangels are?"

"I imagine they've went back to Heaven, too. If they heard that Gabriel left, I really doubt they would have been interested enough to stay down here."

"So before we go hunting Azazel and Abaddon, we need to learn to fight together. Which means we need to trust each other. I'm offering an answer to any of your questions. In return, I'd like the same. Then we hunt nephilim until our fighting styles merge. I won't lie; I keep feeling like you should hang back and let me do the fighting and I know you don't like that…"

"I won't accept it, either…"

"…but it's how I feel right now. I don't want to watch you die. No more death while I'm up here. So I'm opening up my past. Now that I actually *know* all of it, I think you're entitled to know anything about me you think could be helpful."

"And you want me to return the favor afterwards?"

"Yes. That's how we'll trust each other."

Sarah thought for a moment and asked her first question.

"I've always wondered how many powers you have. Will you list them for me?"

"Well… there's ice. That's apparently inherited. I have limited mind reading and hallucination inducing abilities. Neither of them were strong enough to work on Bumalin, or that entire encounter would have gone a lot smoother. I can replicate myself and control the copies. I have lots of insignificant minor demon powers like the ability to counter the powers of other demons and some angels, the ability to see through fog, and so on. I can turn into a huge rage monster and consume other demons. I can teleport when I have Damnation with me. There are probably a few I'm forgetting. Some of them have started to merge and form new powers, but I haven't fully figured that out. How about you?"

"I can blind enemies by overexposure to light. Most demons that touch me will burn. I inherited frost and ice abilities from grandpa. I'm decent with a blade. Honestly, my list sounds kind of depressing next to yours."

"It's not exactly a fair comparison. I'm a weird hybrid of angels and demons. I've found it's a lot easier for me to acquire and keep powers."

"Ok. Next question. How do you feel about Cain's betrayal?"

"I'm angry."

"Leech's death?"

"I'm angry."

"You don't feel sad?"

"Not really. Being sad won't bring them back."

"Neither will being angry."

"I don't like this line of questioning and I don't understand how it's relevant. My turn. What do you think Gabriel told Bumalin? Does it bother you that he's trying to hide something from you?"

"What makes you think he's hiding something?"

"Bumalin's response. 'Does she know?' He's hiding something."

"Well I don't think he is… and I don't like this line of questioning."

"Fair enough. Let's just move on. We both have ice powers. I can't really control mine all that well because I've mostly just had to learn as I go. How about you?"

"It takes some getting used to for few angels that have the power. You have to have a need to slow things down. Make the molecules stop being so quick. Honestly, I have no idea how you've been pulling it off. You're so hot-headed all the time."

"Can you show me? I'll help you hallucinate and then monitor your thoughts to see how you do it."

"That sounds incredibly invasive."

"This is about trust, right? I'd let you in my head but it's just a bunch of angry thoughts and a hunger for more power. Oh and occasionally some thoughts about you that I think you would find invasive and inappropriate."

Shadow grinned and Sarah punched him in the arm.

"Do we have a deal? I promise I'll just be in there to see what you're thinking and feeling when you conjure up the ice."

"Fine. Let's do it."

Shadow placed his thumb on Sarah's forehead and she immediately saw a large yeti running towards her. She initially panicked, but then focused on slowing the yeti's approach. She pointed her hands and ice flew through her veins and out towards the approaching hallucination.

Shadow read her thoughts as this happened and then returned to his own mind.

"Interesting, but I don't think it'll help me. I've just been able to summon the ice when I need it."

"Well I didn't say my way was the only way, but now you know how I do it."

"All the angels do it that way?"

"No. That's just how I learned… and now it's my turn."

"Fine. What do you want to know about my fighting style?"

"I want to learn how to fight with a sword like I've seen you fight. I know you have Damnation now…"

"Sure. I can teach you. I'll use Michael's short blade and you use your sword."

Shadow and Sarah drew their weapons. Shadow replicated himself three times and then backed away.

"My style of fighting involves being quick. I'm not there when their weapon is. I'm not in their line of sight when they expect to see me. Go ahead and put your sword away."

"Then why did you tell me I could use it while you use Michael's short blade?"

Shadow shrugged.

"I haven't taught this stuff much before. Occasionally I'd teach Leech or Lilith a thing or two but never sword fighting. Are you annoyed?"

"Yes."

"Good. Channel that. Not into blind attacks and frustration but into speed. Andddddddd…. Go!"

The three Shadow clones each attacked Sarah from a different angle. She ducked under the blades of the first two but the third scratched her on her arm.

"Get behind them. Get on their side. Find a blind spot. You have to be quick. Think of it like chess. You need to stay several moves ahead. You need to dodge the first attack but then be ready to be out of the way for the second and third as well. Ready?"

Sarah nodded. The three Shadow clones attacked again and she successfully evaded all three swords.

"Good. Now we'll work on counter-attacking."

Sarah went to draw her sword but Shadow shook his head.

"At what point in teaching me how to fight with a sword will you actually… you know… let me use a sword?"

"Counter attack with your fists and feet. Then we'll work on adding the blade."

The three Shadow clones attacked. Sarah evaded their attacks and countered when she could. She tripped one and punched out the other two. Shadow grinned.

"Fine. Now you can draw your sword."

Sarah drew her sword and the Shadow clones disappeared. Sarah looked back at Shadow and saw him facing her with his angel's short blade drawn.

"If you're ready, let's do this."

CHAPTER 15

Aim led his new sniper team silently through the mountains. His new team had shown remarkable progress once he had adequate weapons to train them with and a larger number of demons to select from. They surrounded the small group of Nightmare's demons and found hid behind rocks, desert plants, and whatever else they could find. Aim was eager to feel the true power of his new weapon. As Aim located the minor demon in charge, he placed his crosshairs on the demon's head. He fired. Before the other demons could look for the sniper or react in any way, Aim's team fired and took them out. Aim motioned for his sniper team to move in.

"How many did we get?"

"Seven, Lord Aim."

Aim frowned.

"This is going to take forever."

Jess teleported next to her brother.

"Seems like your new gun is working a lot better than the old one."

"And?"

"And you owe me for helping you get it. I'm basically the *reason* you got it."

Aim addressed at one of his snipers.

"Inventory the weapons and armor. Throw the corpses in the nearest river."

His sniper nodded and went to inform the rest of the team. Aim turned back to Jess.

"And?"

"And I know you have a list of valuable weapons that the Dragon is protecting. I want to know what's written on there as far as mage staffs."

"Not sure. My memory has been pretty bad ever since the… what did you call it? The Aim Clusterfuck Campaign? Yeah… I don't even know if there *are* any mage staffs on my list."

"Come on. You owe me."

"A debt I'd be happy to repay if you'd quit throwing my failure back in my face. I have a competent sniper team now and a much larger army. I'm also working off the death debt I owe to Murmur. Things have changed. Do we have a deal? My information for your word that you'll stop?"

"Fine. It's not really fun anymore anyways. I'll leave you alone about it. What do you have for me?"

"There's a magical staff on the list. Ruyi Jingu Bang… or the compliant golden-hooped rod. It was the magical staff of the immortal monkey king. The Dragon wanted it and took it from him. It was guarded by an army of giants that are supposedly immune to magic and very resistant to physical attacks… so I have no idea how in the Hell you're going to get it. Most of the giants went with the Dragon to Earth. Only three remain at the moment according to my scouts. Good luck making a plan to get it."

"I assume you'll be going with me to retrieve it? You owe me for…"

"Yes, yes. Of course. For White Death. Once we get your magical monkey staff… that's it. You're paid back. Then we go our separate ways and become major demons."

"Do you think the Dragon will ever make us major demons when he returns if he finds out we stole his legendary weapons?"

"Not a problem. We just have to hide them before we go down to the lowest circle of Hell and request to become major demons. He never has to know. We just can't leave anyone alive to tell him. So ideally, you'll need to kill the giants… not just find a way to walk past them and take the staff."

"Any ideas?"

"I'm terrible at planning for this kind of stuff, remember?"

"Come on, Aim. Do you know anything else helpful?"

"Helpful? No. Amusing? Sort of. Apparently the giants stink from miles away. My scouts reported that they had to cover their noses for hours on their way and eventually could even track them purely by the smell. So… there's that."

Jess rolled her eyes.

"Great. Well… I'll let you get back to your tracking and killing. I'll let you know when I have a plan."

Jess approached Murmur and Aim a few days later with a plan.

"So these giants are immune to my magic and extremely resistant to physical attacks. We have to approach it from a physical attack angle. There's three of them. I imagine we only have one weapon that can hurt them."

Murmur kicked his feet up on the table and leaned back in his chair.

"My scythe. So you want me to go in solo and kill all three of them? I'm beginning to sense a pattern. Neither of you want to get things on your own."

"Well I thought about that and this is where I want to discuss our options. We need more scythes. Obviously Shadow's is out. Nightmare and Astaroth won't help us; they'd rather I didn't have a new mage staff. So I think out only option is to look to Leech's and Lilith's scythes. We need to either make a deal and take them or get Lilith down here to help us."

"You think Lilith is just going to hand over her scythe *after* losing her armies? I don't think Lilith will be in a very helpful mood when she makes her way down here. She just lost Leech…"

"…and she just had a baby. I imagine she's on her way back here already. We offer protection. Maybe I can offer her a position as a middle demon. Let's face it, Lilith and Leech were catapulted up by the success of Shadow."

Murmur shook his head.

"Aim has a point. She has no reason to hand over her scythe."

"Then maybe we can ask her to come with us on the mission and kill one of the giants."

Murmur held up a hand to end the conversation.

"I understand that we need scythes. It's pretty useless to speculate how Lilith will react until she comes back down here. Why don't we just wait until we see her and have this conversation with her?"

Aim nodded.

"Sounds like a plan… and I need to get back to tracking and killing demons. I'll see you guys later."

Aim got up and left the room. Jess shook her head.

"I hate even asking her, Murmur. What happened to her really sucks and any way I ask for her help is going to sound really selfish."

"That's what we do in the department of jealousy. We see things we want and we take them. You've never had a problem taking things from other demons or demonesses before."

"It doesn't normally bother me. Asking Lilith to give up her scythe is a lot."

"She may be willing. Death of a loved one changes priorities."

Lilith teleported into the room and grinned at the startled looks on Jess's and Murmur's faces.

"Hey guys. We need to talk."

CHAPTER 16

Jess and Murmur each gave Lilith a hug and then they all sat down to talk.

"I teleported down here to save time. Gangrene is leading Shadow's armies back to Hell. I'm guessing you guys heard about Leech?"

Murmur and Jess both nodded.

"I'm sorry, Lilith. If there's anything we can do…"

"In your case, Jess, maybe there is. I don't accept what happened and I want to undo it if possible."

"Lilith, we're demons. We don't have resurrection powers…"

"I'm not entirely sure Leech is dead."

Lilith put a sack on the table and opened it. Leech's head rolled out on to the table. The eyes were still faintly glowing green.

"He absorbed the lives of a lot of nephilim before he exploded. I think their power has somehow kept him alive…"

Murmur shook his head.

"Lilith, he's dead. Nothing lives after you cut off its head."

"Normally I would agree with you, but I think Leech's case is different. Jess, can you try to summon Leech's spirit so I can talk to him? If you're able to, I'll give up my crazy idea. If not, I want to make a deal with you to try to bring him back."

Jess looked uneasy before she got to her feet. She waved her staff. Nothing happened. She tried again with the same result. Murmur stroked his chin.

"Interesting. Maybe you're right. Maybe the nephilim souls are keeping Leech alive. Jess, go ahead and tell her your plan and then we can work something out."

"First, a little background info. We're stealing the Dragon's legendary weapons while he's on Earth with the majority of his armies. Aim recently acquired White Death, the sniper rifle. I'm going after the compliant staff of the immortal monkey king. I'll actually need its power to attempt to do *anything* to help Leech. His… condition… is beyond anything my current staff could help with."

"Ok… what's the problem?"

"The problem is that the staff is guarded by three giants that can apparently only be killed with scythes. Murmur has one. I need yours."

Lilith slid her scythe across the table.

"Done. I don't want it. My armies abandoned us when we ran into Azazel and the nephilim and I don't want to be a major demon anymore."

Murmur looked confused.

"Your army and Leech's army made their way down here. They joined up with Aim's and Jess's forces claiming that *you* abandoned *them*."

"Nope. They ran the second Azazel showed up with his nephilim. They're cowards. You can have them. I just want to bring Leech back and raise my baby."

Jess attached the scythe to her belt.

"Where is the baby? I wanted to hold her."

"I left her with Raven. I figured this conversation would go faster without any crying. So we have a deal? You take my scythe, armies, and position and you'll help me revive Leech?"

Jess nodded.

"Of course. Anything to help you bring Leech back. Any idea what happened to Leech's scythe?"

"Gangrene has it. You'll have to make a separate deal with him if you want his help. I'm sure there's something you guys can work out. He should be back here soon. Let me know when you have your monkey staff thing and we'll work on bringing Leech back."

Lilith got up from the table, put Leech's head back in the sack, attached the sack to her belt, and left.

Raven started whining again.

"Why can't we just teleport down there?"

"I have an entire army to lead back to Hell, Raven. They can't teleport. We need to walk to a place where all of us can go down."

"What are we going to do when we get down there? Leech is gone and Lilith is done being a major demon. Are you going to take over for Leech with the new army Muan just gave you?"

"I guess it kind of depends. Who are you sticking with? Me or your sister?"

"Why not both?"

"Lilith is going to try to resurrect Leech. I don't think it's going to work. I also have a responsibility to Shadow's forces. Shadow doesn't want to lead them. Muan doesn't want to lead them. They know me and I'm their last hope for a real leader. I have Leech's scythe. I think it's time for me to be the major demon of idolatry."

Raven looked confused.

"This is Shadow's army. Why wouldn't you take over as the major demon of murder?"

"I worked for Leech. I have Leech's scythe. I'm the successor to Leech. We'll work something out when I get down there, but I want Leech's position. It's the only guaranteed spot right now. Lilith is still alive. Shadow is still alive. Leech isn't. I'm going for that spot. I don't want to start a civil war against Lilith or Shadow. That would be suicide. Which brings me back to my question…"

Raven thought for a moment.

"Well I want to help babysit my niece."

"That's fine assuming Lilith stays in Hell. What if she goes back to Earth?"

"You won't follow her back to Earth?"

Gangrene shook his head.

"I'm done. Someone needs to have Murmur's back down in Hell. That's where I'm going and that's where I'm staying. Once the Dragon returns, I'll go to the lowest circle and ask that my position be made official."

"If Lilith goes away, I won't have a cute little baby to play with anymore."

"Well there's an obvious solution to that."

Gangrene winked and Raven giggled.

"Fine. If she goes away, I'll stay with you. I really hope she decides to just stay down in Hell though."

"I don't want to pressure you, Raven. You're a pain in the ass. You're welcome to go with your sister if that's what you really want."

"And you would find yourself another demoness?"

"Sure."

Raven punched Gangrene in the face. His nose started bleeding. He pinched it and continued.

"It was a joke. In all seriousness, though, I don't want to keep you from your family if that's where you want to be."

"I want to say something but it's going to sound cheesy."

Gangrene grinned.

"Go for it."

"You're the only family I need."

Gangrene laughed.

"Wow. That was really cheesy."

Raven knocked Gangrene's hand away from his nose and kissed him. Blood started flowing from his nose again. Neither of them seemed to care.

CHAPTER 17

"He's close."

Shadow and Sarah had been tracking an injured nephilim, that they hoped was Azazel, for days. Shadow could vaguely sense him and they occasionally found spots of blood but the blood became more infrequent as they traveled. The nephilim was obviously healing, even at the high rate of speed he was traveling at.

They continued to practice sword-fighting at night when they assumed their prey was sleeping. Even Shadow had to admit that Sarah was becoming a pro. She was nearing the level of a true master.

"When we find him, I'm thinking we should attack with ice first. I don't think Azazel has ice powers. He isn't a descendant of any of the Archangels that I'm aware of. Even if it isn't a nephilim, no demons have ice and very few angels do."

"It's a nephilim. I'm pretty certain… but I agree with your point. We'll attack with ice first."

As they started trudging through the hills again, a dagger flew through the air and cut Sarah's arm. It wasn't deep and she didn't take time to worry about it. She looked at Shadow as if to say, "Let's do this." Shadow nodded.

Both Shadow and Sarah attacked with ice whenever they saw the creature moving in the shadows. He was quick and neither of them could hit him.

"Why don't you come out?"

"And be attacked by both of you in the open? I don't think so."

It wasn't Azazel's voice, but Shadow felt that he recognized it. He couldn't place it immediately.

"I'm fine with one-on-one against either one of us."

Shadow looked at Sarah, wondering if she would be worried. She looked calm. Shadow realized that she also knew Azazel's voice and knew that this nephilim wasn't him. After Shadow's promise, Scapegoat stepped out into the open. Shadow grinned. The creature was burned in several spots and Shadow could tell that the pain hadn't fully subsided. Leech's final play had kicked his ass along with Azazel's.

"Fine. I choose the angel. Shadow teleports away and watches from a distance or we don't have a deal."

Shadow looked over at Sarah and she nodded. He teleported away and rested with Damnation in his hand. He was ready to teleport back if Sarah needed him. Scapegoat shook his head.

"That's too close. I want you barely able to see us. I don't trust you."

Shadow teleported father away. He sat on a large hill and could still see Scapegoat and Sarah, but barely. Scapegoat nodded approval and drew his blade.

"This sword was crafted by Azazel when he resided in the Heavens and is superior to any weapon of the angels. I will make your death quick and clean and I will take your head to my master. Goodbye, granddaughter of the Archangels."

Scapegoat attacked with speed but Sarah dodged the swipe and kicked at one of his legs. Scapegoat stumbled but was able to regain his footing and turned before Sarah could counter-attack.

"I will not be killed quickly or cleanly. If you're able to kill me at all, you'll die from your own wounds shortly after I do."

Scapegoat angrily charged and Sarah readied herself. Scapegoat skidded to a stop shortly in front of Sarah and cut her arm before turning and running. The cut was shallow but it annoyed Sarah all the same. She pulled a dagger from her belt and threw it at Scapegoat. He knocked it away with his sword.

"Death by a thousand cuts. You have yet to draw blood from me."

"Let's change that then, nephilim."

This time, Sarah charged. Scapegoat disappeared. Sarah didn't want to be taken by surprise, so she froze the ground around her and started building up a wall of ice. She strengthened it on all sides until she was sitting in an icy prison. Sarah sat in the middle and waited. Scapegoat would not be given the element of surprise. If he wanted to attack, he'd have to break through the ice and warn Sarah.

Sarah smelled something burning and saw that her icy fortification was melting. Scapegoat had summoned fire to circle the icy walls and then retreated again. Sarah looked for Scapegoat through the ice but didn't see him. She decided to use a technique Shadow had taught her. She stood, closed her eyes, and waited. Scapegoat attacked and stabbed at her back. Sarah spun, grabbed his sword hand, and began freezing it. Scapegoat cried out in pain and dropped his weapon. He stumbled back several steps, clutching his frozen hand. Sarah retrieved his sword.

"I guess it doesn't matter if I drew blood because I have your weapon now."

Scapegoat summoned flames in both hands.

"Nephilim are resourceful. I don't need a sword to kill you."

Sarah sheathed both blades on her belt and summoned ice in both hands. Scapegoat proceeded to throw fire and Sarah targeted it with precision, throwing ice to stop it. She became focused on the fire and Scapegoat thought she wouldn't notice his attempt to sneak up on her. Scapegoat disappeared and charged again. He summoned fire and placed a burning hand on Sarah's shoulder. Sarah cried out, but drew Scapegoat's blade from her belt, spun, and stabbed Scapegoat through his right rib cage with his own blade. Scapegoat fell to his knees but quickly pulled his sword out and disappeared again. Sarah grinned.

"Was that enough blood for you?"

Scapegoat didn't respond. He knew he was being taunted and didn't want to give away his position. Sarah drew her sword and used her free hand to cool the burn on her shoulder. She continued to look for Scapegoat but saw no traces of where he had run until she noticed the blood in the grass. She started following the trail of blood until she found Scapegoat. He was shifting back and forth between being invisible and lying in a puddle of his own blood. Sarah stepped on his throat. Scapegoat pulled something out of his jacket and then died. A small circular object rolled out of his cold hand. Sarah saw it and started running. She only made it a few steps before the bomb exploded.

CHAPTER 18

Gangrene made his way up the stairs to Murmur's headquarters. Lilith had told him they wanted to make a deal. She seemed to be doing better and Gangrene noted that she was less depressed. Something was driving her. He had no idea what it was, but he was glad that she was feeling better.

A small demon tugged at Gangrene's cloak and pointed down the hall, then ran off to announce that he had arrived. Gangrene entered the room at the end of the hall and realized something. Murmur was doing a lot better than he led them to believe. Many of the legendary items of Hell rumored to be lost were on display in the room. He imagined some of them weren't even fakes.

Murmur sat in Leviathan's old golden throne at the head of a long marble table. Jess was seated next to him. He extended a hand for Gangrene to sit.

"Lilith told me you guys met her at Dagon's. Why am I getting the special treatment?"

"We need your help with something. Jess is going after a new mage staff. It's guarded by three giants who can only be harmed by scythes. We've already made a deal with Lilith. She's in. We need to know if you'll help us."

"What's in it for me?"

Murmur grinned.

"What do you want?"

"It's simple, really. I command Shadow's armies after he renounced his major demon position. I want to take Leech's spot. Major demon of idolatry. I know the traitors from Leech's and Lilith's armies are now under your command. I don't want them back. Fuck them. I want you to recognize my claim until the Dragon returns and support me after he's back."

Jess shook her head.

"My brother, Aim, has already tentatively taken the position of…"

Murmur cut her off.

"With Shadow renouncing his claim, I think we can make something work. You become the major demon of idolatry. Aim becomes the major demon of murder. There's no reason we can't switch things up to make a deal."

"That's a good way to look at it. It's all just speculation anyways. Yes, I have an army and a scythe. There's still the possibility that the Dragon could shoot down my claim to becoming a major demon when he returns. I'm sorry… *if* he returns."

Murmur looked confused.

"What do you mean 'if he returns?' He's the Dragon. I'm not sure he can be killed. We took him on as the Six and weren't able to kill him. You think that Abaddon has a better shot than the rest of us?"

"The only being in existence that could kill the Dragon is Michael. Well… scratch that… Michael and God. God doesn't come down from Heaven to kill things though… so Michael. Abaddon is a combination of Michael and Queen Persephone. An angel and a demon. Nephilim are also generally more powerful and deadly than either angels *or* demons. So there's a real possibility that Abaddon is stronger than Michael. I think he has a good chance of killing the Dragon."

"Interesting. I always thought it was a foregone conclusion that the Dragon would return. If he doesn't, the balance of power tips in our favor. We could march on Nightmare and Astaroth and destroy them."

Gangrene held up his hands.

"Slow down. This is all just speculation. We were talking about a deal to get the monkey stick thing for Jess. I'm in if you agree to my terms. I'm acting major demon of idolatry. I have the best claim with Shadow's army and Leech's scythe. Are we agreed?"

Jess and Murmur both nodded. Jess stood and stretched her arms.

"Enough talk and enough deals. Let's go get Lilith and take care of this. Just the four of us. The three of you fight the giants with your scythes and I'll run in and grab the staff of the monkey king."

Gangrene and Murmur were less enthusiastic, but they both stood. Murmur extended his hand towards the exit.

"Your mission… you lead."

Jess walked out the exit and headed towards Lilith's house.

Lilith had been living in the house of her adoptive father, Panic, for several days. Panic had been killed in the wars of the major demons and had no other family, so Lilith took possession of the small shack. She had known it was possible he would die but had been too focused on other things to care. After losing Leech, Panic's death just added to her sadness. Lucia cried in the other room and Lilith opened a can. The can screamed. She placed the damned soul in a bottle and gave it to her daughter, who sucked contentedly on her meal.

Jess knocked at the door and Lilith let her in.

"I found a spell that should give Leech a chance at returning. It's definitely more than my current staff can handle, though. I made a deal with Gangrene. You ready to take on the giants?"

Raven entered the small house from the back and nodded at Lilith.

"Looks like my babysitter is here. Let's do this and then I'll hand over my scythe. Lead the way."

CHAPTER 19

When Shadow saw the explosion, he immediately teleported to where Sarah was and stood in the path of the fire. The flames ate at his cape and but his armor shielded him from any serious injury. When the explosion finally stopped, Shadow turned quickly and hacked the charred remnants of Scapegoat into several pieces.

"I should have killed you a long time ago."

Shadow turned to Sarah, who was lying motionless on the cold ground. It looked like she had tried to freeze herself before the explosion but was unsuccessful. Her arms and legs appeared to be badly burned.

"I guess the two of you weren't ready to leave the protection of the angels after all…"

In one swift motion, Shadow pulled Damnation from his belt and turned to face the voice. He saw Gabriel frowning at him.

"She wasn't ready to fight a nephilim."

"Agree to disagree. The nephilim is dead. No one knew he was going to suicide bomb her."

"And yet you sent her in anyways instead of demanding the fight for yourself."

"Well I have a couple thoughts. First, you don't know any more about nephilim than I do. So stop pretending this could have somehow been prevented. Second, how about you stop bitching and see if you can help her? I don't have any healing powers. That's an angel's job."

Grabriel kept a tense expression trained on Shadow as he bent down to feel Sarah's pulse. He put his hand over her eyes and muttered some words Shadow couldn't hear. Sarah coughed and her eyes opened briefly but she didn't sit up or say anything. Gabriel lifted her into his arms and Shadow put his hand on Gabriel's shoulder.

"You're not taking her away."

Gabriel turned to face Shadow. His eyes burned with a white hot flame and his voice dropped several octaves and gained a booming, thunder summoning quality.

"You will no longer interfere with my family, demon. She is done here. I should have taken her back when it was clear we couldn't work with your kind."

Shadow raised one of Damnation's blades to Gabriel's throat.

"Put her down, old man."

Gabriel did as requested, but only to draw his sword. Shadow could feel his adrenaline kicking in. There was no one to stop him from killing the Archangel this time. Sarah had closed her eyes again and appeared to be out cold.

Shadow swung Damnation and Gabriel met the attack with his blade. Gabriel punched Shadow in the face. Shadow felt his nose start to trickle blood. He responded by head-butting Gabriel, which drew a similar reaction from the Archangel's nose. Shadow grinned.

"I guess Archangels bleed just like everyone else."

Shadow saw Gabriel summoning ice in his hands and did the same. The two streams of ice met in the middle and started creating a large icicle. While Gabriel continued to shoot ice, Shadow crashed through from the other side of the icicle and kicked the Archangel hard in the gut. Gabriel fell to one knee.

Shadow didn't waste any time. He brought down Damnation swiftly at Gabriel's head. The attack reminded him of the short battle he should have conclusively won against Nightmare in the trials. Surprise registered on his face when Damnation stopped before embedding a blade in Gabriel's neck.

Gabriel had reached up and grabbed one of Damnation's blades with his hand. He brought his forearm down on Shadow's arms and was able to pry Damnation from his hands. Gabriel turned and threw the weapon as far as he could.

"Let's see how cocky you are without your scythe, demon."

Gabriel lunged with his blade and stabbed Shadow through the heart. Shadow cried out in pain before falling to the ground. Gabriel savored the moment only to be punched in the face. He looked at the place where Shadow had fallen and realized that Shadow had cloned himself. The clone vanished when it hit the ground. Shadow grinned again.

"I didn't think that would work on you, old man. I thought you were better than that."

"You still don't have your weapon, demon."

Shadow retrieved Michael's short blade from his belt. He cloned himself again, this time producing five Shadows. They all attacked at the same time. Gabriel stabbed his sword into the ground and looked up at the heavens. Lightning struck and Shadow's clones disappeared. Shadow flew back and dropped Michael's short blade.

Gabriel retrieved his sword and charged. Shadow grasped for the short blade but it was out of reach. He knew he didn't have much time before Gabriel would close the distance between them. Instead of grasping for his sword or attempting to get back on his feet, he stretched his arm in the direction he had seen Damnation fly when Gabriel threw it.

Gabriel stood over Shadow and smiled.

"You will no longer be a plague on my family and an abomination on this Earth."

Gabriel stabbed down at Shadow but his blade was met by Damnation. Shadow climbed the scythe fist over fist until he was back on his feet. He delivered a spinning back kick to Gabriel's chest and Gabriel stumbled backwards several paces.

"Another illusion? I thought I threw that away."

"Ever met a nephilim named Azazel? He liked taking my scythes away from me too. I talked about it with my friend, Jess. Damnation was forged with my blood because I needed a way to make the second blade invisible when I showed my scythe to the Dragon. Jess cast a spell that allows me to recall it because it's a part of me. Azazel can't keep it away from me and neither can you."

Gabriel laughed.

"Clever, little demon. However, all you're doing is delaying the inevitable. I have an offense I've developed over thousands of years. You have nothing but little tricks and an inflated sense of your own power. It's only a matter of time."

Gabriel didn't continue his attack. Shadow could tell he was hesitating. He sensed something else approaching from behind and quickly stepped out of the way. An arrow sailed past him and directly at Gabriel. Gabriel cut it in half with his blade.

"So you've got Remiel hiding in the bushes somewhere?"

Gabriel attacked again and Shadow deflected the blow. As they traded hits, it dawned on him that Gabriel could simply be distracting him while Remiel quietly dragged Sarah away. His theory was confirmed when he looked at the spot where Sarah was and saw Remiel hoisting her onto his shoulders. Shadow continued to fight with Damnation in one hand but lifted his other towards Remiel. Remiel lifted off the ground and moved towards Shadow. When he dropped the few inches back to the Earth, Shadow grabbed his head and quickly planted a hallucination. Remiel loaded an arrow from his quiver and shot it at Gabriel. Gabriel deflected it.

"What did you do to him?"

"Another 'little trick,' as you like to call them. I'm in Remiel's mind. There's not much in there, so it was pretty easy to take over."

Shadow saw a crow land at Sarah's feet. Shadow nodded at it and then continued to attack Gabriel. The crow changed into a bear, lifted Sarah, and ran away. When Shadow saw that they were nearly out of sight, he cut off Remiel's head and teleported away.

CHAPTER 20

Jess, Gangrene, Lilith, and Murmur quietly circled the first giant they had found guarding the staff of the monkey king. The giant had two heads and they seemed to be arguing with each other.

"It's time for a snack."

"No it isn't. We already had a snack. It's time for dinner."

"We haven't even had lunch yet!"

"I can have dinner whenever I want."

"No you can't! Not without my permission!"

The giant's right fist swung up and punched the left head. Jess giggled.

"Alright guys."

Lilith frowned.

"Alright guys… and Lilith. I know it looks like we should just attack the two-headed giant all at once. The other two giants have to be near here though. My plan is for one of you to fight this one and then the other three will move on. Any volunteers?"

Gangrene nodded.

"Yeah… I'd really like to kill this one. Listening to them arguing is giving me a migraine. Who the hell argues with themselves like that?"

Jess nodded.

"Fine. Gangrene can take on this giant and the three of us will move on. Go ahead."

Gangrene started running towards the giant.

"I really need the two of you to shut the fuck up now. I'm tired of listening to you. It's time for you to die."

The two heads looked at each other.

"Can we eat him?"

"Of course we can."

"But is he lunch or dinner?"

Gangrene slashed at the giant's foot with his scythe. It didn't draw blood, but the giant started hopping around and clutching its foot. Jess, Lilith, and Murmur used the opportunity to sneak by unnoticed. After a minute of running, they felt the ground shaking. Jess, Lilith, and Murmur snuck up on the second giant. The giant was larger than the two headed giant and was skipping while chasing a vulture. The ground shook every time gravity brought him down. He was also singing.

"Birdie! Birdie! Birdie! Birdie!"

Lilith put her fingers on her temples.

"Wow. This is worse than that two-headed idiot."

Jess nodded.

"So you want this one then?"

"Sure. Why are the giants so annoying? No wonder they all got sent to Hell."

Lilith ran towards the giant. The giant saw Lilith approaching and changed his direction and his song. He started running at Lilith and yelling.

"Demon! Demon! Demon! Demon!"

Jess and Murmur ran past the second giant. A short time later, they saw a large ball rolling around in front of the entrance to a cave. Jess pointed at it.

"I think that's the third giant."

Murmur looked at her skeptically.

"That rolling ball of fat? It's going too fast. How am I supposed to stop it?"

"You're the major demon. You tell me."

"I guess I'll find a way. The staff is in the cave?"

"If Aim's intel is accurate. So… who knows?"

Murmur grinned.

"Well good luck then. I'll go take on that rolling ball of fat and see if I can put a stop to it."

Murmur ran towards the rolling ball and readied his scythe like a baseball bat. When the ball got close enough, he swung as hard as he could. The ball unfolded itself and fell over. It was the third giant.

"What did you hit me for?"

Murmur wasn't sure how to respond. He decided to answer with a question.

"Why were you rolling around like that?"

The giant scratched his chin and thought for a moment.

"I… I don't know."

Murmur rolled his eyes.

"Talking to you is a waste of time."

"Oh… alright then. I'll go back to rolling around."

Murmur struck with his scythe and Jess ran past them. The cave had very little light but Jess was accustomed to seeing in the dark. She occasionally thought she saw little creatures running around in dark corners but tried to ignore it. She wasn't afraid. When she came to the end of the tunnel, she stepped into a large circular room. A small fire spread in a circle, blocking the way she had come. The light from the fire showed what the little creatures were that had been following her.

"They're cute little monkeys! How adorable!"

The monkeys ran to the center of the room and started climbing on each other. They merged into a larger monkey with a staff.

"I am the immortal monkey king. It's rare that I have visitors. Those idiot giants outside usually annoy everyone away. Who are you and what are you doing here?"

"My name is Jess and I'm… uh…"

"Here to steal my staff?"

"Not steal. I didn't know you existed. I'm a sorceress and I need it for something very important."

"Well… it's mine. Are you going to try to take it from me?"

Jess thought for a moment before responding. She had assumed the staff would just be waiting for her unguarded in the cave. Count on Aim to not find all of the details when it wasn't something he was personally interested in.

"Like I said… I need it. There's a demon that's in between life and death right now. I need to bring him back."

"And you need my staff for the spell. I see."

The monkey king looked as if he was considering the request. After several moments of silence, he shook his head.

"No."

Jess waited for him to elaborate. He didn't.

"That's it? No?"

"Correct. No."

"That's unacceptable."

The monkey king seemed to get a little annoyed with her response.

"No… let me tell you what is unacceptable, Jess. It's unacceptable that the Dragon took away most of the giants he promised would guard me here. It's unacceptable that you somehow got through the three giants that were left. It's unacceptable that you entered my cave and it's unacceptable that you are trying to steal my staff."

Jess readied her staff.

"I guess we don't have anything further to discuss. I was willing to make a deal."

"No. No deals. No. No. No."

"You sound like the giant out there that's chasing a bird. He doesn't have much of a vocabulary either."

The monkey king's eyes turned red.

"No… once again you don't understand your situation. It is you who has a lacking vocabulary. I'm the *immortal* monkey king. Immortal means I can't die. Wandering in here hoping to kill me was incredibly foolish. Attempting to steal my staff was an asinine idea. I will place your rotting corpse at the entrance of this cave with a sign that says 'I was dumb enough to attempt to steal from the monkey king.'"

Jess went with her go-to first attack, corpse hands reaching up from the ground grabbing at anything they could reach and pinning them down. The monkey king flashed briefly and then disappeared. Moments later, Jess felt something fall on her shoulders and hit her hard on the head. She felt dizzy and fell over.

"I won't even need to use spellcraft to slay you. You are a novice. I'm still immensely surprised you made it past the giants given the state of your sorcery."

The monkey king brought his staff down hard, aiming at Jess's head. She brought up both hands in an attempt to block it, unsure of where it actually was because of her dizziness. The staff connected hard with one of her forearms. She ignored the pain and quickly grabbed it with her hand. She started muttering a spell and the staff began to heat up. Fire shot from the staff up the monkey king's furry arm. He kicked Jess hard in the face, threw his staff across the room, and then rolled around in the sandy cave floor until the flames on his arm were extinguished.

"Well that was… unexpected. I guess I misjudged you. I don't come across many demons who can summon flames. It was a miscalculation on my part… one which I won't repeat."

The monkey king ran across the cave and touched his staff briefly before withdrawing his hand. It was still too hot. Jess knew she had a limited window of time to act. She shook her head, hoping to clear her vision, and grabbed at her staff. Jess summoned a snake that slithered over to the monkey king and wrapped itself around his body, pulling his arms to his sides. The monkey king laughed.

"I'm a monkey. My feet work the same as my hands."

The monkey king grabbed his staff, which was now cool enough to handle, with his feet. He cast a spell and the snake turned into a string and fell off him. Before Jess could get back to her feet, the monkey king attacked.

CHAPTER 21

"Were you followed here?"

Muan shook his head.

"I wasn't. We're good."

"We're good until Gabriel comes after us. Why didn't you take out Remiel? He nearly shot me!"

"Couple of things, Shadow. First, I was dropping off your army with Gangrene and then I came back as soon as I could. Second, he didn't almost shoot you. That clumsy oaf couldn't hit the Great Wall of China with an automatic machine gun."

"Right… well… you're the Medic's son. What's wrong with Sarah?"

Muan took a moment to look at Sarah and check a few things. He produced a vial, opened Sarah's mouth, and poured the contents down her throat.

"She's burned pretty badly but I would think she should be waking up any…"

Sarah opened her eyes.

"What… what happened?"

Sarah tried to get up but Shadow held out his hand, letting her know that it wasn't a good idea. She laid her head back on the ground.

"What do you remember?"

"I fought with that nephilim. I think I won. Then I blacked out. Then Grandpa was casting some sort of spell on me."

Muan nodded.

"Right. That makes sense. She looks burned but not enough to be knocked out cold for too long. I figured Gabriel did something."

"What did you give me?"

Muan looked at Shadow, not wanting to answer.

"Muan?"

"A shot of adrenaline mixed with a small amount of cocaine."

Muan held up both his hands in self-defense.

"I want you both to keep in mind that it worked. She's awake."

Shadow waved Muan's statements away. He didn't care. There were more pressing things that needed to be dealt with.

"Why would Gabriel cast a spell to knock you out? Why did he need to get you back to Heaven so badly? I really don't think it was out of concern because you did great in your duel with Scapegoat."

Sarah sat up.

"Wow. Yeah. I can feel that shit you made me drink. It packs a nice kick, Muan."

Muan grinned sheepishly.

"I think I know what it was, Shadow. Grandpa is still trying to keep something from me. I think he might have been worried that I would try to find Bumalin and figure out the memory he stole. It's been bothering me. I think you're right. It was a memory about me."

Shadow nodded.

"Muan? Do you know where Bumalin is right now?"

"Yup. Want me to lead you there?"

Shadow helped Sarah to her feet. She jumped up and down several times and then stretched her legs.

"Yeah… lead the way Muan. We need to figure out what Bumalin knows."

Muan turned into a crow and started flying. Sarah and Shadow followed.

When the demons arrived at the mountain where Bumalin was trying to hide, he looked seriously annoyed.

"Aw… fuck me. I thought I was done with you guys. I didn't tell anyone anything. Why can't you just leave a guy alone?"

"We need you to tell us about the Archangel's memory."

Bumalin rolled his eyes.

"Right. So he can pop out of the bushes and kill me? I don't think so. I'd really rather keep my mouth shut."

Sarah grabbed Bumalin by his cloak and lifted him into the air.

"I nearly died killing a nephilim. Then my grandfather tried to drag me back to Heaven so I wouldn't find out what was in that memory he gave you. After all that… you see that crow up there?"

Sarah paused so that Bumalin could look up. He did and then nodded.

"He made me swallow a shot of adrenaline, drugs, and probably other things he isn't telling me about. I'm not in the mood right now. Tell us what was in the fucking memory."

"But…"

"You have five seconds before my boyfriend cuts your head off. Five…"

"But…"

"Four…"

"You're insane. Crows don't poison angels."

"Three…"

"Come on. Be reasonable. I can give you some other angel's memory. I get angel memories from time to time and…"

"Two…"

"I can't have that Archangel coming back here and…"

"One…"

"Fine. Put me down."

Sarah dropped Bumalin and let him brush himself off.

"You're sure another angel's memory won't…"

"Shadow… kill him."

"No. Ok. Fine. Have a seat and I'll tell you."

Bumalin sat cross-legged in the dirt. Shadow and Sarah sat on a pile of cut bamboo.

"Naturally, I tried to grab the memory of when he became an Archangel first."

"But you said…"

"I lied. I knew it would be a juicy memory and I couldn't help myself. It was blocked off. I couldn't get at it. So I started looking for something interesting… something gossip worthy… something I could use as leverage against the angels."

"And you found?"

"Your birth. Gabriel showed up unexpectedly. Your mother had gone into labor and a demon kept trying to get in and…"

"A demon?"

"Yup. Gabriel threw him out. After your mom had you, she told him not to be angry. Then she revealed that the demon was your father."

Sarah stood and drew her sword. Bumalin held up both hands in defeat.

"You're lying."

"I'm not. I can give you the memory briefly so you can see for yourself… as long as you give it back when we're done."

"Fine. Do it."

Bumalin pulled the memory from a vial and placed it in Sarah's ear. Moments later, she was able to see everything from Gabriel's perspective exactly the way Bumalin had described it. Bumalin removed the memory from Sarah's ear and put it back in the vial.

"I thought you had a demon run off with that."

"Slide of hand. Something this good was worth keeping on me at all times. Now I've held up more than my end of this bargain. How about you guys give me a head start? I need to get the fuck out of here and hide before Gabriel finds out."

Bumalin turned to leave and then turned back to look at Shadow.

"If I see that crow ever again, I will have him killed. Don't follow me. Don't keep tabs on my location. I may not be as powerful as you but I have memories hidden that would destroy both the Heavens and the Underworld. Don't make me use them."

Bumalin turned and ran away. Shadow looked at Sarah with a mischievous look.

"Since when am I your boyfriend?"

"It was the cocaine talking."

Shadow gave her a look that let her know that he wasn't convinced.

"Shut up, Shadow."

CHAPTER 22

Jess knew she was in over her head. The monkey king was toying with her. Any spell she cast was countered by the monkey king. He laughed and ran in circles around the room. Eventually he would get bored and kill her. Her only hope was to last long enough that Lilith, Gangrene, or Murmur had enough time to kill their giant and go looking for her in the cave. She knew even then they wouldn't be able to kill the monkey king. Still, she fought on, wanting to delay her inevitable death.

Jess conjured a banana. The monkey king laughed and ate it. She shot fire from her staff. The monkey king conjured a stick with a marshmallow at the end and cooked it. She was running out of ideas.

"Well… this has been fun but I think your time is up. Would you like to pick the way I kill you? We can go for something really creative."

Jess didn't respond. She backed up against the wall and closed her eyes. It was over. The monkey king laughed.

"No suggestions? Fine. I'll make it quick."

Jess waited. Nothing happened. She thought about opening her eyes but didn't want to risk viewing her own death. Finally, she heard a gunshot.

Jess didn't feel any pain. Maybe she was too shocked and numb to feel it. The monkey king had been true to his word. He made her death quick. Several seconds passed and Jess felt something being shoved into her hands.

"Open your eyes. We have to get out of here."

Jess opened her eyes and saw Aim. Aim was shoving the monkey staff into her hands. The monkey king was lying on the floor of the cave in a daze.

"I shot him with White Death. It isn't going to keep him down for long. Take the damn staff and run."

Jess gripped the staff and Aim started running. Jess lingered. She waved the staff at the monkey king and smiled before casting a spell.

When the monkey king regained consciousness, he wasn't sure what to expect. He sat up and realized that the room had returned to darkness. He started to walk towards the cave's entrance and ran into something solid. He turned around and went backwards, only to run into another barrier. Suddenly, two flames appeared and the monkey king saw Jess standing in front of him, grinning and holding the flames in her hands. His staff was secured on her back.

"I wasn't sure what to do with you after my brother shot you."

"What the fuck did he shoot me with? A cannon? I'm not used to going down like that."

"White Death, the legendary sniper rifle. We picked it up for him before we came here. I hear it packs a punch, even when it hits an immortal. He got you between the eyes?"

Jess looked closer and saw a red mark in between the monkey king's eyes and laughed.

"He used to be a really sucky shot. I have to admit he's really good now. Maybe the best in all of Hell."

"Give me my staff back."

"I don't think so. I like it. In fact, I used it to cast a spell on you. After Murmur killed off Belial, I started reading through the sorcerer's texts and scrolls. There were some great spells in there but most of them were too powerful for my skill level and for my staff. I learned them all anyways on the off chance I would need them someday. There was one I found particularly interesting… one that creates an invisible cage. You can be immortal all you want… you just can't leave the cage I've put you in. I wonder how hungry you'll be in a few hundred years."

The monkey king punched at his invisible barrier and pulled back his hand, shaking it.

"Tell you what… I'll be kinder than you were to me."

Jess took her old staff, broke it in half, and hit the pieces inside the invisible cage with her new staff.

"If you're really the great sorcerer you claim to be, you'll be able to get out of there with a broken staff with limited powers. That… or you can eat it when hunger starts to drive you insane. Whatever you want."

"I'm going to get out of here when the Dragon returns. He'll free me and I will torture you for months before I kill you."

"I wouldn't be so sure that the Dragon cares about you that much. You were an interesting toy in his collection. He found your staff powerful and your immortality intriguing. Both of those things remain the same with you in a cage and a more powerful sorceress wielding your staff. I'm going to try to merge it with my scythe when I become a major demon. Good luck taking it away from me after that."

Jess turned and started to leave. The monkey king screeched.

"Leave me with something. Water. Food. A better staff than this broken stick."

Jess didn't turn back.

"You tried to kill me. I've been more than generous."

As Jess exited the cave, she saw Aim waiting for her.

"What'd you do to the monkey?"

"I gave him what he deserved. A cage."

"Pretty harsh, sis. We even now? I had your back."

"Yes. I'll let the fact that you're a dumbass go for now."

"That's all I ask."

Jess laughed. Murmur, Gangrene, and Lilith approached. All three of them were bloody and covered in dirt. Murmur cracked his knuckles.

"The next time you need a favor, remind me to say no."

Lilith held out her scythe and Jess took it.

"I've held up my end of the bargain. It's your turn."

Jess took her scythe in one hand and her new staff in the other. She muttered words and her eyes glowed red. Both weapons started to heat up and glow. She brought them together and the two weapons fused.

"It's so nice to have a staff powerful enough to tap my full potential. A lot of the spells I used to cast were well beyond the power of my staff and they drained me."

Aim decided he couldn't help himself.

"So Shadow has two scythes and he calls it Damnation. Nightmare has a scythe fused with the berserker staff and he calls it Rage. You have a scythe fused with the immortal monkey king's staff. What do we call it? Poop flinger? Banana slicer?"

Jess waved her scythe and Aim hit himself in the head with the butt of his gun.

"The name isn't important right now. If you start calling my scythe 'Poop flinger' I guarantee bad things will happen to you. Now, Lilith, I have a spell that can enhance Leech's energy stealing power so that he's able to regrow his limbs and body. He'll come back to life. The problem is that we'll need someone powerful enough to fuel his return. I was thinking that Murmur could give it a shot."

Murmur nodded.

"I'm willing to help out. I'm clearly the most powerful demon here so there's no point in anyone else trying."

Gangrene looked like he wanted to say something but decided against it. He decided he didn't want to make a new enemy over his ego.

When Murmur failed, he would show everyone that he was more powerful.

Lilith removed Leech's head from the bag on her belt. The eyes were still glowing a faint green. Jess cast the spell with her scythe and the green light emanating from Leech's eyes grew stronger. Murmur lifted the head. Nothing happened.

"So um… why isn't it…"

Murmur cut his sentence short and dropped to one knee. He grunted as Leech's head stole his energy and strength. After a few seconds, Murmur dropped Leech's head. Gangrene picked it up.

"So clearly Murmur wasn't strong enough. Let me give it a shot."

Once Leech's head started to drain Gangrene's strength, he dropped it even quicker than Murmur. Murmur was breathing heavily, but he grinned up at Gangrene. Lilith hung her head, what little hope she had mostly extinguished. She retrieved Leech's head, put it back in the bag, and reattached it to her belt.

"I guess I know what I need to do. I'm going back to Earth. I'm going to find Shadow. He can help me bring Leech back."

Gangrene fell over but responded in between heavy breaths.

"I'll go… with you…"

Lilith shook her head.

"Murmur, Jess, and Aim need you down here. Aim doesn't have a scythe. Nightmare is dumb, but he's eventually going to figure out that Murmur tricked him. Stay down here and keep the two sides balanced. Thanks for your help, Jess. Good luck running the department of lust."

Lilith turned and headed back towards her house to talk to Raven.

CHAPTER 23

"So what do we do now?"

Shadow shrugged.

"The plan hasn't changed. Kill Azazel. Kill Abaddon. Kill the Dragon. Kill anything that gets in our way."

"We don't know where any of them *are*. How are we supposed to kill them?"

Muan had been running around as a leopard. He was still worried that Sarah wanted to kill him for the concoction he used to bring her back. He turned back into a demon and held up both hands in a defensive manner.

"I'd like to speak because I have a lead. If you're going to hit me, slice me up, or throw things… Please tell me now so I can turn back into a leopard and run away."

Sarah smiled and spoke through gritted teeth.

"You have a lead for where we can score more cocaine? Is that what you have a lead for?"

Muan sighed.

"Right. You're clearly still pissed. I'd like you to remember that I *did* save your life though."

"No. Shadow saved my life and he didn't inject me with anything. That's how you save someone's life, Muan. You get in the way of what's about to kill them. You don't force a cocktail of 'Muan's best drugs and booze' down their throats."

"There was barely any booze. Small bit of adrenaline. It was mostly drugs."

Sarah started advancing towards Muan but Shadow cut her off and held her back.

"Let's hear your lead, Muan."

"I think I know how we can locate Azazel."

"We're listening."

"Well you killed Scapegoat. Scapegoat worked for Azazel. If he had something on him that *belonged* to Azazel, I can create a potion that will lead us to him. I think. My dad did it a few times. I've never made it on my own."

"Shouldn't be a problem though, right Muan? It's probably just meth mixed with marijuana and crack. Maybe some chili pepper for flavor."

"Wow. I didn't know angels had such a hard time letting things go."

"I'm not an angel. I'm a nephilim. I can be as pissed as I want."

Shadow hit Damnation against the ground and the Earth shook.

"Enough. We should follow Muan's lead and go find Azazel. Since I know where Scapegoat died, we can just save time and teleport back. Come on."

Sarah and Muan each placed a hand on one of Shadow's shoulders. He teleported the three of them back to the site of Scapegoat's death. Muan started searching among the small chunks of burning remains.

"It needs to be something that was clearly Azazel's. If you see any kind of mark that leads you to believe that…"

"What about Scapegoat's sword?"

Sarah pulled the sword from her belt.

"He told me it was forged by Azazel in the heavens."

"Sure. That'll work if you're ok with me grinding it up and putting it in the potion."

Sarah sheathed the weapon on her own belt.

"I kind of like it. Let's call that our backup plan. I'd like to keep it if I can."

Muan nodded and the three of them started searching. Sarah thought she saw something on Scapegoat's shoulder.

"Help me get his armor off. There's some kind of mark on his right shoulder blade. Maybe it'll help us figure some things out."

Shadow and Muan removed Scapegoat's breastplate. They looked at the marking and then at each other. They looked disturbed.

"I don't get it. What does it mean?"

Shadow looked at Muan. He assumed Muan could explain it better.

"That's a devils tongue marking. Black speech. It's a mark we use to…"

Muan looked at Shadow and Shadow nodded as if to confirm that he should continue.

"… a mark we use to brand our slaves. Demons in training who never make it beyond that rank. They're sometimes marked by minor demons, middle demons, and major demons. It basically just confirms that Scapegoat was Azazel's slave. It actually explains a few things, like why he never tried to escape and why he did everything Azazel told him to without question."

Sarah looked at Shadow, hoping she knew the answer to what she was about to ask.

"You never… marked anyone… like that. Did you?"

Shadow shook his head.

"Everyone who worked for me did so of their own free will. Branding marks isn't my style. I have to admit that I almost feel bad for the guy. He could have done pretty well if he wasn't enslaved by a creature of Azazel's power. Scapegoat probably could have climbed up to the rank of middle demon in Hell without any issues."

"Can we cut the marking off his shoulder and use it in the potion?"

Muan nodded.

"I'm sure it was accompanied by a powerful spell. Scapegoat was Azazel's property. It should work."

Muan approached Scapegoat's corpse with his knife. Sarah turned away as he started slicing into scarred flesh. He put it in a small bowl that he produced form under his cloak and mixed in several ingredients from vials and bottles. When he was done, he poured the potion on the ground. Sarah looked confused.

"Why did you pour it out? Did you mess something up?"

Muan shook his head.

"Just wait for it."

"Wait for what?"

The spilled potion rose up into the air and formed a black dog. The dog didn't look at them. It just started running. Muan pointed at it.

"Follow the dog. It'll take us to Azazel."

"Muan, you're really creepy. You know that, right?"

Muan grinned.

"What you call creepy, I call awesome. Witch doctors are awesome. Now start running. We can't let the dog get too far ahead of us."

Muan turned back into a leopard and started running after the dog. Shadow and Sarah followed. After a few minutes of running, the dog disappeared. Muan went to the spot where it had vanished and looked confused.

"That doesn't make any sense. It should have kept running until…"

Shadow saw a flash of light in the air above Muan's head. It was descending towards him. He shoved Muan out of the way and brought Damnation up to meet the blade. He recognized his opponent.

"Raphael. So you didn't go home with Gabriel. Attacking me was a stupid move."

Raphael backed up several paces and laughed.

"I only come to Earth for one reason. To hunt demons. That's all the three of you are. I found out Gabriel's secret from Bumalin. I'll start with the small witch doctor. Then I'll cut Gabriel's bastard offspring in half. Finally, I'll pierce Abaddon's son through the heart with my blade. Gabriel was protecting you but he isn't here anymore."

Sarah and Muan started advancing towards Raphael, weapons in hand. Shadow held up his arms and they stopped. He pointed Damnation at Raphael and grinned.

"My scythe hasn't had the opportunity to bathe itself in Archangel blood yet. Thank you for the opportunity."

CHAPTER 24

Gangrene had been waiting outside Lilith's house for what felt like hours. Raven and Lilith were still inside, hugging and crying. He had thought about entering several times but he knew how crazy the half-sisters could be when they were emotional. He sat on a rock outside and polished his scythe, hoping they would hurry up. When he heard something shatter inside the house, he jumped up and ran inside.

"What's going on? Is someone attacking you?"

Gangrene scanned the room and saw Raven breathing heavily and the shattered remains of a vase on the floor.

"Gangrene, tell my sister she's not going to Earth alone. We're going with her."

"I already offered. She said no. She wants me to stay down here and help Murmur."

Lilith raised her hands in submission.

"Hey. There's no need to throw things. Let's just sit at the table and have a mature discussion about this. I'm willing to listen if the two of you are."

Gangrene and Raven stood where they were in stunned silence. They had never heard Lilith say the words "mature discussion" before and neither of them had any idea how to respond.

"I made some tea. It'll help calm everyone down. Sit at the table and have a cup."

Gangrene shook his head.

"I'm perfectly calm. There's no need to…"

Lilith cut him off, shrieking.

"Sit at the damn table and drink the tea!"

Raven and Gangrene sat at the table. Raven was still pouting.

"We can drink all the tea in Hell but it isn't going to change the fact that you aren't going back to Earth with my niece to look for Shadow. Not without us. I talked to Gangrene a while back about letting you go if it came to it… but I can't do it. I hate all of my other sisters. I can't let you leave."

Gangrene raised an eyebrow.

"You're taking your daughter back up there? I think I'm going to have to agree with Raven. That world is crazy enough right now with all the nephilim running around, not to mention the Dragon has most of his forces up there. I'm going to have to insist that…"

"How do you like the tea?"

Gangrene and Raven looked at the table at the cups Lilith had placed in front of them.

"Lilith, tea isn't going to change my mind either. It's irresponsible to take an infant…"

"Try it. The two of you need to calm down before we discuss this."

Raven looked at the tea.

"It's a trap."

Lilith laughed.

"How is this a trap?"

Raven looked over at Gangrene and then back at her sister.

"You're trying to drug us so that you can run away."

Lilith looked at the floor.

"Well shit. Why couldn't you just drink the tea?"

Gangrene stood, looking outraged.

"You were seriously trying to drug us so you could sneak away?"

"That was Plan A. I guess I'm going to have to resort to Plan B now. Jess…"

Jess entered the house from the back entrance. She waved her scythe and four shadowy figures crawled up from holes that appeared in the floor. They grabbed Gangrene and Raven's arms and took their weapons.

"Sorry about this, guys. Lilith and I made a side deal since I wasn't able to bring Leech back. No hard feelings. Just business."

Jess turned and left. Lilith went to Lucia's room and wrapped her in a blanket. Raven and Gangrene continued to struggle to free themselves.

"I'm really sorry guys. The next time I ask you to drink tea, please just do it."

Lilith carried Lucia outside and placed her in the saddle addition Leech had designed to securely carry the baby when Lilith went riding. Lilith then mounted Keshi and rode towards Jess.

"Hey, Jess. One more quick favor."

"We already made our deal, Lilith. I don't owe you anything else. They're going to be pissed enough that I just did what I did. You realize Gangrene is a major demon now, right?"

Lilith shrugged.

"So are you. Thanks to me. I handed over my scythe. I know you've been helpful but I want one more favor."

Jess sighed.

"What is it?"

"I want you to cast a spell to make my horse talk. I've always wondered what he's thinking."

"I can't do that."

"Can't or won't?"

"Pick one."

"Why not?"

"Because no demon sorcerer has ever been insane enough to come up with a spell to make horses talk."

"Can the angels do it then? I can ask one of the angel sorcerers when I make it to Earth."

"I don't know. I've never asked one. I don't know if you know this or not, but most of us don't get along with demons well enough to chat with them."

"Fine. If I can't have that then I want a different favor."

"I never agreed to give you a favor. Our deal is done. Bring Leech to Shadow and he should be able to draw enough strength to come back... plus I just attacked your half-sister and a major demon. No more favors."

Lilith looked at Jess like she was going to scream. Jess returned her agitated look.

"What? What else do you want?"

"A spell of protection for Lucia."

Jess softened a little.

"Well that's way less stupid than making a horse talk. Of course I can do something like that."

"Curse her green blanket so that anyone that picks her up other than a demon will have their life force stolen."

Jess nodded and cast the spell.

"Cool. Thanks, Jess. I'm off. Tell Gangrene and Raven not to be too pissed. Tell them it was all my idea and you didn't want to help but I threatened to kill you."

"But you didn't threaten to kill me..."

"Oh good. You never got my note. Forget I said that. Just tell them it wasn't your fault."

"What note?"

Lilith kicked Keshi and the horse started sprinting. Jess watched them go and tried not to laugh.

"That girl is fucking insane. I hope she stays safe up there."

CHAPTER 25

Shadow started circling Raphael and Raphael started circling in the opposite direction. Sarah tried to diffuse the situation.

"Raphael, please don't do this. I won't tell Grandpa. Just go home. We don't have a problem with you."

"You'll address me as Archangel Raphael and I don't care what Gabriel has to say about this. One of his bloodlines is corrupted. He doesn't have the strength to do anything about it so I'm doing him a favor by cutting off the mutilated branch. He has other sons and daughters to succeed him if he ever tires of being an Archangel. Why he chose you as his favorite never made sense to most of the angels anyways."

Shadow snorted.

"You angels really are an upscale bunch… talking about lineages as if we were all horses. Tell me, Raphael. Is the fact that your blood is pure going to make a difference when I spill it all over the ground?"

"Silence, abomination. Michael should have killed your father the moment he found out that he existed. I will not allow your mixed-breed race to continue. I must restore order. You don't stand a chance against me. The last time I was here, I captured Asmodeus and threw him back in Hell."

Shadow chuckled.

"I killed Asmodeus. So I guess I finished the half-ass job you did. You're welcome."

"Your arrogance will be your downfall, mutt."

Sarah shook her head.

"I'm not going to watch this. This is wrong."

She turned and ran. Shadow didn't even turn to watch her leave. Raphael placed his fingers in his mouth and whistled. A white stallion engulfed in white flames started charging in Raphael's direction. Raphael was able to jump into the air and mount the horse without it slowing down. He charged after Sarah. Shadow turned to Muan.

"I really hate to ask this but we don't have any horses here with us. We need to cut him off. Do you mind?"

Muan turned into a moose. Shadow gave him an annoyed look and he turned back into a demon.

"What? I don't like being a horse. I can run at about the same speed as a moose… plus I'll have antlers. That's way cooler."

"Fine. Moose it is. Let's go."

Muan grinned and turned back into a moose. Shadow climbed on his back and Muan ran after the Raphael. Several minutes later, they caught up to a perplexed Raphael. His horse was nowhere in sight and he was searching the area.

"Where did she go?"

Shadow dismounted and Muan changed back into a demon.

"Sarah's too bright to be tracked down by you. She wanted to get away and she did. It really reveals you for the coward that you are. I'm your most difficult opponent and you chose to run from me to prey on Gabriel's granddaughter. Pathetic."

"Are you in that much of a hurry to die, young creature? Very well. I will grant you your death wish. Before I do, we need to find a way to keep your pygmy friend occupied."

Raphael pointed at a nearby tree. The tree's roots pulled out of the soil as if they were legs. The tree creature started advancing towards Muan and Shadow. Muan wasn't sure how to respond. The tree crept forward until Muan finally pointed at the tree and looked at Raphael.

"That's messed up. What the hell is wrong with you angels?"

Muan turned into an elephant and started charging the tree. Shadow turned his attention back to Raphael.

"I didn't need his help."

"It doesn't matter. I don't trust your kind. It's better to keep your little friend occupied. Now go ahead and take a free shot."

Raphael held out his arms, exposing his armor. Shadow charged and swung Damnation with all of his might. Raphael brought up his shield just in time to meet the strike. The shield split in two and both Raphael and Shadow flew back several paces.

To avoid Raphael, Sarah had run into the forest and hid. She had made it ahead of the Archangel's horse and had climbed a tree. Once inside, she pointed her sword at the heavens and shot ice directly up. Gabriel appeared within seconds.

"What's wrong? Why did you signal me?"

"Raphael found out what I am. He's been following us and he tracked down Bumalin. He tried to kill me and Shadow is fighting him right now."

Gabriel didn't have time to respond. The two were interrupted as an elephant crashed through the forest, smashing an uprooted tree against the ground with his trunk. Gabriel waved his hand and the tree burst into wood splinters. The elephant turned back into Muan, gasping for breath.

"Sarah! Shadow's taking him on. I'm pretty sure he's going to kill Raphael. Should we let him?"

Muan noticed Gabriel.

"Oh… hello. Didn't know you were here."

"You think Shadow should kill an Archangel?"

"I think it's an option after all the things he said. He isn't going to stop. If he didn't have such an intense desire to kill us, he would already be back in Heaven spilling the secret you've protected for years."

"Then we only have two options. We either kill Raphael or…"

"Grandpa!"

Sarah looked shocked.

"There's another way we could end this and spare his life. Muan, turn into a bird and find Bumalin. Now."

Shadow and Raphael continued to battle. Since Shadow's armor used to belong to Michael, it had done its job admirably and blocked all incoming shots from Raphael. However, Raphael had managed to knock Shadow's right gauntlet off and cut his right hand deeply with his blade. Shadow had lashed out after the hit and punched Raphael hard in the face. He followed it up with a slash from Damnation. Raphael stumbled back with a broken nose and a cut across his left eye. The two continued to circle each other while they caught their breath.

Gabriel ran out of the forest and stood next to Shadow. Raphael couldn't believe it.

"You side with these traitors? I will have you stripped of your rank! You will be an outcast with the rest of them! Michael will throw you from the heavens for this…"

"I'm not here to side with anyone. I'm here to put an end to this. Shadow is doing something admirable and you need to let him continue his mission."

"I'm going back to Heaven right now."

Gabriel closed the distance between himself and Raphael. He tripped Raphael and brought his head down hard on the solid ground. He then held his sword to the Archangel's neck.

"Do not teleport away. We're discussing this."

"You attacked me! How dare you…"

Shadow walked up to Raphael and punched him across the face as hard as he could. The Archangel blacked out. Gabriel looked at Shadow disapprovingly.

"We couldn't trust him. He would have teleported away the second he stopped bitching about how unfair life is and whatever the hell else he was saying. I kind of tuned out."

Gabriel looked like he had more to say, but Sarah and Muan arrived followed by a frightened Bumalin.

"What part of leave me the fuck alone do you guys not understand? I want nothing more to do with this asshole. I barely escaped the last time *after* he got the information he wanted. He wanted to torture me!"

Gabriel nodded.

"I understand. We're giving you a chance to take your revenge. You can take any memories from him related to nephilim. When you're done, I don't want him to even know what a nephilim is. It's either that or we have to kill him so…"

Bumalin crossed his arms.

"I like the kill him option. That would be revenge."

Muan walked up to Raphael and kicked him in the face.

"I'm with Bumalin on this one. This asshole made me fight a tree. A fucking tree! Who the fuck does that?"

Bumalin hit Muan hard across the back and laughed.

"Listen to the little witch doctor. We should just put this asshole down right now."

Sarah shook her head.

"Do either of you comprehend the amount of attention it would draw if we were to kill an Archangel? Grandpa's right. Wipe his memory and wash our hands of this whole thing. We don't need to give any other angels another reason to hunt us. Shadow, what do you think?"

Shadow thought for a minute, knowing that whatever he said wouldn't sit well with one side. He didn't want to be the deciding vote but he knew what he had to do.

"As much as I would like to kill him, it's an unnecessary distraction. He's in our way. We don't need more angels getting in our way because we killed him. I need to kill Azazel, Abaddon, and the Dragon. I don't need this guy's armies coming down here and becoming obstacles. Bumalin, wipe his memory."

"Can I wipe all of your memories? I'm really fucking sick of being involved with this mess. I keep running away and either you or someone you pissed off keeps finding me. My life was so much simpler before all of this."

"You're welcome to come with us. We'll protect you."

"No. I'll wipe his memory of nephilim and then all of you need to seriously stay the fuck away. Seriously. No more. Do we have a deal?"

Gabriel nodded and shook Bumalin's hand.

"Before you do this, the same conditions apply. Raphael has a blocked off memory. It's similar to the one I have. The memory of when he became an Archangel. Don't try to take it. I'll know if you do and I'll have to kill you. Understood?"

"Sure. Whatever. I don't care what happened on the day you guys became Archangels. Just let me do this so I can leave."

Bumalin reached down and placed his hand on Raphael's forehead. He extracted several memories and put them in a vial. He turned to leave but turned back and faced the group one more time.

"Seriously. Stop looking for me. I don't want to see any of you ever again."

Bumalin turned and ran away. Muan looked at Shadow.

"Want me to follow him?"

Shadow grinned.

"No. We can find him again if we need to. Let him run away for now."

CHAPTER 26

When Keshi crossed the border between Earth and Hell, Lilith decided to rest. It was more riding than she was used to since she had taken her mother's scythe and could teleport where she wanted to go. Lucia was also cranky. Lilith produced a bottle from her bag and Lucia sucked contentedly on the soul of a departed thief.

Lilith wasn't sure what to do now that she had made it to Earth. She was used to following Shadow and Leech. Both of them were much better at planning. She preferred to act impulsively and then deal with future consequences as they came. She had gotten her way. Gangrene and Raven hadn't followed her to Earth. It dawned on Lilith for the first time that in being selfless for once and letting Gangrene and Raven stay in Hell to support Murmur, Jess, and Aim, she may have ultimately screwed herself and her daughter.

Lucia put the bottle down and started to shiver. Lilith realized that they hadn't come to Earth in the same way Leech had taken them. She didn't know where they were exactly, but she knew that they weren't in the Caribbean. The land wasn't completely ice but it was snowing. Lilith wrapped Lucia in another blanket. She knew young demons, and she assumed young nephilim, weren't as immune to the elements of Earth as they would be when they grew up.

Fire. That's what she needed. She needed to figure out how to start a fire. It should be simple enough. She'd seen Leech do it. She'd seen Jess do it. Her kid needed some warmth. She looked up at Keshi.

"Everything would be easier if you could talk to me."

Lilith fumbled through her bag and found the rocks Leech had used to start fires. She also found Leech's guns. She considered gathering some sticks and flammable material and then shooting them. After she gathered some twigs and stacked them in a pile, she pointed the gun. Before she fired, she realized that it probably wasn't a good idea to discharge a firearm close to her child. She moved Lucia, but then abandoned the idea altogether.

Lilith next tried the rocks from Leech's belongings. She hit the rocks together and produced sparks. After hitting them together several times near the sticks, nothing happened. She put the rocks back in the bag. Lucia looked like she was about to cry.

"It's ok. I'll figure it out. Give me some time."

Lilith removed a short staff from her bag that Jess had given her. It was about a third the length of the Monkey King staff. She also found a short book of essential spells. She hoped it started on the level of an absolute beginner. As she thumbed through the pages, she realized that it had pictures of simple wand movements and simple spells. She turned the pages until she found an entry labeled "Fire." She spun the staff in a circle around her pile of sticks, double-checking that she had the movement right.

"Ignis."

The sticks caught on fire and Lilith had a small fire going within minutes. Lucia watched the flames dance with fascination. Lilith replaced the handles of her whips with the small staff so that she could not only send flames down the whip, but other things as she practiced and learned new spells. Lilith and Lucia continued south for a few days. Lilith could feel the presence of a nephilim. She wasn't sure that it was Shadow, but didn't really know what else she should do so she continued to follow it.

It was about four days after they arrived on Earth that their luck took a turn for the worse. Lilith had created a fire, as was the routine, and Lilith, Lucia, and Keshi were about to go to sleep for the night when Lilith heard a noise that sounded like a branch snapping. Lilith was up within seconds, her whips in hand. For the first time in a long time, she was actually afraid. Lilith picked up Lucia and moved her closer to the snoring Keshi before looking for the source of the noise. After a few minutes of searching, she thought she saw a blade illuminated in the moonlight. She struck at it with one of her whips, but it was gone before she connected with anything solid. After another minute of silence, Lilith started to wonder if she was imagining things. She had kept Keshi and Lucia in her sight the entire time but decided to head back and keep them closer. She walked quickly but switched to a full-speed run when she heard Lucia start crying and saw Keshi jump to her feet. When she arrived back at camp, Lilith saw an angel holding Lucia and trying to simultaneously nurse an injury on her right hand.

"What the hell did you do to that blanket? It's like the thing bit me!"

"Give me my baby back and I'll let you walk away uninjured."

The angel grinned.

"Not going to happen, Lilith."

"You know who I am?"

"Indeed. I also know that this is the child of Leech the angel slayer. We've been tracking you for days."

"Why do the angels care what I'm doing?"

"Nephilim are an abomination and we're here to put you down."

"You keep saying 'we.' I only see one of you."

The angel grinned again.

"Just know that there's an entire army of angels on your tail. The commander will be very interested in the scouting report I prepare later tonight."

"That's not going to happen."

Lilith prepared to strike, but the angel scout dropped Lucia before she had a chance. The angel's hand burst into flames. Lilith acted swiftly, wrapping one of her whips around Lucia before she hit the ground and pulling the baby towards her. She was able to catch the crying infant and held her in one arm while she prepared to strike again with her other hand. Before she could make a move, the angel had run off.

CHAPTER 27

Gangrene pointed his scythe at Jess's neck as soon as he entered Dagon's.

"This is unforgivable. You *attacked* me. I'm not just going to let this go."

Murmur stepped in front of Gangrene.

"You're mad at the wrong person. Everyone from Vixen's lineage is insane and you know it."

"Oh so now you're insulting my girlfriend too? Did I strike a nerve, Murmur? Are you banging Jess and developing *feelings* for her?"

Murmur huffed and Jess almost thought she saw smoke coming from his nostrils. She pushed him backwards and shoved him towards his chair. Murmur didn't fall in to it, but kept his eyes on Gangrene. Jess put her scythe on the table.

"I'm sorry, Gangrene. I really am. Let me explain my side of things before you threaten to slice me up. Fair enough?"

Gangrene stomped over to the table and sat down. Jess looked at Murmur.

"You sit, too. It doesn't help when you're staring at him menacingly. All of us need to be on the same page."

Murmur reluctantly sat but he kept his eyes on Gangrene and his hand rested on his scythe without gripping it. Jess sat as well.

"Again… I'm really sorry. Let's clear up a few things though. First, I didn't attack you. I restrained you. If Lilith had asked me to attack you, I would have said no."

"A technicality. One which I really don't care about right now."

"Second, you should have known something was coming. Her whole 'I'm going to knock them out with tea' plan was fucking ridiculous. I told her as much when she explained it to me."

"We're not talking about what Lilith did. That's an entirely different conversation that I'll have with *Lilith* the next time I see her. Yes, I'm pissed at her… but I'm pissed at you, too. Why don't we stay on *that* topic?"

"Fair enough. Then you need to understand where I'm coming from. Lilith lost her army. Lilith lost Leech. Lilith made a deal where she gave up her scythe and her major demon position *after* she helped me get my new mage staff. I tried to bring Leech back and failed. So I still owed her and she pointed it out to me. It's even a possibility that even *Shadow* doesn't have enough strength to spare to bring Leech back.

So I'm sorry, but I did what needed to be done to keep control of my armies and my scythe. You would have done the same in my position."

Murmur nodded.

"Not only that, these nephilim problems don't concern us. You're one of us, Gangrene. You're a demon. We need you down here to keep Nightmare and Astaroth…"

"I'm not a fucking chess piece! I won't be forced to stay down here because it suits *your* plan! I've worked with Shadow and Leech. They have my respect. Give me one fucking reason why I should respect *you*!"

Murmur took his hand off his scythe and took a long drink from his mug. He wiped his mouth with the back of his hand.

"I don't have a great answer for you. Right now I'm not asking you to respect me. I just need you to trust me and to help me. Why should you trust and help me? Because Shadow did. Because Leech did. Because I helped both of them enough times and all of us benefited. I have a plan, Gangrene, and you're an important part of it. If you're really that worried about Lilith then I understand. Go to Earth. See how she's doing."

Murmur had put it all on the table, hoping Gangrene wanted to hear his plan and didn't just stomp off. He was having a hard time reading Gangrene's expression.

"Fine. Let's hear it."

"We can preemptively attack Nightmare and Astaroth. Even with the four of us, we'll need the element of surprise. Their armies are huge. Once we kill them, we have the Dragon make the three of you officially major demons when he returns."

"That puts me as the odd man out again. Jess and Aim worked for you as middle demons for a long time. They'll do whatever you say. What's to stop the three of you from turning on me?"

Jess looked confused.

"Why would we? You aren't the enemy here. Nightmare and Astaroth picked this fight."

"I know Murmur's history. Shadow and Leech both told me how he became a major demon. Does a middle demon named Tannin ring any bells?"

"He embarrassed me. What I did to him was retribution. I deserved Leviathan's spot."

"So you still think you didn't do anything wrong. How can I work with you? If I go over to Nightmare and Astaroth, we could crush the three of you for sure. Aim doesn't even have a scythe yet."

Murmur put his hand back on his scythe but Jess touched his arm and shook her head.

"You'd be in the exact same position after you won only it would be worse. Nightmare hates Shadow and Leech. They'd kill you the moment you had served your purpose."

"So what you're saying is I should take my army to Earth and find Shadow and Lilith. That way you dumbasses can work all this shit out for yourselves and I don't have to be a part of it."

"Don't be like that, Gangrene. We're friends of Shadow and Lilith. We wouldn't turn on you."

"Based on what? I still don't see why I should trust you. I may have his scythe, but I'm not Leech. I'm not Shadow. I'm stuck in a really shitty situation down here and it's making me want to go to Earth."

"What can we do to make you stay? How can we earn your trust?"

Gangrene got up from his seat.

"I'm not sure right now. I'll get back to you."

Gangrene walked out and headed towards Lilith's house. Raven had claimed it as her own until her sister returned.

Aim walked slowly with his arms behind his back as he watched his sniper team train. They were able to hit their targets with a kill shot about half the time. They were getting better. He no longer thought of them as a disaster. He saw his sister approaching and walked in her direction.

"Well? How did it go?"

"Not great. He said he might even go to Earth. You need to be ready to take him out if he attempts to leave."

"And you're ok with that?"

"Bare minimum we need his scythe. If he leaves, Nightmare and Astaroth will crush us without it. I'd say shoot to injure but if we can't take him alive…"

"War is a bitch. I know it sucks but it has to be done. Murmur is right. He needs to help us one way or another."

Jess hesitated, but then nodded.

"I know. It would be a good idea to watch him 24/7 from now on. We can't let him sneak up to Earth."

Aim nodded and called his sniper team over to him.

"Guys, we have a mission. Get the rest of the army and then follow me."

CHAPTER 28

"I'm not going back!"

Sarah pointed Azazel's heavenly sword at Gabriel. She liked the feel of it, it was a powerful weapon. Gabriel brushed it aside and looked disappointed.

"You're being disrespectful. I've let you run around down here with Shadow long enough. Raphael nearly killed all three of you."

"No he didn't. He never found me when I ran off, Muan never even fought him and I still believe Shadow could have killed him."

"This is not up for debate, young lady. I have to protect you. You're coming with me."

Gabriel tried to grab Sarah's arm but Shadow got in the way.

"As long as I'm here, this *is* up for debate. All three of us are fine. Sarah only called you down here so I wouldn't kill an Archangel. I appreciate your help. Wiping his memory was a good idea. I don't think the alternative would have been so bad though. Raphael is an absolute asshole."

Shadow almost continued with "reminds me of all the Archangels," but decided not to say that out loud. Gabriel looked like he was losing his patience.

"I know you're trying to do a good thing down here, Shadow, but I have to protect my granddaughter. You even know why now. If anyone else finds out she's a nephilim…"

"I'll kill them. Problem solved."

"I'm sorry, but this is still not up for debate."

Shadow knew he couldn't convince Gabriel that he would protect her unless he told a lie. Fortunately, he was very good at lying.

"You're right. It isn't up for debate because she's carrying my child. She's staying with me."

Muan's jaw dropped open and stayed there. Sarah's eyes went wide with shock. Gabriel looked angrier than Shadow had ever seen him.

"I'm going to give you one chance to take that back. Tell me you're lying."

Sarah walked up next to Shadow and locked her fingers with his. She put a hand on her stomach.

"I had hoped you would be happy for us, Grandpa. You'll have another great-grandchild. An extremely powerful one. It kicks up a storm."

Gabriel drew his sword.

"I am going to kill you. There's no stopping me this time."

Shadow didn't draw Damnation. He held up a hand and stood where he was.

"I understand that you're angry."

"You don't know the half of it, boy."

"Talk a minute to think about this. She can't give birth to a *nephilim* in *Heaven*. Then her secret would be out for sure. I imagine our kid is going to look a little more like a demon than its mother. You have a safe way to explain that?"

Gabriel stopped.

"Then what do you propose? I have to get back to Heaven and watch Raphael. On the off chance Bumalin didn't get everything, I need to be there to stop him from saying anything."

"Sarah stays with me. Naturally she won't fight anymore. Muan will be her permanent bodyguard and I will watch them both. I will give my life to stop anything from harming her. You have my word."

Gabriel thought this over.

"Fine. Just know that I am NOT OK WITH THIS!"

Gabriel's voice boomed and shook the Earth. Muan fell over backwards.

"Your have my word, Gabriel. She will be safe here with me. Maybe one day I can even call you 'Grandpa.'"

Sarah squeezed Shadow's hand tightly.

"Don't push it. Now's not the time for jokes."

Gabriel turned his back on them and ascended back to Heaven without another word.

Muan approached Sarah with his head hanging in shame. He refused to look up.

"I am so sorry I made you take drugs. I was trying to save your life. I had no idea you were pregnant. Please forgive me."

Muan kneeled at Sarah's feet. Shadow burst out laughing and Sarah tried to hide the smile that crept across her face but ultimately couldn't. Muan looked up.

"You guys are taking this way better than I thought you would. So she's not pregnant, is she?"

"No, Muan, I'm not. Shadow took a gamble and told a lie. It was the only way to get Grandpa to go back to Heaven without me."

"Fine. I want to be the bodyguard when you guys actually have a kid though. Deal?"

Shadow and Sarah exchanged an uncomfortable look. Muan laughed.

"Alright. Back to business. Muan I actually have a job for you. I've been sensing that Lilith is back on Earth. She's getting further and further away from us. I don't know where exactly she is but I know it's somewhere cold. I'm guessing she can't sense me as strongly. My powers are developing faster. I need you to find her and get her here. I don't know why she's back on Earth but I want to make sure she's safe. She actually has a kid that we need to protect."

Muan nodded.

"No problem. I'll find her."

Before Muan could transform, Sarah put her hand on his shoulder.

"Muan, how do you keep tracking everyone down?"

"I… uh… I'm just a good tracker."

"I'm sure that's true, but you're abnormally fast at finding people. Are you using that potion you showed us that lets you track angels and demons?"

Muan looked back at the ground.

"No…"

"Tell me the truth."

"Ok fine. It's been helpful, hasn't it?"

"I don't recall giving you anything to use to track me… so how have you been doing it?"

Muan turned into a crow and flew away. Shadow laughed.

"Uh oh. Little thieving Muan has been caught."

"You're ok with this?"

"I knew he stole something from me a while back and I knew what he was using for. Made him good at getting stuff back to me. Not a big problem. He probably doesn't have anything of yours because you've been with me for a while now."

Sarah looked like she wanted to ask something but she was silent.

"You want to talk about something else?"

"Yeah. How did that lie come to your head so quickly?"

"Does it matter? It worked. Gabriel bought it."

"Do you want kids someday?"

"Fuck no. I'm going to be a target for the rest of my life. It's bad enough that I have to protect you and a kid…"

"Woah. Hold on there, buddy. You *don't* need to protect me. The fight with Scapegoat was a fluke. I was winning. I can protect myself."

"I'm not saying you can't… it's just better if I…"

"If you what? I just told you that I don't need your protection."

"Did I strike a nerve when I said you were pregnant?"

Sarah didn't respond. She turned away from Shadow and crossed her arms. Shadow thought for a minute about what he should say because the last few things he had said had not helped the situation.

"Look, I didn't know you thought about stuff like that…"

"Oh shut up. Don't flatter yourself. You're just so *infuriating* sometimes. I want kids someday but I'm not having them with *you* so just forget about it. You're an ass. Forget we ever had this conversation."

Shadow knew joking around was probably a bad idea, but he didn't see how he could make it any worse at this point.

"Changed my mind. I want to knock you up now. I can see it means a whole lot to you and…"

Sarah flipped him off.

"Come on… you know you want to be the mother of Shadow, Jr. It'll be awesome. He'll be running around all the time with ice in his hands and teleporting and…"

"Did I strike a nerve when I said I didn't want to have kids with you?"

Shadow grinned and Sarah fought hard to stay mad at him. She walked away quickly so Shadow wouldn't see her smile.

CHAPTER 29

Lilith had been trying to figure out how the angel's hand had burst into flames for days. She still had no clue how it happened. As she returned from a small town, having collected a soul from a recently departed lawyer, she felt something warm on the back of her neck. She carried Lucia in a backpack, so she was immediately worried. She took the backpack off and saw that Lucia's hands were on fire. The baby didn't appear to be in pain and was actually giggling. Lilith clapped the fire out with an old rag and Lucia started crying. Lilith finally figured it out.

"Can you make fire without a spell?"

Lucia looked up at her mother. Lilith put the rag away. Lucia held out her hands and both of them erupted in white flames. She started giggling again.

"Well I guess you can start the fire at night from now on."

Lucia clapped and the fire went away. She looked like she was about to cry but Lilith loaded the human soul into a bottle and gave it to Lucia. Lucia sucked contentedly on her lunch.

"Damn. Didn't know she could do that. That's really cool."

Lilith had been following a feeling for days that a nephilim was nearby. She hoped it was Shadow but was prepared to be wrong. She had been brushing up on her attack skills and minor spells from the book Jess had given her. At this point, she knew she was close and could reach the nephilim within a day.

That night, before she went to sleep, Lilith saw something glowing in the moonlight. As she looked closer, she realized it was a set of eyes and they were moving closer. She reached for her whip but then she saw another pair of eyes and then another.

She grabbed Lucia, hopped on Keshi and rode as fast as she could away from the spot. The ground rattled, Keshi stumbled, and Lilith and the baby went flying into the air. Lilith was able to land with Lilith on her feet, but Keshi rolled before lying still on the ground.

"What kind of coward attacks a mother and her child at night?"

"Normally, I would be glad to kill you in the daylight. We're pressed for time."

Lucia lit a fire in her hands and Lilith recognized the Archangel, Uriel.

"I see. The angel kind of coward. Makes sense. A demon would at least have the balls to challenge me to a fair fight."

"You know that's a lie. A demon would have stabbed you in your sleep."

"And you were about to…?"

Uriel laughed.

"Fair point. We don't deal fairly with nephilim. You're part of a plague that needs to be wiped from this Earth. My scout told me we were close. I'm glad I finally caught up to you."

Lilith glanced at Keshi. The horse was still down. Uriel wasted no time. He drew his sword and moved in quickly for the kill. Lilith shielded her daughter and waited for the end. When Uriel struck, his blade was met by another blade. Something around the same size as Uriel struck at him and shoved him back. Lilith could also hear the angel army running around in panic. She saw what was happening, but didn't quite understand it.

She recognized the two creatures attacking the angels but couldn't remember their names or where she had seen them before. One of them was putting angels to sleep. The other was raising sleeping angels from their sleep and turning them against their fellow angels. A majority of the army turned and ran. Uriel saw his army retreating and gritted his teeth. He pointed his sword at the creature that had saved Lilith's life.

"This isn't over, Samael. We haven't forgotten your treachery."

Uriel disappeared. Samael helped Lilith to her feet.

"Are you ok?"

Lilith just stared at him.

"We're not here to hurt you. In fact I'm…"

"You're my father."

Samael looked surprised.

"I was going to say I'm familiar with nephilim. I was going to wait until you knew me a little better before revealing that I was your father. How did you find out?"

"Does it matter? I know. You let my mother take me back to Hell and I had a slight angelic tint to my countenance so she threw me out. I was raised by a minor demon named Panic. I would say thanks for saving me, but I feel it's you're still in my debt, not the other way around."

"I would agree… and I would like to make up for it. I've wanted to come meet you many times but being tied to me would only make you more of a target. I know you were looking for nephilim and I believe you were drawn towards my sons. They're your half-brothers. Lilith, meet Hypnos and Thanatos."

"Right. Now I remember. They saved me and said they were doing it as a favor to Shadow. I'm…"

Lilith looked at Thanatos.

"Maybe I took a hit to the head… but I'm pretty sure Leech killed you."

Thanatos laughed.

"The nephilim of death does not die. I laugh in the face of death."

Thanatos pulled out a mirror and laughed at his own reflection. Lilith noticed Lucia yawn loudly. Hypnos nodded.

"I apologize. That was probably my fault. She's just a baby nephilim and I tend to have that effect on lesser creatures. I'm Hypnos, the nephilim of sleep. In the past, I have pursued angels and demons that were pursuing you and your friends and put them down long enough for all of you to escape. You were even unaware that some of them were pursuing you."

"Wrong. Shadow is aware of everything that's going on."

"I stand corrected. I don't really understand the limits of Shadow's powers. I'm not even sure that he does."

Lilith looked back at Samael.

"Hypnos I'm ok with. He's polite. Thanatos is weird and I don't like you either."

Hypnos tapped Lilith on her shoulder.

"Might I hold the young one? I don't have any nieces… or I didn't. I didn't really have any nieces before… just now."

"Alright, but just you. I don't want the 'whatever the hell of death' over there touching her."

Thanatos was oblivious. He was still holding a mirror in front of his face and chuckling at his reflection. Lilith handed Lucia over to Hypnos and she promptly fell asleep in his arms. He rocked her back and forth.

"Uncle Hypnos. So cool. Thanatos, can you believe we're uncles?"

Thanatos looked over at Hypnos and put the mirror away.

"I want to hold her next."

Lilith shook her head.

"Nope. Not happening. Now someone explain to me what's going on here."

Samael sighed.

"I'm sorry we had to finally meet like this… but we're here to help. Not only you… but your friends as well. I believe in what Leech and Shadow were doing to put an end to Abaddon's chaos."

It dawned on Lilith that Samael was probably a powerful fallen angel. She removed Leech's head from the sack and held it out to him.

"I imagine you're very powerful. I need someone powerful to help me bring Leech back. I don't know where Shadow is. Can you help me?"

Samael grabbed the head with one of his large hands. He fell to one knee as the head started to drain his strength. A ghostly body appeared under Leech's head and Lilith clapped her hands and jumped up and down with joy. Her joy was short-lived. Samael dropped Leech's head and it rolled on the ground. The body disappeared. When Samael got back to his feet, he was breathing heavily.

"I'm… sorry, Lilith. I don't… seem to have the strength… I had when I was… younger."

Lilith retrieved the head and put it back in the sack.

"It was a long shot. I just figured it was worth a try. That's why I'm trying to find Shadow. He can bring Leech back."

"We're here to help you. We can track Shadow and take you to him."

Lilith turned to go, but Samael placed a hand on her shoulder.

"Before we do that… can I hold my granddaughter? I promise I'll be very careful."

Lilith looked at him skeptically.

"You can trust me. I tried to bring Leech back. We stopped the angels from killing you. I promise you that we're here to help."

Lilith considered her father's words briefly, then took Lucia and placed her in Samael's arms. Samael looked tried to stop the grin from spreading across his face, but he couldn't.

CHAPTER 30

Aim and his snipers had been watching Gangrene in shifts. They had a few false alarms where they thought Gangrene was on his way to Earth but he always returned before leaving Hell. Aim started to wonder if Gangrene knew that they were watching him. Gangrene was acting suspicious this morning. He stepped outside of his tent and put on a hooded cloak. He immediately started making his way towards one of the portals to Earth.

Aim had considered killing Gangrene and taking his scythe. He could make up a story and convince Murmur and Jess that it was necessary. As long as he could hide the truth, no one would be the wiser. With Gangrene's forces added to his own, Aim would command an army larger than any in Hell apart from the Dragon's forces.

"Follow him. If he even gets close to the portal this time, we're surrounding him and taking him down. I'm tired of allowing him such a long leash. He's clearly planning to go to Earth."

Aim's sniper team nodded and started packing up their gear. They were ready to go in less than a minute. Aim mounted a horse and took off. His snipers followed.

Gangrene had known that he was being watched since his last meeting with Murmur and Jess. He had even spotted his tail on several occasions and was convinced that he had lost them completely at least twice. Gangrene was convinced that he knew a lot more ways to get to Earth than Aim, Jess, or Murmur did. He had considered making a run for the surface, but he couldn't sneak his army up there. Last night he had come up with a plan to deal with his tail permanently. He hoped it was just one of the three. He didn't want to deal with Aim, Jess, and Murmur simultaneously, but he figured he wouldn't have to. One of them had to be preparing for war with Nightmare and Astaroth.

As Gangrene approached the portal, Aim stepped out from the shadows and blocked his path. He pointed his gun at Gangrene's face.

"Good morning, Aim. Just you following me? Your sister and the big guy busy with other things?"

Aim was unsure how to respond. Playing mind games was not one of his skills.

"I don't need them to deal with you. You're making a run for Earth. I was told I could take you out if you tried."

"I don't believe that. I've tested you a few times. You've never stepped out and confronted me. Thanks for confirming it's just you though. That makes me a lot more confident in my response."

Aim felt a slight tinge of fear creep up his spine, but he held his hand steady on the trigger.

"You don't have a response. I caught you by surprise."

Gangrene laughed and drew his scythe.

"Wow. I thought you were better than that. I guess your team never told you that they completely lost me at least twice. They were probably scared to report it. I've known you were following me… and you know what else? I hope you try to kill me. I'm capturing your sister as we speak."

"You're a liar. Jess is fine."

"Is she? Doesn't it bother you that my army hasn't intervened and tried to cut you off?"

"We caught you by surprise. You aren't going to talk your way out of this."

"Then take your shot. Make it a good one, though. I trained under both Shadow and Leech. If you miss, I will kill you."

Gangrene adopted a defensive position and hoped that Raven could deliver on her promise to capture Jess. There was no other way to diffuse the situation without death.

Gangrene had given Raven the sword he took from Scapegoat and told her to lead his armies towards Jess. The plan was to capture her and take her alive to the portal Gangrene would be slowly approaching. She was nervous. Gangrene could be dead or in serious trouble by the time she made it back. She could fail at capturing Jess. Jess could kill her. Above all, she missed Lilith and her niece.

"So… I don't really have a great plan. I'm going to try to talk Jess down and get her to come with us willingly. She let Lilith escape from us a while back and I think she's still feeling guilty. We're only going to attack if she makes the first move. Gangrene will be alright until we get back."

One of Gangrene's soldiers stepped forward and bowed his head briefly in Raven's direction.

"All due respect, is that really our best plan? It would be easier to take her by surprise and bind her. Take her staff. Run her back to Gangrene. Gangrene can only last so long against a group of snipers trained by Aim. Aim isn't running around with a broken rifle now, he has White Death from the Dragon's personal collection."

"What's your name again?"

"Adder, my lady."

Raven noticed that some of the demons had nodded as Adder was speaking. She was slightly concerned.

"We'll go with my plan, Adder. You'll march at the back of the army."

"But…"

"Back of the army. Now."

Adder started to draw his sword but saw Raven's blade start to glow a red-orange. He took his hand off his weapon and let it fall back into its hilt. He started stomping towards the back of the army, grumbling.

"Any other problems?"

Raven's question was met with silence.

"Good. We're almost there. Let's get this done and get back to Gangrene."

CHAPTER 31

"What the hell are those things?"

Sarah pointed at the army they had found. The demons painted themselves, snorted chemicals, and didn't wear any kind of cumbersome armor. She also heard a lot of yelling and fighting amongst the ranks.

"Berserkers. Nightmare converted his entire army into berserkers as well. They're part of the Dragon's army. They used to be led by a demon named Bloodlust, but I heard he was killed by Nightmare. It makes sense, because Nightmare has the berserker staff and he fused it with his scythe. That's how he made the demon scythe, Rage. Azazel crafted it for him."

"So the Dragon is somewhere nearby?"

"I don't think so. I don't really sense him anywhere near us. I wonder if maybe we should ask them."

Shadow got up to walk towards the berserkers, but Sarah grabbed his arm.

"Why would you want to do that? They might kill you or take you to the Dragon."

"I really don't think he's around. I want to know what they're doing. If the Dragon is around, I need to kill him anyways. Besides, I've always wanted to learn how they fight. It'll be worthwhile to talk to them."

Shadow stepped out from his hiding spot and approached the army. He was immediately surrounded. A large demon stepped out to meet him.

"Shadow of the nephilim. What on Earth possessed you to walk into our camp?"

The demon noticed Sarah trailing Shadow and laughed.

"With an angel, no less. Give me one good reason why I shouldn't kill you both and bring your corpses to the Dragon."

"I can think of a few. First, you can't kill me. I have the armor of Michael the Archangel. I've fought the Archangels Gabriel and Raphael and neither of them could kill me. Second, I can always teleport away. I may not be a traditional demon anymore, but I still have my scythe. Third, I'm just here to talk. I don't sense the Dragon anywhere around here and I want to know where he is."

"You want to kill him?"

Shadow nodded. The demon extended his hand and Shadow shook it.

"I am Adrenaline. I took command of the berserkers after Azazel killed Bloodlust, the commander before me."

Shadow looked confused.

"Azazel killed Bloodlust? The rumor in Hell is that Nightmare…"

"Nightmare was fighting him at the time. Azazel snuck up behind him and stopped him. Otherwise, Bloodlust would have destroyed Nightmare before he fell over and died. He was headless and still the berserker staff fueled his rage. He continued to fight on."

"So… you're ok with me killing the Dragon?"

"Yes. I would like you to kill him."

"Why?"

"Ever since Nightmare took our staff, we are no longer in the Dragon's favor. It's not like Nightmare can control us or anything like that, but he still doesn't trust us anymore. He has us hunting nephilim while he marches towards Abaddon with the rest of his armies. So at this point, he doesn't really care what happens to us. We failed to protect the berserker staff and are now a disgraced order."

"I see. Well I know that Nightmare has fused the berserker staff with his scythe. I don't know how you'll ever get it back."

Adrenaline looked at the other berserkers and they all shook their heads.

"The loss of the staff won't be a problem forever, but I won't tell you why, Shadow. We don't trust you. Our purposes may align, but we know you're only after power. My turn to ask some questions. Why are you traveling with an angel?"

"She's the granddaughter of the Archangel Gabriel and she's helping me kill the creatures we've come here to kill."

"And they are?"

"Azazel, Abaddon, and the Dragon."

The berserkers screamed and yelled at the mention of Azazel.

"We have been following Azazel hoping to kill him as well. We heard a rumor that your friend, Leech, had already killed him."

"No, unfortunately. Leech injured him very badly, but he got away. I'm going to kill him for Leech."

"Then two of our enemies are the same. Why do you hunt Abaddon?"

"He's my father. I need to put him down. I can't let him destroy this world. It's my responsibility to stop him because no one else can."

"Admirable. We don't often consider responsibility. Our emotions are much simpler. You kill one of us and we kill you… even if it means another of us dies in the process. Bloodlust should have defeated Nightmare and Azazel needs to die. So now you have your information. I'm not sure how it helped you, but we will let you leave without trying to kill you. You are not our enemy, Shadow."

"Information is not all I was seeking. I'd like your help. I'd like to learn how you fight so I can incorporate the techniques into my own fighting. If necessary, I need to be ready to keep fighting on to kill my foes even if I fall down dead in the end. I've heard of berserkers who fought well past when they should have died. I need to learn how to fight like that and I don't think Nightmare did it the right way."

Adrenaline spit on the ground.

"The berserkers under Nightmare's command are an abomination. They know nothing of our ways or how to channel the rage."

Sarah stepped forward.

"I would like to learn with Shadow."

Adrenaline spit on the ground again.

"We don't train angels. No exceptions. We only spare your life for Shadow's sake."

"We should talk in private, Adrenaline. There's something you should know."

Shadow looked around.

"I won't tell you in front of your entire army."

Adrenaline nodded.

"Back to training!"

The berserkers reluctantly dispersed and resumed training.

"Well? Go ahead then."

"Sarah isn't an angel. She's a nephilim like me. If you're willing to train me then you should be willing to train her."

"The Archangel Gabriel mixed bloodlines with a demon? You lie."

"Not Gabriel. One of his children. It's a secret few know and I will seal it with your death should you ever tell anyone."

"Can you prove it?"

Sarah and Shadow had been practicing a few demon spells in case Sarah had need of them. She summoned ice in her left hand and fire in her right, careful to not let any berserkers other than Adrenaline see her powers. Adrenaline smiled and looked at Shadow.

"Amazing. Your secret is safe with me as long as you rid us of Azazel and restore our name. We will train you."

Sarah stepped in between Shadow and Adrenaline to confirm what he was saying.

"You'll train *both* of us?"

"Both of you. It's not every day that we get to work with nephilim descended from Archangels."

CHAPTER 32

Hypnos had asked Lilith if he could continue to carry Lucia and Lilith had agreed, as long as he didn't hand her over to Thanatos. Thanatos still creeped Lilith out. While Lilith still didn't fully trust them, she felt much better with Samael and her half-brothers around. At least she knew she wouldn't be caught off guard again. The group had been following Samael's lead for several days now. Samael stopped suddenly.

"What's wrong?"

"The angels are still following us. Uriel never went back to Heaven. I think we need to deal with them before we continue towards Shadow."

"There are four of us and a baby."

"You're right. I know it's not fair. We're far more powerful than they are. We don't really have a choice, though. They're going to keep following us until they can ambush us again at night. Angels are generally cowards like that."

Lilith giggled.

"Aren't you an angel, Samael?"

"A fallen angel. There's a difference."

Lilith figured now would be a good time to approach what was likely an uncomfortable subject. She didn't care. He owed her an explanation.

"Why did you hook up with Vixen? That still doesn't make any sense to me. I thought angels weren't drawn in by lust."

"Angels can be tempted and I was obviously not the first to…"

Samael shifted uncomfortably.

"Was it simply an attraction based hook up?"

"Pretty much. I was also curious what it was like to be with a demoness. I like new experiences. I…"

Samael looked over at Lilith and saw that his discomfort was amusing her.

"So this is how you're going to get back at me? Fine."

"Just having some fun. We can move on to easier topics. When did you find out she was pregnant?"

"A few months later. I had spies watching her. They confirmed that she was with child. Of course, I didn't know if it was mine or not."

"When did you realize I was your daughter?"

"Shortly after you were born. I saw you and I tried to take you from her. I almost took you to Heaven. I was talked out of going through with that idea. The angels would have killed you. You look too much like your mother. I returned you to Hell and…"

"You thought Vixen was going to take care of me? She was a vain, jealous…"

"I knew she wouldn't."

Samael hung his head.

"I tried to protect you. After I was cast out of Heaven for my sins, I watched over you every time you came to Earth."

"A lot of good that did me. Did you know I grew up with a minor demon named Panic? I had no real family. All of Vixen's children were jealous of me. I was alone almost all the time."

"I know about all of that."

"How could you know all of that?"

"Because I hired Panic to take care of you and I blackmailed your mother to keep your identity a secret. I didn't want word getting out that you were a nephilim."

Lilith stood and scrutinized Samael. Her instincts told her that he was lying.

"You hired Panic to protect me?"

"I did. He reported to me on a regular basis and told me how you were doing. He sent me pictures. He even stopped me from marching down there and taking you up here to Earth once. He was a good guy and a credit to the race of demons."

"Where's your proof? Can you prove any of this?"

Samael removed a folder from his bag and handed it to Lilith. It was filled with letters in Panic's hand-writing and pictures of Lilith from when she was younger.

"Do you want to know why I got kicked out of Heaven?"

Lilith sat back down and returned the folder to Samael.

"I told them I had a daughter that was half demon, but I refused to acknowledge it as a sin. They told me to deny loving you and that the whole thing could be forgiven. I couldn't do it. I walked out on the angels and came to Earth… then I had your brothers with another demoness and waited."

"Waited for what?"

"For the right time to let you know who I was. To let you know that even though you made your own friends, you always had a family that loved you, too."

Lilith could feel the tears rolling down her cheeks. She scooted next to Samael and hugged him.

"Protecting me is going to be hard."

"Why's that?"

"I'm kind of insane and I act on impulse. I think I get that from Vixen."

Samael laughed.

"No, my child. You get that from both of us."

The next morning, Lilith sat down with Samael, Hypnos, and Thanatos to plan their attack on Uriel and his angels. Samael took the lead.

"What we have to do is capture or kill Uriel. They'll scatter in fear if we can pull that off. Nothing short of that will get them to stop. Any thoughts?"

Lilith looked at her half-brothers.

"Question. How far-reaching are their powers?"

Thanatos was holding something under his cloak and looking at it from time to time. He would grin when he saw it. Lilith assumed it was a mirror. Hypnos answered her question.

"We have to come into contact with them. Our powers only work through touch. They multiply after contact, though. If Thanatos touches someone long enough, he can kill them and I can put angels and demons into comas."

"That's too bad. Leech's powers were long range and more amplified than that."

Thanatos took this as a personal insult.

"Trust me, Lilith, we're more powerful than Leech ever was."

"That's hard to believe considering the fact that Leech took out an entire nephilim army and severely injured Azazel on his own."

"I would have killed Azazel."

"Then why haven't you? You've had plenty of opportunities!"

Lucia started to cry when she heard her mother raise her voice. Hypnos started rocking her in his arms.

"Enough, guys. You're upsetting my niece."

Thanatos looked like he wanted to continue but Samael looked at him and shook his head.

"We will not insult the memory of one of the most powerful demons to ever walk the Earth. Leech was every bit the fighter that his grandfather was."

Lilith was immediately distracted by the tangent.

"You knew Baal?"

"Fairly well. Fought him plenty of times. He even gave me something to remember him by."

Samael removed his gauntlet and revealed a long scar across his palm.

"Did you give him something to remember you by?"

Samael grinned.

"Of course. Long scar across his lower back. We're scar buddies."

Lilith giggled. Thanatos looked like he wanted to get back on the subject of who was more powerful. Hypnos spoke before he had the opportunity.

"My powers are growing. Anything in my general vicinity tends to be more tired and I can put this little angel to sleep without touching her."

Hypnos tickled Lucia and she giggled. She grabbed his hand and it started to turn red. He pulled his hand back before she could fully set it on fire. Hypnos grinned sheepishly. Samael took control of the discussion back.

"I do think we have a way to win this without too much effort. I still have an angel's ring of distraction. Lilith can wear it and I think she's powerful to make the entire army look at her. Once all eyes are on her, Hynos and Thanatos can put everyone to sleep or down for good. I'll take on Uriel while the three of you deal with the army. Join me when you're finished and the four of us will take on Uriel."

Samael reached into his pocket and produced an angel's ring of distraction. He handed it to Lilith.

"I'm distracting enough as I am."

Samael laughed.

"Then this will just amplify your natural abilities. Trust me, it'll help. I don't think you've distracted an entire army before… and angels are harder to distract than demons."

"I won't need it."

"Then wear it to humor me. I'm not doing this unless I know you'll have everything you need to be safe."

Lilith sighed and put on the ring of distraction.

CHAPTER 33

Raven approached Jess with her weapons secured on her belt and her hands in the air.

"I have an army with me, but I promise I just want to talk."

"Well that's… unnerving."

"We couldn't think of another way to do this. You see… Gangrene and I know that Aim has been stalking him and it's at the point where Aim is trying to kill him now."

Jess grabbed her scythe. Raven didn't draw her weapon.

"He's still deciding what he wants to do. The problem is that Aim is going to try to kill him anyways. So I'd like you to come with me and talk your brother out of what he's trying to do. There's still the possibility that this can end peacefully."

Jess grabbed her scythe, spun Raven around to face Gangrene's army, and held her scythe's blade to Raven's throat.

"Back off. All of you."

Raven nodded.

"Do it."

Gangrene's army marched back several paces and waited.

"So this is how you want to play this? Gangrene will kill your brother if you hurt me… and then he'll come for you."

"Gangrene can't kill me and he can't kill Murmur."

"Maybe not, but he's comfortable playing a waiting game. Shadow could kill you both. Leech could kill you both once Lilith brings him back. Guess who they would side with if you kill me?"

"You know I don't want to do this, Raven, but Gangrene isn't leaving us a choice. If he leaves with his scythe and his army, Nightmare and Astaroth will slaughter our armies and then all three of us. It's self-preservation. That's all. We just can't let him leave."

"He wasn't planning on leaving until he caught Aim following him."

"Let's just go to Gangrene and Aim and work this whole thing out. My army is coming with us."

Jess hit her scythe against the ground and her demon army started to crawl out of the sand. Jess waved her scythe and Raven's hands were bound. She placed the scythe's blade on the small of Raven's black and nudged her forward.

"Take us back to Gangrene. We'll sort this out."

Aim had attempted to shoot Gangrene three times. Gangrene had blocked the shots with his scythe. He still had the feeling that Aim wasn't really trying to kill him yet. Aim was still afraid and he had good reason to be.

The truth was that Gangrene and Raven were leaning towards respecting Lilith's wishes and staying in Hell until they discovered that Aim was following them. Gangrene couldn't let something like that pass. It was too disrespectful to his position and his army would think he was a coward if he didn't respond appropriately.

Gangrene had waited long enough. He either needed to kill Aim or take him prisoner. He was worried that Jess might have killed Raven. Gangrene started advancing towards Aim. Aim shot the ground immediately in front of Gangrene.

"Don't come any closer."

Gangrene froze for a moment and then took a few more steps. Aim took another shot at the ground in front of Gangrene.

"I'm warning you, Gangrene. Don't do anything stupid. I *will* kill you."

Gangrene took another step and Aim shot him in the foot. Gangrene closed the distance between them and grabbed both of his hands. Aim's hands started to sizzle and melt. He cried out and dropped his gun. Gangrene spun around and placed his scythe's blade on Aim's neck. All of Aim's snipers trained their weapons on Gangrene.

"What did you do to my hands?"

"Melted them a little. It's going to be difficult to shoot anyone for a while."

"What the fuck, Gangrene?"

"You shot me in the foot. I couldn't give you anymore leash. It's time we go see your sister and see if we can still resolve this without me slitting your throat."

"It would be the last time you ever saw your girlfriend."

Gangrene looked down the sandy hill and saw Jess walking behind Raven. Raven hands were bound behind her back. Gangrene saw his army next to Jess's army.

"So do we trade and then battle this out? If I can't get Raven back, I will cut his throat right now and then take his gun. This won't end well for you, Jess."

"I don't want to kill her. We just couldn't let you leave."

"I wasn't planning on leaving until I caught this dumbass following me. Now there's no way I can trust you. You, Aim, and Murmur can kiss my ass!"

Gangrene's army cheered approvingly.

"Nightmare and Astaroth have to be watching this. Whoever wins this fight will still lose. They'll move in to finish off the weakened victor."

"So what do you propose?"

"We trade and then I'll leave with Aim. Our armies will go with us. We won't keep a tail on you anymore. If you want to go to Earth, we won't stop you… but no bloodshed right now. Do we have a deal?"

"The next time I see this asshole following me, I will disintegrate his hands for good. As it is, he's not going to be able to shoot his gun for a couple of weeks. You know what else?"

Gangrene stepped forward and picked up White Death.

"I'm keeping this. It's an annoyance tax for having to deal with the two of you."

"That's not part of our deal."

"I didn't agree to a deal yet. The two of you tried to have me killed and then you kidnapped Raven when she came to talk things over with you. You're lucky I'm not giving you your brother back in three pieces. Those are my terms. If you don't agree, I'll put the two of you down, put your armies down, and then flee to Earth. Once I find Shadow and Leech, I'll be back to take our Murmur. So do we walk away from this or do we end this hear and now?"

"I'll make the trade. Keep the gun."

Aim turned to face Gangrene.

"I don't agree to this. That's *my* gun."

"I didn't ask for your permission, broken sniper. I was negotiating with your sister. Now get the fuck out of my sight before I change my mind."

Gangrene shoved Aim. Aim tripped and fell backwards down the hill, rolling the last few feet. Gangrene's army laughed and cheered. Jess nudged Raven with her scythe and Raven started walking forward. When she came to Aim, she helped him to his feet and Aim returned to his sister. Gangrene kept White Death trained on Jess and Aim until they were out of sight.

Raven kissed Gangrene on the cheek.

"One of your demons wanted to kill them. Did I make a mistake?"

"Nope. You made the right call. I'd trade a bullet in the foot for a legendary weapon any day. We came out way ahead on this."

CHAPTER 34

Once they had been painted with the customary markings of the berserkers, Shadow and Sarah began the training process. Adrenaline started each of them off against one of his berserkers. If they won, he made them face off against another and then another. Sarah made it through about five before she collapsed. Shadow showed no signs of tiring.

"This is when it counts. When you don't have anything left to give. I'll be your next opponent."

Adrenaline was tossed a long stick from one of his berserkers. Sarah used the stick she had been given to slowly climb back to her feet. Adrenaline immediately tripped her. Shadow cloned himself and made the clone continue fighting his opponent. He came over to Sarah's fight to watch. He didn't want to interfere but knew he was going to if they hurt her beyond what he could stand to watch. Adrenaline circled her as she struggled back to her feet.

"Your opponents will not be as forgiving as I am. They will not go easy on you because you've defeated five in a row. So after each opponent, you need to get angrier."

Adrenaline struck again. Sarah tried to raise her stick to blow the incoming blow but she was too slow. Adrenaline struck her hard across the face. She didn't fall, but she stumbled and fell to one knee.

"There's a rage inside all creatures that can help you when you have nothing left to give. It's as powerful as any power ring or drugs we can give you. Ignite that fire and we will show you how to enhance it."

Adrenaline struck again, but Sarah blocked the blow with her stick. She began circling in the opposite direction of Adrenaline. He smiled at her.

"Good. You're angry. Now… do you have enough in you to put me down?"

Adrenaline struck quickly at Sarah's left knee and then kicked her legs out from under her. She fell. Shadow stepped forward to intervene but Adrenaline placed his stick in Shadow's path.

"You need to go back to your own fight."

"No I don't. My clone is doing just fine."

"Sarah will get this and I can't have you here. She needs to learn this on her own. By attempting to intervene, you're denying her the power we can grant."

Sarah got back to her feet.

"It's fine, Shadow. I want to learn. Go back to your fight."

Shadow nodded and fused with his clone. He continued fighting. Adrenaline leaned over Sarah again.

"When you're actually out there fighting, you're not always going to have Shadow to run in and save you. There will come a time when it's all up to you. Either you win the fight or you die. He's going to be up against challenges that will test the limits of his strength."

"I can do this."

Adrenaline decided to change tactics and get meaner.

"No, I don't think you can. It was a mistake to think that an angel can learn how to fight like a demon. You don't have it in you."

Sarah swung with her stick and Adrenaline stepped out of the way. She struggled to keep her footing and not fall down again.

"Pathetic. I guess the 'moral superiority' is all the angels have because you sure as fuck can't fight."

Sarah struck at Adrenaline's face, but he deflected the blow easily.

"Do you even know how to be mad? Are you forgiving me as I'm saying this shit? Wow. If that's all Heaven can produce, the Archangels are more of a joke than I realized."

Sarah attacked and swung several times. Adrenaline blocked each incoming attack and tripped her again. Sarah went down hard.

"Does it bother you that Shadow pities you? That he runs in to fight your battles? That he doesn't think you can take care of yourself? Is that all you are? A pathetic creature that exists because of the pity of the strong?"

"Shut up."

"Oh… did I finally strike a nerve? It's about fucking time. Stop forgiving me and fight!"

Sarah struck and Adrenaline countered the hit. He struck her hard in the legs. Instead of going down, Sarah used the momentum to complete a backflip and came at him again. She struck hard with her stick at his jaw. He wasn't expecting it and Sarah drew blood. She smiled.

"Is that angry enough for you?"

Sarah saw Adrenaline's eyes go red. He hit her twice in the abdomen with his stick and then delivered a roundhouse kick to the right side of her face. Sarah had to struggle to stay conscious. Adrenaline extended a hand and helped her back to her feet.

"That's all it should take to set you off. One strike. One connection. It should anger you to no end. Every time your enemy hits you, it's a personal insult that should make you stronger. If it helps, keep repeating the words in your head that set you off until you don't need them anymore."

"So are we done for the day?"

"You're still standing. I'll throw you back into the rotation. Here's a chance to apply what I just taught you. Find your limits and then ignore them."

Adrenaline put Sarah's stick back in her hand. He walked towards his tent and tapped one of the berserkers on the way. The berserker took Adrenaline's stick and went to fight Sarah. Sarah had the berserker down before Adrenaline reached his tent.

Adrenaline gave orders to have two at a time face off against Shadow. Then three. Then four. Ultimately, Adrenaline realized that Shadow may not have limits. He didn't want Shadow to realize this. It would boost his ego and get in the way of developing fury. Once four failed, Adrenaline sent in five berserkers at a time.

CHAPTER 35

"Uriel, it's time for you to go home. I'll give you a chance to walk away before I kill you and slaughter your army."

Uriel laughed.

"Do you think the threats of an outcast are going to scare me off? We knew you were coming. My army should be finishing off your mixed-blood children and wiping your stain off this Earth as we speak."

"You had your chance. I'll make sure to explain that to anyone who comes to investigate your death."

Samael started by casting a spell that set a blinding light around his sword. Uriel laughed.

"You can't blind an Archangel with light."

Uriel felt a stabbing pain in his lower left shoulder blade. He turned and swung his sword. There was nothing there.

"I wasn't going for a blinding light. I was going for a distraction. You angels are so limited in your thinking process."

Uriel removed the dagger from his shoulder and saw that Samael had retrieved his sword. He had left it in the ground and attacked from another angle while Uriel was looking at the sword.

"Looks like I drew first blood. Not bad for an outcast, right?"

Uriel attacked and Samael blocked the attack with his blade. Uriel followed it up with a head-butt. Samael stumbled back several paces before he regained his footing. He could feel blood streaming down from his nose. Uriel charged again, but Samael was ready this time. He cast a tornado that sent Uriel hurling back into the air. He then pulled his bow from his back and shot an arrow at the airborne Archangel. It connected with Uriel's shin.

When Uriel landed, he broke the arrow. He pointed his sword at Samael and lightning shot out of the point. It hit Samael square in the chest and he flew backwards through the air. Uriel moved in for the kill, but Hypnos, Thanatos, and Lilith arrived. Uriel turned and ran.

"Coward!"

Lilith and Thanatos stayed with Samael while Hypnos ran after Uriel. Uriel slowed his pace and turned on Hypnos. Hypnos pulled a dagger from his belt.

"Looks like he beat you up pretty bad. Here's a parting gift from the nephilim."

Hypnos threw the dagger. Uriel spun and the dagger barely grazed his cheek. He was ready to counter attack when he felt his strength start to leave him. He was suddenly very tired. Hypnos grinned at the Archangel as he turned and ran. When he made it back, Hypnos looked at his brother.

"What do you think? Is he going to make it?"

Thanatos shook his head.

"The attack wasn't fatal. He'll live. At least… I think he'll live. I'm honestly not sure. We should have made it back here sooner."

Lilith paced back and forth with Lucia.

"Is there anything we can do?"

Thanatos shook his head a second time.

"He's beyond my ability to do much of anything. That was an Archangel that shot lightning at him. He has to win this one on his own."

Steam looked at the two corpses on the floor and laughed. He had a dead demon on the left and a dead angel on the right. He prodded them both with his boot to make sure they were actually dead. No reaction. Steam stepped over their bodies and approached the cockpit of the airplane.

Steam was an outcast from both the angels and the demons. His mother was a minor demon and his father was a minor angel. He had lived with his father briefly before being thrown out of the Heavens. He tried to live with his mother, but was thrown out of Hell for being too much of a light source. After being rejected from Heaven and Hell, he made his way to Earth. Steam was mostly a scavenger, tracking angels and demons and then feeding off of the souls they find.

Both an angel and a demon had been deployed to deal with the pilot of the airplane. He had been contemplating suicide. The angel was sent to talk him out of it. The demon was sent to talk him into it. After the angel and demon fought at the front of the plain, Steam moved in and finished them both off with his sorcery and then stabbed them both several times with his short blade. He knew he had a rare opportunity. If he talked the pilot into bringing the plane down, he could feed off the souls of the passengers for weeks. After reading the intel in the pockets of both the angel and the demon, Steam approached the pilot and whispered in his ear.

"She *is* cheating on you. You daughter is actually your neighbor's daughter."

Steam saw the pilot shift uncomfortably. He went in for the kill.

"Bring this plane down. Go down with a boom. You have nothing to live for. No one loves you."

The pilot started to sweat. Steam switched to his other ear and was ready for another round when he felt a strong feeling. He had occasionally felt it when he was getting too close to nephilim, but never this strongly. Steam felt a strong headache followed by a pressing urge to jump out of the plane. He stumbled back several steps and fell on his knees. When Steam made it back to his feet and stumbled towards the pilot, he couldn't remember what he was supposed to be doing there. The need to jump out of the plane was too strong. Steam made his way to the plane's emergency exit and jumped.

Lilith continued to pace back and forth. Hypnos wore a solemn expression on his face and wasn't acting like himself. Thanatos was moving through the sleeping and injured angels and cutting their heads off with an axe. Lilith stopped pacing and Hypnos saw that she was watching Thanatos with a curious expression.

"He does stuff like that when he's nervous. The death calms him down. He must be pretty worried about Dad."

"How is he even still alive? Leech fought him a while back and I thought he killed him."

"Honestly, I'm not sure he can be killed. He's not crazy powerful or anything, but I've thought he was dead several times before, too. He always comes back."

"Interesting. Well… he still gives me the creeps."

"Lilith, we're all a little weird. I'm not sure if you've noticed, but most angels and demons think you're…"

Lilith looked angrily at Hypnos as he chose his words very carefully.

"…slightly insane."

Lilith laughed.

"That was very polite of you, Hypnos. I know that I'm batshit crazy. I just get nervous around a creature who calls himself the nephilim of death, especially with my newborn daughter."

"He's harmless to us."

"That's not how he seemed when…"

Their conversation was interrupted by a creature dropping out of the sky. Lilith and Hypnos both cautiously approached. The creature started to get to his feet when Thantos charged with his axe. The creature didn't move. As Thanatos swung his axe, it went right through him. The creature grabbed the axe and wrestled it away from Thanatos.

"Woah! Calm down. I'm not here to hurt you guys."

Lilith took the axe back from the creature.

"Who are you and what do you want?"

The creature put his weapons on the ground and stepped back with his arms up.

"The name's Steam. I just had a really weird feeling that you guys needed my help and that I should come down here."

Lilith raised one eyebrow.

"Come down here? Where were you?"

Steam grinned.

"On a plane. I jumped."

Steam's grin turned into an annoyed expression.

"Aw shit! I was going to bring that plane down and eat for weeks! This fucking sucks!"

"Why did you feel like you needed to come down here? We don't need any help…"

"I'm not sure. Can I get my stuff back now? I swear I won't attack you."

Lilith pulled out her whip and lit it on fire.

"Not just yet. Tell us who you are. I still don't understand why you came here."

"Before I answer that… I need to know. Are you guys angels or demons?"

Lilith looked at Hypnos, unsure how to answer. Hypnos responded by taking the axe from Lilith and giving it back to Thanatos. Thanatos returned to slaying angels, no longer interested in the conversation.

"Neither. We're nephilim. I'm Hypnos. This is my sister, Lilith. Fair warning, don't fuck with us. My brother and sister may be crazy, but I will defend them to my last breath. That goes double for my niece and my father."

"Well that doesn't make any sense. Generally, when I sense other nephilim my instincts tell me to run the other way."

"You're a nephilim, too?"

"Yup. Mom's a demon and Dad's an angel. I can't live in either place so I live here. I kill angels and demons after tracking their prey, but I don't mess with other nephilim. You can trust me. We're not going to have any issues."

Lilith looked at Hypnos and Hypnos nodded. He thought Steam was probably alright. Lilith pointed at Steam's weapons.

"Go ahead. Take them back. I'm still not sure why you're here but…"

Steam gathered his belongings and made his way towards the tree under which Samael was resting.

"What happened to this guy?"

Hypnos put his arm in Steam's path, blocking him from moving any closer.

"That's my dad."

"An angel?"

"Was almost an Archangel."

Steam looked impressed.

"So this is Samael? I've heard the stories. This guy's a legend. Never thought he'd still be alive. I figured the angels would have hunted him down by now."

"Well that's what they just tried to do. The Archangel Uriel was hunting my sister and fought my father. Dad got in some good hits and Uriel ran away."

"He got hit with lightning, didn't he? That's gotta hurt. I can try some remedial first aid if you'd like."

Hypnos looked to Lilith. Lilith nodded.

"Sure. What do you need?"

"Just some water. I can convert it into steam and run it over the char marks on his armor. It should help. I've used it on myself a few times and it always makes *me* feel better."

"Go for it then."

Steam drew some water from a nearby river and heated it with his hands. The steam floated towards Samael's armor and then slowly started to coat his wounds. After a few minutes, a loud explosion interrupted the nephilim and everyone looked to the nearby hills. Steam grinned.

"Fuck yeah! The pilot brought the plane down! There's going to be a ton of food over there. Everyone ready for some food?"

Lucia heard the word 'food' and started to clap her hands excitedly.

CHAPTER 36

"So what do we do now? We're kind of… stuck down here without any friends. If we head for Earth again, Jess, Aim, and Murmur will attack this time. We can't ally with them because of the way things went down. We don't really have any options and it's making me nervous…"

Gangrene nodded, acknowledging Raven's comments. He had a solution, but he knew she wasn't going to like it.

"We could always have a meeting with Nightmare and Astaroth."

Raven looked at Gangrene with wide-eyed disbelief.

"Hear me out. We could meet with them and agree to side with them. When the battle starts, we take my army and flee to Earth. Everyone will be preoccupied with the war. No one will be watching for us to leave."

"You're seriously considering siding with the assholes who fought against Shadow, Leech, and Lilith?"

"Not really. It's a strategy… and it's honestly the only good strategy we have at this point. We need Murmur, Jess, and Aim off our backs. Our other option is to sit down here until one side wins the war and then comes for us. That doesn't sound very appealing."

"But the thing is…"

A demon arrived and bowed in front of Gangrene.

"General Nightmare and General Astaroth are ready to meet with you, if you'll follow me."

Raven slapped Gangrene across the face. The messenger demon looked horrified and brought his eyes back to the ground.

"You set up a meeting without talking to me!"

"Better to ask forgiveness than permission. I knew you weren't going to agree with me… but babe… it's our *only* good option. All other roads lead to death. You know I'm right."

Gangrene got up to leave. Raven turned away from him.

"You'll see it was the right thing to do when you see your sister again."

Gangrene followed the messenger demon to Nightmare's headquarters. He was escorted inside a large stone building and led to a room on the third floor.

"A drink while you wait, General Gangrene?"

"Not thirsty. I also don't trust Nightmare and Astaroth to not poison me."

"You sure? We have a lovely witch from the 17th century. It's aged nicely."

"Fine. Bring two glasses. If I'm going to have a drink, you're going to have some with me."

The messenger demon went away and returned with a bottle and two glasses. He handed one glass to Gangrene and poured a portion of the damned soul in both glasses. Gangrene took both glasses and poured them down the messenger demon's throat. When he didn't die after a few minutes, Gangrene took the bottle from him.

"17th century witch, huh? Nice."

Gangrene took a long drink. He hadn't had anything quite that refreshing in a long time. A few minutes later, the door to Nightmare's conference room opened and Gangrene entered. Nightmare and Astaroth were already waiting.

"Gangrene. Glad you decided to meet with us. With you on our side…"

Gangrene held up his hand and took another swig from the bottle.

"Nothing is decided yet. I heard what Murmur, Jess, and Aim had to offer and then they pissed me off. Now I'm willing to hear what you have to offer."

Nightmare pointed to a seat across from Astaroth. Gangrene took it.

"We don't have any hard feelings. You were trained by Shadow and Leech and they're both powerful demons. Obviously we aren't willing to work with either of them, but we'd be willing to cut you in on the spoils after we kill off the three pretenders. What you do after that is your call. I'm not going to pretend that we have to be buddies and rule as three kings…"

Astaroth cut in.

"Two kings and a queen."

"Right. Well we don't have to rule Hell together. Those three just need to be put down. I heard about Aim's attempt to kill you. How's your foot?"

"You don't need to remind me that they're assholes. I still came out way ahead from that whole thing though…"

Gangrene removed White Death from the strap around his back and placed it on the table. He pointed it at Nightmare. Nightmare looked hungrily at the weapon.

"I had heard that Aim was running around with that. I guess he isn't anymore."

"I told them it was the only way they walked away alive. It would have been a bloody battle, but I think I could have put both Jess and Aim down."

"Well there's no need for bloody battles if you join with us. With your demons added to ours, we would outnumber Murmur's combined forces by about five to one. We could end this whole ridiculous nonsense quickly."

"Didn't you meet with Murmur and offer to side with him initially? Didn't you ask him to kill a demon you made look like Muan? Now you've turned on him. I wonder what's changed or if the two of you are just…"

Astaroth slammed her fist down on the table.

"*We* didn't turn on him. He lied to us. He was never going to back us against his buddies."

Nightmare looked at Astaroth with an expression that told her that she needed to cool down. Gangrene and Murmur had some of the same friends. Nightmare waved Astaroth's comment casually away with his hand.

"It's a moot point now. I hear Shadow, Leech, and Lilith are all on Earth now and they don't want to be major demons anymore. Good for them. You also need to remember that when we had a common enemy, even Shadow and I were able to work together."

"The legion ring. Leech told me about that. What was it like fighting the Dragon?"

"The Six becoming Legion was the most power any of us has ever felt. The Dragon didn't frighten us at all when we were merged as that abomination. Given enough time, we would have killed him. It's too bad that things happened like they did… but we're getting off topic."

Gangrene grinned.

"I know we are. I just wanted to hear your side of that whole legion experience. I had heard the story from Leech but I wanted to hear the other angles. Astaroth, what did you think of it?"

"I agree with Nightmare. We were a being of raw power. Of course, I didn't get to control more than a small part of Legion and Shadow took that away from me before…"

Nightmare grabbed Astaroth's knee under the table and squeezed hard. She stopped her story and then looked furiously back at him. Gangrene watched the exchange with amusement.

"Well I have to admit that Nightmare really is the most talented liar in Hell. It's pretty obvious Astaroth still hates Shadow and I imagine Nightmare feels the same way. I've been meaning to ask, why didn't you ever avenge your son?"

Astaroth tightened her grip on her scythe.

"You know… the one Cain killed. Venom? Cain broke his neck so loudly that everyone in Hell could hear it. It echoed."

Astaroth was up from her chair and across the room in seconds. She swung at Gangrene with her scythe. Gangrene blocked the blow with his own scythe and kept his other hand on the trigger of White Death, which was still pointed at Nightmare.

"Well that tells me what I needed to know. I came here to find out if the two of you are capable of putting your emotions aside to work with me. It's pretty clear that you aren't. I'll show myself out."

Nightmare stood and drew his scythe.

"I'm afraid we can't allow you to leave, Gangrene."

CHAPTER 37

"Today we learn how to utilize the power contained in the drugs we use."

Sarah and Shadow were sitting in front of Adrenaline with several other berserkers in training. Adrenaline tossed a small leather bag to both Sarah and Shadow. Sarah sniffed its contents and stuck out her tongue.

"This smells like chili pepper mixed with lots of other terrible stuff. It's supposed to make us fight harder?"

"Take a sample. Snort it."

Sarah plugged one nostril and sucked a small amount of the powder up her nose. It burned. She was about to blow it out when she felt an odd sensation in her head. It was as if the neural pathways were connecting faster. Movement around her was slower and she had more time to react. Her muscles felt stronger. She could see openings to attack. She looked at Adrenaline before hopping to her feet.

"I'm ready. Tell me what I need to know."

Adrenaline grinned.

"The first thing you need to know is that the drugs are more powerful than you realize. There's a reason I asked everyone…"

Sarah fell over.

"…to sit."

Some of the berserkers in training chuckled behind her. Shadow suppressed a grin.

"I appreciate your enthusiasm, Sarah, but this is something we can't rush. Your body has to adjust. It will take time."

Shadow tossed his drugs back at Adrenaline.

"I don't need this. I'm in control of enough power without throwing this into the mix."

Adrenaline threw it back at Shadow.

"You may change your mind with what we have planned for today."

"And what might that be?"

"A free for all. Everyone is going to adjust to the drugs over the next few hours and then we'll give you more. Every demon in training against every other demon in training. Anything goes. Please try not to kill each other, though. We have a hard enough time finding recruits."

The demons adjusted to the drugs over the next several hours and then Adrenaline refilled the small bags he had given them. He started pacing with his hands clasped behind his back.

"No weapons. No spells. If I see either, you will be immediately disqualified. The winner will go one on one with me. If you defeat me, there is an additional prize."

Shadow gave a half-grin to the remark.

"Which is?"

"Win and find out. It could enhance the powers of even someone like you."

All of the demons got up and handed over their weapons and armor to the berserkers. Shadow wrapped Michael's short blade in his cape without anyone noticing. They all painted their faces, took their drugs, and waited for the signal.

"Go."

Shadow was immediately attacked by three berserkers in training. They held his arms and the third one put him in a headlock. Sarah wound up and delivered an uppercut to his jaw. Shadow tasted a small amount of blood. He had bit his tongue. He shot an angry but amused look back at her.

"Fight to win, right? We're not friends in here."

Shadow spit blood from his mouth.

"I see."

He pulled his arms together and the two demons holding his arms cracked skulls. There was a loud noise and they fell over, unconscious. Shadow jumped into the air and used the downward force to flip the third demon over his shoulder. He adjusted his positioning and came down on the demon's throat with his elbow.

Sarah was taking on two at once and Shadow decided to exploit this. She was expertly dodging their attacks and countering with kicks and punches. Shadow saw a brief opening and went for it. He delivered a roundhouse kick to her left side. Shadow a couple of her ribs crack and she stumbled but didn't lose her footing. She charged him but he stepped out of the way and tripped her. She went down hard and Shadow finished off the two demons she was fighting. When Sarah got back to her feet, she realized what she needed to do.

"None of us can win until Shadow goes down. We need to attack together."

Even in their enraged state, Sarah's words made sense to the demons. They all stopped fighting and attacked Shadow. Shadow dodged as many of the incoming attacks as he could, but it was too much for even him. The last thing he saw before he lost control was Sarah charging at him. Shadow turned into a rage monster. He grew in size and ferocity and lost all control. He pounded several demons with his fists and squashed them. Sarah turned to run. The rage monster scooped her up into his massive fist and opened his mouth, ready to consume her.

Adrenaline started clapping slowly. The rage monster turned to see that the berserker commander was wearing his armor and held Damnation in his right hand. The rage monster threw Sarah to the ground and went after Adrenaline. Adrenaline held his ground. As the rage monster punched, Adrenaline carefully aimed and struck back with Damnation. The rage monster started to bleed from a large gash in his hand. It made the monster even angrier. From somewhere deep within, Shadow's mind turned back on and decided to take control. Rage and power were not the answers here.

Shadow changed back to his normal form. Adrenaline looked confused.

"You're not going to keep coming at me as a rage monster?"

"No. The tricks you've taught us are pretty cool and there's definitely a time for them. Now is not one of those times. That's my weapon and my armor. I can't beat you as a rage monster without killing myself in the process. My mission is too important to let that happen. So now that I have a clear head, I know to do this."

Shadow held out his hand. Damnation began to shake. Adrenaline grabbed the weapon with both hands, but it sailed into the air and into Shadow's open palm.

"It was a trick I watched Azazel do once. I decided to learn it after he used it against me. No one can take Damnation away from me. It's infused with my blood and it will always come back."

"So we have a stalemate then. I know what I'm wearing. This is the armor of Michael the Archangel. Even with Damnation, you won't be able to kill me."

Shadow grinned.

"We could always find out."

Adrenaline nodded.

"Very well. Give me a moment to prepare a new weapon."

Adrenaline looked to one of his berserker demons and nodded. The berserker produced a staff wrapped in cloth. He unwrapped the cloth onto his hand and then tossed it to Adrenaline. Adrenaline pointed the staff at the fallen demons that Shadow had killed. Markings began to appear on the staff and glow a bright red. The souls of the demons left the remains of their corpses and joined with the staff. Adrenaline pointed his new weapon at Shadow.

"Is that…"

"It's another berserker staff. We've been working on it since Nightmare stole the last one. If you defeat me, I will trade it to you in exchange for a promise."

"What promise?"

"That's not important right now. You haven't defeated me."

Shadow held Damnation in his right hand and summoned ice in his left.

"Let's go then."

Adrenaline struck as soon as the words had left Shadow's mouth. He hit Shadow twice across the face with his new berserker staff and then hit him hard under the jaw with an uppercut. Shadow flew backwards through the air. When he landed, he felt dizzy. He could see three Adrenalines approaching him and couldn't focus the image into one. Adrenaline raised the berserker staff over his head and swung down hard. Shadow brought Damnation up to meet the attack, but wasn't ready for Adrenaline's follow-up. Adrenaline spun and hit Shadow hard in the back of the head with the berserker staff. Shadow went down. He tried to push himself up, but Adrenaline kicked him hard in the ribs. He went down again. When Shadow looked up at Adrenaline, Adrenaline swung down forcefully with the berserker staff. Shadow blacked out.

CHAPTER 38

The nephilim slowly made their way towards the plane crash. Hypnos and Thanatos carried their father on a stretcher Lilith had conjured from a spell in her book. Lilith carried Lucia and Steam formed water into different balloon animal-like formations to keep the infant entertained. Lucia smiled and tried to grab at the water animals.

As the group made their way towards the fallen plane, a large explosion sent them all flying backwards into the air. Lucia went sailing out of her mother's arms, but Steam caught her. She started to cry and Steam attempted to calm her. Lilith got to her feet, drew her whip, and lit it on fire.

"Who's there?"

A demon stepped into view. He wore a black hat that was tilted down to hide his face, a black trench coat, and held what appeared to be a rocket launcher over his shoulder.

"These are my souls. You guys can find somewhere else to scavenge."

Lilith shook her head.

"Steam brought down the plane. These are our souls. My father is injured and my daughter is hungry. You have one chance to leave."

"You don't know who I am, do ya?"

"No. I don't much care, either. I've killed too many demons to remember all of their names. That's a 'no' to my offer to walk away then?"

"I ain't a demon, lady. Well… not all demon. I got a little angel in me. That's how I'm able to make my trench coat do this…"

The stranger tucked the rocket launcher in his trench coat. The weapon disappeared inside and seemed to no longer exist. He pulled two swords out of his trench coat.

"I'm known as Weapon. I collect a lot of things. I store them all in my coat. Most of my collection is weapons. For instance, I'll add your whip to my collection after I kill you. It looks like it's made of sturdy stuff."

"I'm Lilith, the daughter of Samael and Vixen. You don't want to piss me off. I'm friends with Shadow."

The stranger waved one of his swords around, pointing at the other nephilim.

"Which one of them is Shadow? I'll kill him, too."

"You've seriously never heard of Shadow?"

"No. I'm starting to think I know your little friend over there, though."

Weapon pointed one of his blades at Steam.

"He's run off with a couple of my scores before. I hate thieves. I'll be adding his head to my collection."

Hypnos was checking Samael for any further injuries from the explosion. Thanatos was focused on Weapon. He ran at Weapon, ducked under the blades as he swung them, and placed his palm on Weapon's forehead. Weapon staggered backwards a few steps and then fell to the ground. Thanatos picked up one of Weapon's blades and brought it up to kill him.

"No!"

Thanatos looked at his half-sister with a confused expression.

"We shouldn't go around killing nephilim if we can help it."

Thanatos threw the sword hard into the ground near Weapon's head and stomped off. Hypnos cautiously approached his sister.

"Honestly, I'm really surprised Thanatos listened to you. You may want to be a little less forceful with him. I know he's strange, but he's also very powerful."

Lilith raised both eyebrows.

"So you were fine with what he was about to do?"

"Yes. We don't know this guy and he attacked us. I'd say that's enough to justify putting someone down for good. Explain to me why you don't agree."

"Shadow is going to need help. This war is a problem for all of us. Angels, demons, nephilim, and humans. We didn't kill Steam and he's been alright so far. We need the nephilim on our side. We never should have hunted them."

"*We* never did, Lilith. *You* did."

Lilith looked at the ground.

"I know. I regret it. I'm trying to make up for it. Shadow needs all the help he can get."

"You can start by treating Thanatos like you treat me. I know. He has no idea how to do things properly. He's odd... but that doesn't mean you can just keep treating him like that. Why do you keep doing that?"

"Because I'm afraid of him. I don't know how to..."

"Lilith, do you trust me?"

"Of course, Hypnos. I just can't..."

"Take my word for it. He wants to protect you. He wants you to be safe. You have *no reason* to fear him. I know he was probably... off... when he was sent to bring you to us. There was no good way to approach that situation, though. We weren't sure if we could trust Leech. From what you tell me about him, we should have. It would have saved us a lot of time and a bunch of problems."

"Fine. I'll try."

Lilith went to Steam and took Lucia from his arms. She walked in the direction she had seen Thanatos going.

Thanatos was sitting on a rock. He had no idea how he had messed up this time, but it had clearly pissed off his sister. He searched his brain for how he could have done it differently. The search came up empty. He had killed before and Lilith had never objected. He pulled a mirror out from his cloak and looked at his reflection, but couldn't bring himself to laugh.

"Thanatos?"

Thanatos looked up. Lilith was standing there with his niece. He looked back down.

"We should have killed that guy. I don't want him to hurt the baby."

"Do you want to hold her?"

Thanatos gave her an awestruck look. He excitedly shook his head yes. Lilith cautiously placed Lucia in Thanatos's arms. He gently rocked her back and forth.

"Do you think she'll like my mirror?"

Thanatos shifted Lucia into his left arm and looked in his mirror. He laughed at his reflection and then handed it to Lucia. She looked at herself and giggled. Lilith couldn't help but smile.

CHAPTER 39

Gangrene's mind quickly reviewed all of the exits he had seen on his way up. He kept his scythe pointed at Astaroth and White Death pointed at Nightmare.

"We can still walk away from this. No one has done anything that we can't overlook yet. I'm leaving. We can resume discussions at some other time. I won't keep going after…"

Nightmare continued to slowly walk towards Gangrene with a smile on his face. It made him uneasy and he moved White Death up so it was pointed at Nightmare's head.

"Stop moving. I can kill you if I have to."

Nightmare laughed.

"I doubt it. Regardless, you can't kill both of us. We need your army, Gangrene."

"I guess it's a good thing I brought them with me then. They're surrounding this place as we speak."

Nightmare laughed again.

"No they aren't. Who do you think you're trying to lie to? I'm the major demon of lies."

Astaroth slowly pulled back her scythe and moved it over her shoulder with both hands, readying a strike. Gangrene saw the move out of the corner of his eye.

"None of that. I'm serious. I'll kill you."

Astaroth swung her scythe. Gangrene reacted instantly. He fired White Death right as Nightmare started running towards him and then brought his scythe up to block Astaroth's attack. He then aimed White Death at Astaroth, praying he had hit Nightmare and stopped him in his tracks.

"Well I guess we're past any point of reconciliation. So…"

Gangrene fired White Death at Astaroth's head. She threw a glass bottle in the path of the bullet. The bottle shattered and smoke started to flow into the room. Within seconds, Gangrene was having trouble seeing anything more than a few feet in front of him. He scanned his surroundings, but saw no trace of Nightmare or Astaroth. He kept White Death and his scythe ready.

"That was very s-s-s-stupid."

Astaroth hissed out the final word. Gangrene saw a dark, snake-like form slither in front of him. He took a shot with White Death, but the shadow was already gone.

"Have you ever been hunted by a s-s-s-snake before?"

Gangrene could sense Astaroth slithering behind him. He turned and swung with his scythe. Nothing was there.

"S-s-s-silly little demon."

"Show yourself. You're fighting like a coward."

"Are you s-s-s-scared?"

Nightmare jumped out from the smoke and swung at Gangrene. Gangrene blocked the attack with the barrel of White Death, but Nightmare kicked him hard. Gangrene flew backwards across the room and dropped his weapons when he hit the wall. Astaroth sprung out from the smoke, lunging at Gangrene's neck with her fangs. Gangrene scrambled for his weapons. His hand locked onto something and he swung it hard at the springing snake. He didn't score a perfect hit, but his scythe's blade lodged in Astaroth's neck. Gangrene could feel White Death with his left foot. He put his foot under the gun, kicked it into the air, and grabbed it. Before Astaroth could struggle free from his scythe, Gangrene fired White Death and blew off her head. Nightmare emerged from the smoke and saw Astaroth's headless corpse. His scythe and eyes started glowing red.

"What did you do?"

Gangrene attempted to ready his weapons to keep Nightmare back, but Nightmare punched him hard in the face. Gangrene could hear his nose break and warm blood came gushing out of his nostrils. Nightmare struck again with his fist. Gangrene blocked the attack, but Nightmare followed it up with a swing from the butt of his scythe to Gangrene's chin. Gangrene knew Nightmare's scythe had been fused with the berserker staff and he knew that Nightmare was angry enough that he would continue to fight, even past death, until Gangrene was put down. He knew he had no other option. He had to run. Nightmare attacked again. Gangrene brought White Death up and fired. He didn't wait to see the aftermath. He turned and ran. Nightmare followed.

"Gangrene doesn't leave this place! Capture him and bring him back here!"

Gangrene was nearly to the entrance when he felt something wrap around his leg. He turned and saw a demon sorcerer and the chain he had conjured. It was slowly winding its way up Gangrene's leg and had reached his knee. Gangrene turned and fired White Death. The shot missed, but it distracted the sorcerer. Gangrene hacked at the chain with his scythe. The scythe cut cleanly through the chain. He ran out the entrance.

When Gangrene made it outside, he almost wished he was back inside. He was staring at the combined forces of Nightmare and Astaroth. This was a no-win situation. He knew he was going to die. He wiped the blood from under his nose with his sleeve and readied his weapons to face them. Gangrene was going to go down fighting.

"That's what happens when you stick your nose in where it doesn't belong."

Gangrene turned and saw Raven grinning at him. She handed him a piece of cloth, which he tore, rolled up, and stuck up his nostrils to stop the bleeding.

"So you couldn't just let me come here and die, huh? You're getting way too attached, babe. I'm not sure if I'm ok with this."

Raven punched him playfully in the shoulder and then walked past him. Gangrene saw that she had brought his entire army with her.

"I don't really care what you're ok with. I wanted you and now you're mine. Deal with it."

Raven pointed at the combined armies of Nightmare and Astaroth.

"Kill the motherfuckers who injured your general!"

Gangrene's army charged. Raven and Gangrene charged with them. Nightmare ran out of his headquarters with an enraged look on his face.

"Kill Gangrene! He doesn't leave this place alive!"

One of the demons in Astaroth's army looked confused.

"Where is General Astaroth?"

Nightmare pulled a knife from his belt and threw it. It landed in the demon's throat. He fell over and bled into the sand. Nightmare didn't wait for anyone else to question his commands. He ran at Gangrene and attacked.

CHAPTER 40

Shadow sat straight up and held out his hand, willing Damnation to fly into his open palm. He heard something moving around in the sand next to him. He looked down and saw his scythe with all of his armor. He was in no immediate danger. When he laid back down, he realized what a terrible headache he had.

Sarah entered the tent and saw Shadow with his hand over his forehead.

"Didn't know it was possible for you to get your ass kicked."

"It isn't. The guy had my armor and tried to take my weapon. I was basically fighting a less powerful version of myself after wasting a significant amount of energy on beating up the rest of you."

"So it's a loss with an asterisk next to it in the record book? A loss is a loss, Shadow."

"Did I… what happened when…"

Shadow closed his eyes, hoping that he could form the question he needed to ask.

"What did I do when I became a rage monster?"

"You don't remember?"

"Only bits and pieces."

"Well… you attacked everyone. You nearly killed me. It was pretty terrifying."

"Adrenaline has a new berserker staff. I'm guessing no one outside of this group knows it exists. We need to take it so that…"

"You seem to have enough power when you're angry. That thing turns you into a kamikaze weapon. I think you'll do just fine without it."

"My father is the son of the Archangel Michael. Do you think it's going to be easy to put him down? I mean… I'll completely ignore the fact that he's my father. I can do that. I know I mean nothing to him and it's easy for him to mean nothing to me. I'm just talking about the sheer amount of power that he has available to him here on Earth."

"After seeing what you did, I'm not going to let you have the berserker staff."

Shadow grinned.

"You're going to stop me?"

"I don't want you to die. So yes. I'll stop you."

"I can't be stopped. I always…"

"Win? No you don't. In fact, I think I'll go ahead and take your armor. You aren't using it and…"

Shadow jumped out of the bed and grabbed Sarah's wrist. She pushed him away.

"It was a joke. It wouldn't even fit me. It's way too big."

"This is important. Not just for me, but for everyone. I already sacrificed Leech to this stupid mission and I won't let anyone else take the same risk. I need to guarantee that Abaddon goes down for good."

"Why? Why is this your responsibility?"

"It isn't. It's Michael's responsibility. It's Persephone's responsibility. It's the Dragon's responsibility. The only problem is I don't trust any of them to actually *do* anything about it. I can't live in a world where…"

Shadow's head started to throb and he laid back down.

"I can't let anything happen to Lilith. I can't let anything happen to Leech's kid. I can't let anything happen to Muan… but most importantly, I can't let anything happen to you."

Sarah sat down on the bed next to him.

"Most importantly? Why am I the most important?"

"You just are. Stop pushing it."

"Why can't you just say it?"

"Because I'm a demon. Demons don't say things like that."

"Wrong. You're a nephilim, not a demon, and I heard Leech say things like that to Lilith all the time."

"Leech is fucking dead now. That's what being soft got him."

Sarah waited a few moments before responding.

"You don't mean that."

"I mean it. I never took all of this seriously because I knew I had my friends with me. Well no one is going to be there with me when I face off with Abaddon. I won't sacrifice anyone else to this bullshit. I'll face him alone, I'll go berserk, and I'll end him. That's all there is to it."

"Nope. I'll be there."

"No you won't."

"I don't like it when you go off on tangents. It's very sad that Leech died. That doesn't mean he was soft. Why am I the most important?"

"Because I fucking love you, you asshole!"

Sarah tried to prevent the onslaught of laughter she felt creeping up her face. Shadow saw her reaction.

"Oh wonderful! I say the stupid shit you want me to and you're ready to laugh at me! Why don't you just get the fuck out of here?"

"I can't."

"Why not?"

"Because I fucking love you too, you asshole!"

Shadow tried hard to suppress the laughter. Neither of them lasted very long. They both started laughing. Shadow ended it abruptly by sitting up and kissing her. Sarah got into the bed with Shadow, got on top of him, and took off her clothes.

Sarah waited for the fall of night before she slipped her robes and armor back on. Shadow was sleeping peacefully next to her. She was nearly tempted to abandon her plan and couldn't help but feel bad about what she knew she had to do. She needed to keep Shadow alive. She couldn't let him attack his father with suicide being his way to guarantee victory.

Sarah slipped out of the tent and made her way to the small cave where she suspected Adrenaline was keeping the berserker staff. She snorted a small amount of the drugs from her pouch and waited for the effect to hit her. It didn't take long.

Sarah took down the guards watching the cave entrance without any issues. She saw the berserker staff briefly before something hit her hard on the right side of her face. She felt blood streaming out of her ear. When she looked up, she saw Adrenaline standing over her.

"This isn't yours. This is our gift to Shadow."

"I don't have time to discuss this with you."

Sarah drove her sword into the ground and whispered a prayer. Her sword started to glow and became brighter and brighter until Adrenaline could no longer see. Sarah used the distraction to slip past him, grab the berserker staff, and run. By the time Adrenaline could see again, Sarah was gone.

CHAPTER 41

Weapon looked at the group of nephilim with annoyance.

"Can I have something to eat or are you guys just going to let me die in these chains?"

Thanatos was making funny faces at Lucia. He stopped long enough to respond.

"You tried to steal from us AND you're a cranky asshole. No one feels bad for you."

Steam was roasting one of the souls from the airplane over a fire he had started.

"I'll give you something to eat when you admit that this was my airplane and you have no right to anything on board. These are all my souls that I share freely with my friends."

Weapon rolled his eyes.

"Fuck it then. I'll just die in these chains I guess."

Thanatos handed his mirror over to Lucia. She giggled at her reflection.

"Can you die a little quieter then? I'm trying to play with my niece."

When Samael finally awoke, he saw Hypnos and Lilith standing over him.

"How long was I out?"

Before Hypnos could answer, Lilith pulled her father in for a hug. He winced.

"Oh, sorry. I forgot."

"Uriel shot lightning, didn't he? Wow. It's been a while since someone has tried to 'bolt' me to death."

"We found a couple of nephilim and a plane with dozens of evil souls to…"

Hypnos cleared his throat loudly and Lilith looked up at him. He shook his head.

"Oh right. Angels don't eat evil humans. I'm sure there were some good ones that you can have for a snack if you're feeling…"

Hypnos shook his head again and cut her off.

"You were out for a few days, Dad. We found two nephilim, Steam and Weapon. Steam is alright. He tried to heal you. Weapon is in chains because he tried to steal the airplane from us and then he attacked us."

"So why didn't one of you put that Weapon guy down?"

Lilith frowned.

"Because we shouldn't be killing nephilim if we can avoid it. Not anymore. Shadow's going to need some help and nephilim are powerful. Weapon hides all sorts of cool shit in his coat. He has a rocket launcher. I think I saw a mouse trap. There's a few clocks. He had a cool collection of butter knives…"

"The asshole shot us with a rocket launcher, Dad. Thanatos was about to put him down, but Lilith told him not to."

"Where's Thanatos?"

"Playing with my daughter. They're sitting by the fire over there next to Steam. Weapon is in chains. He could be useful, daddy. Why don't you let us keep him?"

"Lilith, he isn't a puppy. Weapon is a dangerous…"

"Oh can I have a puppy? I want a puppy too."

Hypnos exhaled loudly.

"Lilith, you're going to annoy him to death. Stop it."

"But I've wanted a puppy for a long time."

Samael looked at Lilith for several seconds without speaking then turned to Hypnos.

"Is the area secure? No angels or demons patrolling? Are we sure Uriel won't attack us again?"

Hypnos grinned.

"I took care of that. He's going to be drowsy for a while courtesy of a parting gift that I threw at him. It grazed him as he was thinking about turning back and fighting. I could tell it was effective. He won't be coming back without reinforcements."

Samael tried to push himself to his feet, but he fell back over.

"I want to meet Steam. Bring him here."

Hypnos nodded and ran off. Lilith looked like she was deep in thought.

"What's wrong?"

"Oh I was just thinking about what you said. I want both, but if I can't have you spare Weapon's life AND a puppy, I think I'll go with sparing Weapon's life. Shadow needs all the help he can get."

Samael chuckled.

"Well I can tell you put a lot of thought into that."

"I did. I've really wanted a puppy ever since you said I could have one a few minutes ago."

Samael sighed and shook his head. Lilith pouted.

"That's what Leech used to do when he thought I was being annoying."

"Wow. I definitely did *not* think you would use that as a bargaining chip. Fine. We'll keep the nephilim alive for now and decide what to do with him later. Also… I never said you could have a puppy."

"That's how I heard it. I guess you need to speak more clearly in the future."

Hypnos returned with Steam. Steam nodded at Samael.

"Glad you're awake. Especially if Archangels are hunting us now."

"What makes you think you're a part of us?"

Steam brought his hands up defensively.

"I didn't mean to imply anything. Just the general term. They're in the area. They're around. If I'm around, they're not going to care whether I'm with you guys or not. I figure it's better to have Samael and his crazy children on my side."

"Why are you here, Steam? I heard you brought down a plane…"

"I just scavenge for the most part. Steal souls from angels and demons. Up on that plane, an angel and a demon were fighting over the pilot. I took them both out and then brought the plane down. For whatever reason, I was drawn here. Maybe it was just the fact that four nephilim were here. Had I known that beforehand, I wouldn't have jumped off the plane. I try to stay away from other nephilim. I don't plan on causing any trouble… especially when other nephilim are involved."

"So what do you want from us?"

"Nothing. I'll stick around and help if I can. If you want me to leave, I can do that too… but please tell me right now. I'd like to run the fuck away if you'd rather not have me and angels are hunting you in this area. I'll also take the souls on the plane with me. Those are mine."

"My daughter seems to trust you. What's your take on the other nephilim, Weapon?"

"That guy's an asshole. I still think we should kill him and be done with it. Lilith said we're not going to do that. If we kill him, I call dibs on his magic weapon coat thing."

"If we join with Shadow and help him assault Abaddon and the Dragon…"

"I can fight, if that's what you're asking. I don't really know how to fight with a team, though… and I'm definitely not helping anyone take on Abaddon or the Dragon directly. I'll kill demons. I'll kill angels. I'll stay the fuck away from the powerhouses you just mentioned."

Lilith cut in.

"Not a problem. None of us is going to take on those two directly. That's what Shadow is for. He can kill anyone or anything."

Steam decided to make his point one more time.

"Again… I'm just a harmless scavenger. I'm not sure what brought me here, but I'm not here to hurt anyone. I'll fight against your enemies if you guys can keep me safe. I've heard the stories. You defied the Archangels and you're still alive. I imagine this is a good group to be in. Especially if you can take on Uriel and live to tell the tale."

Samael nodded his approval.

"You can stick around. Go with Hypnos and bring the other nephilim here. I want to talk to him."

Thanatos appeared, clutching his nose and dragging Weapon by a chain.

"This asshole headbutted me and tried to run away. Lucia lit his coat on fire and I used the distraction to bring him down. I vote we kill him now."

Lilith looked concerned.

"Where is Lucia? You just left her by the plane?"

"Of course not."

Thanatos turned around to reveal Lucia's head and arms peeking out of a backpack. Samael turned his attention to Weapon.

"Why did you attack my children?"

"They wanted to take the souls I found."

"So you decided to use a rocket launcher?"

"I'll admit I was leaning towards a machine gun or an automatic rifle, but I hadn't used the rocket launcher in a while and it just felt right. Sometimes you just need to launch a rocket to deal with a problem. I thought this was one of those problems. Turns out I should have went with something else."

"What will you do if I let you go? Will you try to take the souls back?"

Hypnos and Thanatos opened their mouths to protest but Samael raised his hand to silence them.

"I'd leave. I know who you are and the souls are no longer worth fighting over. I've also heard you guys talking about Uriel being in the area. I want to get out of here."

Samael grabbed his sword and slowly got to his feet. He walked towards Weapon and cut the chains.

"Go. If I see a rocket or anything like it headed this way, I will stop it and I will kill you."

"Hey… no problem. I'm gone."

Weapon got to his feet and ran away. Lilith looked angry.

"You didn't even ask him if he wanted to fight for Shadow and help us."

"I said I would spare his life and I did, but there's no way he would want to help us."

Hypnos cut in.

"I want to track him down and kill him. He's still a threat and…"

Samael shook his head.

"Nope. We're done discussing this. Let him go."

A crow landed next to Lilith and turned into Muan.

"Finally. You guys have been running all over the place. It's been really annoying."

Lilith looked concerned.

"Is Shadow alright? He didn't go after his dad without us, did he?"

"No. Just told me to find you and bring you back to him. I um…"

Muan looked around.

"… I'm just supposed to bring Lilith and her kid back. Who the hell are all these guys?"

Thanatos pointed an axe at Muan.

"We're coming too. Shadow's going to need all the help he can get and I'm not leaving my niece. Lead the way, little monkey demon."

CHAPTER 42

Gangrene parried the first several shots from Nightmare and realized that he needed to slow him down. The berserker staff in Nightmare's scythe, Rage, was adding to his power as his anger increased and Gangrene knew Nightmare would eventually kill him if he could keep ramping up like that. He tossed White Death over to Raven and returned to blocking Nightmare's attacks. After two more blocks, Nightmare hit Gangrene's scythe hard enough that it flew out of his hands. Nightmare brought his scythe up to finish off Gangrene. Gangrene closed his eyes.

Raven waited to make sure she had the shot and then fired. Her aim wasn't perfect, but Nightmare took a hit in the shoulder. It delayed him for a brief second and Gangrene rolled out of the way just in time. He scrambled to his feet and started running towards his scythe.

"We can't do this. We need to turn around and get out of here. Sound the retreat, Raven."

Raven shook her head.

"We'll be fine. I have a plan. You just need to hold him off for a little longer."

"That's the problem, Raven. I *can't*. He's about to go into full on psycho mode."

Raven scanned the horizon and looked disappointed.

"Just a little longer."

Gangrene retrieved his scythe and turned to see Nightmare charging at him again. No trash talk, no commands to his army. Gangrene knew he was impossible to stop at this point. The next time Nightmare charged, Gangrene got out of the way in time and counterattacked. His scythe pierced Nightmare's armor around his left wrist and he ran it up his arm. Nightmare started to bleed, but he didn't even stop to notice it. He punched Gangrene hard in the face and Gangrene went flying through the air. When he landed, he was barely holding on to consciousness. He looked for Raven, but didn't see her anywhere. He heard White Death fire somewhere in the distance, but it didn't affect Nightmare. His scythe went up high in the air and came crashing down towards Gangrene's neck. Gangrene shut his eyes and embraced his impending death.

Murmur got to Gangrene just in time to block Nightmare's swing with his own scythe. Jess was only a few steps behind and she swung her scythe hard at Nightmare, knocking him back several steps.

Gangrene opened his eyes and saw Aim standing over him, extending a hand. He took it and Aim helped him to his feet.

"Your girl convinced us that this was the best way to take Nightmare down. I never thought you'd be able to kill Astaroth, though. Well done, Gangrene."

"Raven arranged all of this?"

"Yup. She called you a stubborn ass, presented her plan, and then promised I'd get White Death back. No hard feelings about the um… time I tried to kill you?"

"I guess we're even since the three of you saved my life. I'm still not happy about not being included in the planning. What if I didn't make it out of there alive?"

"We were standing by. I had a clear shot in through the window. Jess was ready to teleport Murmur in there to get you out if necessary. Trust me, everything was planned for. We didn't include you because it couldn't look staged and we figured there was probably a little bad blood between us still."

"You shot me in the foot, asshat."

"Yeah… I'm sorry about that. I promise I'll never shoot you in the foot ever again."

"Right. Well I have an army to lead."

Aim held out his hand. Gangrene looked confused.

"What?"

"My gun. I want White Death back."

"Oh Nightmare took that from me. You're going to have to get it back yourself. Good luck, Aim."

Gangrene punched Aim in the shoulder and took off running to help his army. Aim called out after him.

"That's not funny, Gangrene! Where the fuck is my gun?"

As Gangrene ran down the hill to join his army of demons, he passed Raven. He grabbed her arm and she started running with him.

"Aim wants his gun back. You're not giving it to him. It's yours now."

"You could have just gotten me flowers and an 'I'm a dumbass for not listening to you, Raven' card."

Gangrene laughed.

"Fine. Give me the gun back and I'll get you a card and flowers."

"No it's ok. I want the gun now."

Aim saw Gangrene run off with Raven and noticed that White Death was strapped to Raven's back.

"Son of a bitch. Now what am I supposed to…"

Jess appeared next to Aim and handed him a scythe.

"Stop complaining and fight. It's going to take all three of us to keep Nightmare at bay."

"Where'd you get this?"

"Astaroth's corpse. Stop bitching about your gun. We need your help."

Aim nodded and joined in with Jess and Murmur as they held Nightmare back from the rest of the battle.

CHAPTER 43

Adrenaline woke Shadow in the middle of the night. He looked panicked. Shadow wondered if he was about to be attacked and reached for Damnation.

"It's Sarah. She stole the berserker staff."

"That's not possible because she's…"

Shadow checked the side of the bed where Sarah had been sleeping. He realized he had been played.

"Do you have anyone tracking her?"

"I have all of my berserkers out there looking for her. Shadow, we need to get that staff back so you can take on Abaddon. It's the only way."

"Yes. I know. He's too powerful and all that shit. Kind of irrelevant if we don't find her, isn't it?"

A berserker demon entered the tent and bowed.

"Apologies, Lord Adrenaline and General Shadow. There's a group of… well… I'm not exactly sure what they are. One seems to be an angel… there's a crazy demoness… I… a crow led them here and then turned into a small demon. He said he knows you, General Shadow."

Shadow smiled.

"It's Muan. He brought Lilith here. Perfect."

Shadow muttered a few words and his armor and weapons attached themselves to him. He grabbed Damnation and went out to meet them. As soon as he exited his tent, he was knocked back in by Lilith jumping at him for a hug.

"I've missed you, Shady. I'm so glad you aren't dead yet."

Shadow laughed.

"I'm glad you're not dead, too. Where's the baby?"

Thanatos approached and Shadow gripped Damnation.

"I remember this guy. What is he doing here?"

"My niece is in my backpack."

Thanatos turned around. Shadow cautiously removed the sleeping baby and rocked her back and forth. He turned to Lilith.

"Niece?"

"Long story. I found my father and apparently Hypnos and Thanatos are my half-brothers… and they're going to help us fight! Surprise!"

"So… that time you guys came down to Hell to help 'me' out…"

Hypnos nodded.

"We were really down there for our sister. We couldn't let her die down there. We used the time to educate you on nephilim and our family ties remained a secret. We couldn't risk Lilith being outed as a nephilim. They would have killed her."

"But you were fine with spreading that rumor about me?"

Thanatos shrugged.

"Sure. You're not our sister. Unless there's something Dad forgot to tell us…"

Samael stepped forward and extended his hand.

"Good to meet you, Shadow. I'm Samael. I met your father a long time ago when he ascended into the Heavens to find Michael. Powerful guy. It's too bad that the torture…"

Hypnos cleared his throat loudly. Shadow grinned.

"Well good to know putting your foot in your mouth is a family trait. I always wondered where Lilith got that."

Shadow saw Steam standing behind everyone else.

"I know everyone now but this guy. Who are you?"

Lilith walked behind Steam and shoved him forward. Steam looked nervous and didn't say anything. Lilith rolled her eyes.

"This is Steam. He's happy to meet you."

"Another nephilim?"

Steam leaned in to Lilith's ear and whispered.

"He looks scary as fuck. What if I say the wrong thing and he kills me?"

Lilith rolled her eyes again.

"Shadow… Steam wants you to promise not to kill him before he'll talk."

Shadow grinned.

"I generally don't make promises like that. Who knows what the future holds? There are so many reasons I can think of that would make me want to kill you, but if it'll make you feel better…"

Lilith nodded.

"…I promise not to kill you. Take note that I'm lying. I still haven't even promised not to kill Lilith and I've wanted to at least a dozen times."

Lilith giggled. Steam reluctantly extended his hand. Shadow shook it.

"The name's Steam… Lord… General… King… uh… Shadow. Your majesty. Your honor."

Steam leaned back over to Lilith.

"What am I supposed to call him?"

Shadow laughed.

"Well he's terrified. Fine. We'll figure all of this out in the morning. All of you will need to meet Adrenaline and the berserkers. For now, I think we should all get some sleep. I've had enough interruptions for one night."

Lilith looked around.

"Where's Sarah?"

"That's a long story, too. Let's just put it on hold for now."

Lilith looked like something had just dawned on her and removed Leech's head from the sack on her belt. Shadow looked at her like she was crazy.

"Why have you been carrying around Leech's head? Lilith… this is a whole new level of…"

"We can bring him back."

"What do you mean? He's dead, Lilith. We don't have time for false hope right now."

"No. It's not false hope. When he took on Azazel to save us, he consumed a small army of nephilim with his parasitic touch. Took all of their energy in. I had Jess cast a spell on his head. He can come back if he can siphon off power from someone powerful enough to…"

Samael cut her off.

"Shadow needs his strength to fight Abaddon, Lilith. Maybe we should hold off on…"

Shadow shook his head.

"No. No waiting. What do I need to do?"

Lilith hesitated.

"This is going to hurt. It'll drain you. Are you sure?"

Shadow nodded.

"Let's do it."

Lilith grabbed Shadow's hand and put Leech's head in his open palm. Nothing happened. Lilith looked confused.

"I don't understand. It usually just…"

Leech's eyes started to glow green. Shadow yelled out and fell to his knees. Blood started to trickle down his nose and out of his eyes. Lilith started to cry. In a panic, she tried to take Leech's head back, but Shadow stopped her with his free hand.

"No. Let me finish this."

Shadow slowly got back on his feet. He tried to tighten his muscles and bear the pain, but he called out again in agony. A green form started to crawl down Leech's head. It formed a neck, then a torso, and slowly crawled out until arms appeared. Lilith continued to cry.

"Daddy! Help him!"

Samael sadly shook his head.

"I can't, sweetheart. Shadow is stronger than I am. He has to do this alone."

When the green mist formed Leech's toes, it became a solid body. Leech started to breathe again, but didn't open his eyes. Shadow let go of Leech's head and fell into unconsciousness.

CHAPTER 44

After Weapon left the nephilim that had captured him, he made sure everything was still in his coat. The process took a long time, because his coat held every weapon in his collection and some other items he found useful. When he finished, his stomach growled.

"Damn it. I need to find something to eat. Those assholes took everything in my plane."

Weapon saw a nearby town and started slowly walking towards it. He made it several steps before he remembered that he had faster modes of transportation. He set his coat on the ground and slowly pulled a motorcycle out of one of the larger inner pockets.

"Should have grabbed a few souls when I saw those idiots coming and taken off on this thing… I just never get a chance to use the rocket launcher anymore."

When Weapon made it down to the small town, he packed his motorcycle back in to his coat and pulled out a pair of pistols. Weapon started making his way down a quiet residential street. It was night, so any angels and demons in the area were likely bored and didn't have their guard up. Weapon entered the first house he came to because he smelled death inside. An old man sat in a recliner. His drink had spilled on the floor and there was no breath coming from his mouth. It looked like the guy had drank himself into sleep and wasn't going to wake up. Weapon retrieved the old man's soul and took a big gulp. Dirty cop. Perfect to take the edge off of his growing hunger. He stored the rest of the soul in a jar in his coat and moved on.

Weapon left the house and walked across the lawn of the next house up the street. There were toys on the lawn. Children. Weapon grinned. While he couldn't take the children yet, there were probably some angels and demons inside and he was fine with killing and eating them. Weapon spotted a door with a poster of a heavy metal band on the door. Probably a teenager, so there was likely an angel and a demon inside. Weapon walked through the door and saw the angel and demon struggling. The demon was winning. Weapon pulled a short sword from his coat and jammed it up the demon's spine. The demon arched his back and then fell over dead. The angel looked relieved until he saw Weapon standing over him, demon blood dripping off his blade.

"No! Please don't! I won't cause any trouble. You can take whatever you want."

Weapon rolled his eyes and cut the angel's belly open. He then hacked the angel and demon into manageable pieces, wrapped them, and stored them in his coat. He cleaned his blade and remembered the toys in the front yard. They didn't belong to the teenager. There was a younger child in the house somewhere. Weapon put his short sword back in his coat and pulled out a shotgun. After he stepped back into the hall, he saw the door next to the teenager's room. It had flower stickers and cartoon characters all over it. Weapon readied his shotgun and ran in. As he scanned the room, he saw an angel kneeling on the floor and praying. She opened her eyes, looked up at Weapon, and grinned.

"I heard the angel call out in the other room. I just finished saying a prayer to the Archangel Uriel. He's still in the area and he knows you're here now."

Weapon pointed the shotgun at the angel's head.

"Well then fuck you and fuck your noisy friend in the other room. Uriel won't find anything when he gets here other than angel and demon blood on the floors. I'll be taking your corpse with me in smaller, manageable pieces."

The angel looked disgusted.

"You're a savage. Curse you and all of the nephilim."

Weapon laughed.

"I didn't know angels could curse."

Weapon fired the shotgun and the angel's head exploded. As he was hacking up the remains, he heard footsteps downstairs.

"Shit."

Weapon abandoned his future meal and made his way out of the window. The angels entered the room shortly after he left and saw the remains of their sister on the floor. The middle angel ordered her corpse be covered and then taken outside. He also called for a messenger. The messenger angel bowed.

"Lord Cassiel, what would you have me do?"

"We were brought here by a prayer to Archangel Uriel. Get a message to him. Everyone has been killed. I suspect a nephilim. I'll be pursuing him and taking him down. No reinforcements needed."

The messenger angel wrote out the message and Cassiel stamped it with his ring. The messenger angel bowed and left. Cassiel followed him out of the house and then turned to his army.

"There's a nephilim in this neighborhood somewhere. We're going to find him and then rid the world of his abominable soul. This will be no different than the other nephilim we've killed. We're doing the Lord's work here. Those creatures are worse than the demons.

Report to me when we have him captured and bound. Go with God, my brothers and sisters."

Minor angels began organizing search parties and the angels spread out, searching the neighborhood.

Weapon watched Cassiel's speech from a rooftop three houses down from where he had killed the angels and the demon. He held his hand over his heart in mock appreciation.

"Those angel speeches. They always get me going. Sometimes when they call me a plague enough times, I even want to kill me."

Weapon pulled a pair of binoculars out from his coat and zoomed in on Cassiel. He was an angel of medium build and the only thing that separated him from the other angels was the fact that his blonde hair glowed a little brighter and his robes were a little whiter, if such a thing was possible. Weapon was about to return his binoculars to his coat and run away when he noticed something odd on the angel's belt. He zoomed in even further. There were heads attached to Cassiel's belt. Nephilim heads. Weapon knew a few of them.

"Well fuck. I guess I should have given this guy a little more credit. He's a special kind of asshole. Didn't know the angels were *successfully* hunting nephilim now."

Weapon returned the binoculars to his inside coat pocket and made a run for it.

CHAPTER 45

When Gangrene made it to his army, he summoned messenger demons and prepared a message for his middle demons. He told them to cut a path towards an exit to the Earth and to not get pulled any deeper into the battle. The messengers nodded at the message and took off to deliver it. It was up to Murmur, Jess, and Aim now. He had equaled the playing field for them by killing Astaroth and that was enough.

Gangrene and Raven jumped into the battle and started cutting down the remains of Astaroth's army. They were nearly through to a cave with a portal to the surface when the ground started to shake. Gangrene grabbed one of his minor demons by the shoulder and killed his opponent.

"What's making the ground shake like that?"

"It's been happening off and on since we started fighting, General Gangrene. The rumor going through our ranks is that it's the gateway twins. Culsans and Culsu. They were in Astaroth's army and are likely to succeed her now that she's dead."

The ground shook again as soon as the demon finished his explanation.

"They're getting closer. Should I get Lord Ghoul down here?"

Lord Ghoul was one of Gangrene's middle demons. The minor demon obviously fought for Lord Ghoul. Gangrene shook his head.

"No. I'll deal with the twins. Just be ready to run to the surface. We're getting out of here as soon as possible."

The minor demon nodded and returned to the battle. The ground rumbled again. A large beast-like creature ran in front of Gangrene and split into a demon and a demoness. The demon drew two swords from his belt and the demoness summoned fire in each hand. They each pointed at Gangrene and alternated speaking.

"We've been waiting for you, Gangrene."

"You're a coward and we're here to kill you and take your scythe."

Gangrene grinned.

"Do you guys *plan* coordinated speeches? Do I get a one-liner from each of you every time I say something? I really don't have time for that long of a conversation."

"Surrender now. Fall on your sword."

"Die with honor. You can't win."

Gangrene spun his scythe and attacked. Culsu started throwing fire, but Gangrene was able to expertly dodge the attacks. Culsans attacked with both blades and Gangrene was able to block everything with his scythe. He didn't notice Culsu sneak around to his back, though. She fired off two fireballs and his back began to burn. He unlatched his breastplate and cape and threw them on the ground. His back was slightly singed, but the pain just increased the adrenaline flowing through his system. He attacked Culsu, but she summoned a shield of fire and kept retreating while throwing fire in his path. When he had nearly caught her, he felt a stabbing pain in his right shoulder. He spun around and saw Culsans smiling at him. One of his swords was sticking out of Gangrene, close to the shoulder blade. Gangrene removed it and broke it on his knee.

Gangrene was starting to regret not asking Lord Ghoul to join him. He remembered that Raven was somewhere nearby and called out her name. He played defense against the gateway twins until he could hear gunfire getting closer. It sounded like White Death.

"Hey babe. There are two of them and they're starting to piss me off. Flip a coin?"

Raven looked at the gateway twins and shook her head.

"No coin. I get the hot chick. She looks yummy."

"Fine. Whatever. Just kill her. We need to get out of here."

After dodging several fireballs that Culsu hurled her way, Raven struck with her whip. She was able to wrap it around Culsu's throat and then yanked on it hard. Culsu went flying through the air until she was only a few feet from White Death. Raven fired and the bullet penetrated Culsu's eye and lodged itself in her skull. She fell over, dead. Raven looked disappointed.

"That wasn't as fun as I wanted it to be. I think I'm going to steal her clothes. It's the least she can do for me since she wasn't willing to fight very hard."

Raven removed Culsu's clothes and then ran off to continue fighting. Culsans began circling Gangrene, driven by fury but determined to not launch a foolish attack. Gangrene started circling in the opposite direction.

"Your girlfriend is kind of insane."

"I know. I'm into it. Your sister is kind of dead."

Gangrene hoped this would provoke an attack, but Culsans just smiled and kept circling. Gangrene felt someone tap him on his shoulder. It was the minor demon he had talked to earlier.

"We're through to the cave, General Gangrene. We've started sending the armies through. Shouldn't be long now."

Gangrene nodded.

"I'll be there shortly. Get everyone through."

Culsans launched himself into the air with his blades overhead. Gangrene aimed his scythe and sliced upwards. Culsans was able to land part of his attack, as each blade had sunk into Gangrene's shoulders, but neither wound was very deep. Gangrene managed to cut Culsans in half. He pulled his scythe back and ran towards the cave. A few moments later, he was on Earth with his armies.

"We need to find the Dragon. I need to be officially named a major demon. After that, we have two choices. We can side with Shadow and fight his father or we can head back down to Hell as the new official department of idolatry. I want my tent built right now and I'd like to see all of my middle demons inside within the next ten minutes. Get it done."

Several demons scurried off to build Gangrene's tent and the rest of them started bandaging and cleaning injuries. Ghoul approached Gangrene and asked if he could have a word in private.

"What's up?"

"If you're hoping the middle demons will back your play to help Shadow, know that it's going to be close. Half of the middle demons want to head back down to Hell and finish off Nightmare's army to share in the spoils of war. Just… be ready for that when it comes up."

"I haven't made a decision yet. I could seriously go either way. My real loyalty is to my armies. If everyone decides to head back down, we'll head back down."

Ghoul smiled as if he was pleased with Gangrene's answer.

"I guess I'll see you in ten then."

CHAPTER 46

Shadow jolted awake and looked around the room. He saw the tear-streaked face of Lilith.

"Did it work? Did we bring him back?"

"I… I don't know. He keeps yelling in different voices and different languages and he won't open his eyes. Whatever that thing is… it isn't Leech."

Shadow could feel his pulse racing and recognized the effect. He saw a needle on the table next to him. Lilith connected the dots for his drug-hazed mind.

"Adrenaline was here. We couldn't get you to wake up. He injected you with berserker drugs. They worked. Quickly."

"Great. How long was I out?"

"Three days. Adrenaline told us all about your berserker training and how Sarah ran off with the new berserker staff. I'm sorry, Shadow. If I had known..."

"It's fine. We had to try."

Shadow got on his feet and waited for his surroundings to stop spinning.

"Wow. I need to stop getting my ass kicked. It really doesn't feel good."

Lilith didn't respond. Shadow put his hand on her shoulder. She turned into his shoulder and started crying.

"Hey. It'll be alright. He's alive again. We just need to figure out the next step to bring him back. This is just a minor setback. The hard part is over. Have you tried showing him his old guns and axe?"

"That didn't do anything."

Shadow looked down at Leech and saw what Lilith meant about him changing voices. He also seemed to occasionally shoot fire from his hands and there were scorch marks on the table he was bolted to.

"Has Samael tried anything? Or your brothers? Do they have any ideas?"

Lilith stopped crying long enough to shake her head.

"Have you shown him your daughter?"

"I'm not exposing her to him like this. I don't know what he's capable of right now."

"Tell me again the details of how he died."

"Fuck you."

"Lilith, it'll help. Stop feeling sorry for yourself and help me bring him back."

"Fine. I'll try. Our armies abandoned us and he didn't want Azazel to hurt us… so…"

Lilith started sobbing again and Shadow helped her along.

"He ran around in the sand and drew a circle around the nephilim…"

"Yes… and then he sucked in their souls. He took all of their strength and power. Then he ran at Azazel and exploded."

"He sucked in their souls. Isn't that what has kept him barely alive all this time? Leftover power?"

"I guess so. I guess they're a part of him now. That's what Jess was saying anyways. It doesn't really matter though because he's useless like this."

Shadow dug around in his pocket and pulled out the large black ring he had taken from Cain's hand. He showed it to Lilith.

"Ugly jewelry isn't going to make me feel better right now. I'm too upset."

"No. It's not for you. It's for Leech."

Lilith looked confused.

"You're giving Leech a ring?"

"The legion ring. The ring we used to combine the Six into Legion. That's why he's speaking in different languages and cycling through powers. They're fighting for control in there. We need to unify them so that Leech can take over. He'll become the dominant soul and come back to us."

"That's crazy."

"It'll work. It has to. I can't keep siphoning off my strength with no payoff. I already lost the berserker staff and the angel who I thought was my friend. I can't lose Leech. Not again."

Shadow walked over to Leech and put the legion ring on his right hand.

Leech stood in the middle of a pit, surrounded by all the nephilim he had destroyed. He didn't know why, but he could finally see them.

"This is my body and I'm in control here. All of you need to submit and let me take over."

His request was met by a chorus of laughter.

"Listen to me. We have the potential to be powerful. More powerful than Azazel. Maybe even more powerful than Shadow. I need all of you to stop fighting for control. Submit your will to mine and we can move on."

One of the nephilim came clearly into view and spoke to Leech.

"You killed us. Why would we submit to you? It would be so much more entertaining to torment your loved ones until this body expires. It's called revenge, Leech. You don't have control anymore."

"I'll make you a deal then. Choose a champion from among your ranks and I will fight him. Or her. Whatever. If I win, I get complete control. If I lose, the nephilim can take over this body. Do we have a deal?"

"We pick the location."

"Sure. Fine. Anything is better than this pit we're in right now."

Leech and the nephilim were suddenly in a swamp.

"When we win, we will destroy you and then kill Lilith and your daughter."

"You won't win."

A vine crept out of the swamp and wrapped itself around Leech's ankle. Several other vines started crawling their way towards his other limbs. Leech looked around, hoping for something to cut them with. Suddenly, his back felt heavier. He reached back and retrieved his axe. A few minutes later, he was free of the vines. The vines, grass, and bushes crawled away from Leech like snakes and gathered into a large beast-like creature.

"Remember our deal, Leech. They die when we win."

Leech tried to use his parasitic touch, but nothing happened. He closed his eyes and imagined his guns were attached to his belt. When he opened his eyes, they were exactly where he had imagined them. He pointed at the swamp creature and started firing.

CHAPTER 47

Weapon knew the angels were tracking him, but there was nothing he could do to slow them down. He had to get out of the area quickly and find Shadow. If the idiotic group of nephilim that had captured him was right, being around Shadow and Samael was the safest place to be right now.

Weapon wasn't using his motorcycle because it made too much noise and would be a dead giveaway. He had decided to roll down the street on a skateboard he had pulled from his coat. There weren't many situations where the skateboard was preferable to his motorcycle, so Weapon was enjoying the change of pace.

Weapon moved in the direction his senses told him to. He had been able to track down other nephilim before and tracking was made easier by the fact that there were several of them in one location. As he neared the group, he saw a much larger force than he expected. He pocketed his skateboard and hid out in the bushes with his binoculars. When he zoomed in, he confirmed his suspicions. Berserker demons. Lots of them. It didn't make any sense because he also felt that the nephilim were very close.

"Maybe they were captured."

As Weapon said it, he could tell it sounded ridiculous. Samael and his children weren't captured. They could take care of themselves. He didn't know what the situation was, but he knew they were in there. He decided to approach the camp, but clearly signal who he was in case they saw him from a distance.

One of the berserker demons on guard duty made his way quickly to Adrenaline. Adrenaline had been explaining some berserker techniques to Thanatos, as he played with his niece.

"There's something approaching. He has a large weapon of some kind, but we're unsure what it is."

"Send a band out to capture it."

Thanatos stood.

"I'll lead them out there. We may need to kill this thing and I haven't killed anything in a while. My hands are starting to get… *itchy*."

"Sure. Let Thanatos lead a group out there. Bind the creature and bring it in alive if you can." Thanatos nodded and delivered baby Lucia to Muan. He grabbed his large axe and started walking towards the approaching creature. Several berserker demons followed him.

Weapon saw the small band approaching. He grabbed his binoculars again. He could see a few berserker demons being led by Thanatos.

"Shit."

Weapon recalled that Thanatos had tried to kill him and didn't know if he would try again when separated from Lilith. After all, she was the only one who argued to spare his life. He decided to send a warning. He aimed at an area somewhat to the right of the approaching band and fired his rocket launcher.

Thantos saw the rocket explode and immediately knew who he was dealing with. His only remaining decision was what to do about it. He still wanted to kill Weapon, but knew that Lilith would be mad at him if she found out. She didn't want them killing nephilim anymore. If he killed Weapon, she would probably stop letting him babysit his niece and he didn't like that thought.

"It's a nephilim named Weapon. He has a rocket launcher. I don't know why he's here. He told us he was going to leave us alone. I'll try to disarm him and we'll bring him in alive. If he resists at all, attack from all sides and put him down. He's a dangerous little fucker."

The berserkers nodded and fanned out so they could encircle the approaching nephilim. When they came close enough, Weapon rested the rocket launcher on his shoulder.

"What up, Big T? I need to talk to Lilith and Shadow, if he's here."

"Put the rocket launcher down."

Weapon opened his coat and Thanatos shook his head.

"On the ground. Not back in the coat. Take your fucking coat off while you're at it."

Weapon placed his rocket launcher on the ground and then stepped back several paces to remove his coat.

"I'm just here to talk."

"You fired a rocket at us. Again."

Weapon rolled his eyes.

"That didn't count. I missed on purpose. It wasn't even close to you guys. I just wanted to give you a heads up that it was me so you wouldn't shoot me before I got a chance to talk to Shadow and Lilith."

Weapon removed his coat and draped it over his arm.

"You going to try to kill me, Thanatos? 'Cuz if you are, I'm going to keep my coat. If you want to kill me, you'll have to take me down fully armed."

"Lilith wants you alive. Put the coat on the ground and step back."

"You're not answering my question. *Lilith* wants me alive. Does that mean you aren't going to kill me?"

"Not today. Now put the fucking coat on the fucking ground and step the fuck back."

Weapon grinned.

"That's all I needed to hear. The first part… not the chorus of 'fucks.'"

Weapon folded his coat and laid it on the ground before backing away. The berserker demons retrieved the coat and the rocket launcher. Thanatos grabbed Weapons arms and shoved them behind his back before tying them together. He shoved him with his axe towards Shadow's tent. When they made it to Shadow's tent, Thanatos poked his head in.

"It's that Weapon asshole. He's back and he fired a rocket at us again."

Thanatos withdrew his head and shoved Weapon inside. Lilith looked amused.

"Shadow, this is Weapon. He's the nephilim I told you about. He likes to hide stuff in his coat."

Thanatos entered and dropped the coat on the table. He placed the rocket launcher in a chest of weapons and then shut and locked it, knowing his niece would be curious. As he looked back at the table, he saw Lucia already getting in to the coat and searching its inner pockets. He rushed to the table to pick her up. When he pulled her out of the coat, she brought a wrapped demon arm with her. Thanatos unwrapped it and let her chew on it. Weapon shook his head.

"What is it with you guys and stealing my food? That was supposed to be my dinner."

"Maybe if your go-to reaction wasn't 'I'll fire a rocket,' you wouldn't have issues like that as often."

Thanatos took Lucia out of the room. Shadow picked up the coat with curiousity.

"How much can this thing hold?"

"Not sure. Don't even know if it has a limit."

"And you made it yourself?"

"Gift. Look… I'm not here to be interrogated. I ran into one of Uriel's patrolling bands and I'd like to help you kill all the angels. Or all the demons. Or whatever. I forgot what your mission actually is. I just know it's not safe out there right now and I'd rather hang around you guys until things settle down."

"And why should we trust you? Samael told me you wanted nothing to do with us."

"That was before I found out you were with them. I figure this is the safest place to be right now. Having your own personal berserker army is just the icing on the cake."

"They aren't mine. You still haven't answered my question."

"Give me a chance. You'll learn to trust me and I can be useful. I have at least moderate skill with every weapon in my coat."

"How many weapons do you have in your coat?"

Weapon thought for a minute.

"You know… I don't remember anymore."

Lilith pulled a chainsaw out of one of the coat's pockets.

"Why don't you prove it to us?"

She turned to Shadow.

"We can set up a bunch of targets and have Weapon give us a demonstration."

Shadow nodded.

"I like it. Show us what you can do and maybe you'll be worth keeping around. Meet us outside in five minutes."

"Is anyone going to cut me free?"

"Yup. In five minutes."

Shadow and Lilith assembled a bunch of targets and straw men. Lilith cast a spell on a few of them to make them move. Weapon was able to hit them with every item he pulled from his coat, including regular weapons like knives, guns, and his rocket launcher, but he also landed killing blows with a kayak paddle, a spatula, and a tire iron. Shadow and Lilith decided to let him stay.

CHAPTER 48

Gangrene met with his middle demons and presented what he hoped would be a compelling speech in favor of helping Shadow. He tried to find ways to appeal to their self-interest since he knew loyalty would be a failing argument. Then he called for a vote. Four middle demons voted to help Shadow and five voted to return to Hell. Gangrene could have voted himself and then made the decision when the results were a tie, but he let the vote stand.

"We'll go to the Dragon, I'll become a major demon, and then we'll return to Hell to claim our share of Astaroth's and Nightmare's armies and treasure."

As the middle demons filed out, Raven looked angry.

"We've discussed this before, Raven. We have to put ourselves ahead of Shadow and your sister. I have to do what's best for my armies and the department."

"And you think your middle demons know what's best? You're their leader. You decide what's best. You could have overruled their vote."

"And had five middle demons plotting to kill me the second we start fighting on Shadow's side? I don't think so. The other four only voted to help Shadow because they knew it's what I wanted. They'll be fine with returning to Hell."

"Fine. You want to be a major demon. I know we've already discussed this. We have to do what's best for us… but Gangrene…"

"Yes?"

"Find a way to help them anyways."

"Like how?"

"You'll think of something."

Within a few days, Gangrene had tracked down the Dragon and his armies. When they entered the camp, they were stopped by one of the giants.

"No one comes in unless they have a scythe. The Dragon isn't interested in talking to anyone else right now."

Gangrene's middle demons put their hands on their weapons and waited for Gangrene to give them a signal, but he shook his head.

"Wait outside."

Raven tried to enter with Gangrene, but the guards shoved her back.

"I'm going in, too."

"You can't. I have to do this alone."

"Not gonna happen, Gangrene."

Gangrene waved Ghoul over.

"She doesn't follow me in. You'll keep her outside the Dragon's camp. Understood?"

Ghoul nodded and motioned for several minor demons to come forward. He pointed at Raven. Raven looked furious, but the demons were able to drag her away without any further resistance. The giant turned and led Gangrene to the Dragon's tent. When Gangrene entered, he saw that the Dragon looked uncomfortable on his throne. Gangrene kneeled.

"I am Gangrene, successor to the fallen major demon, Leech. I was a minor demon under Shadow and a middle demon under Leech. My position as major demon of idolatry is uncontested. I have the support of the nine middle demons in my army. I request that my position be made official."

"This couldn't wait until I was back in Hell."

"Apologies, Great Dragon, but it couldn't. The demons are at war. Leech and Astaroth are dead. Shadow and Lilith have renounced their positions and their armies. I want the official powers that come with the scythe. I need to put an end to what's going on down there."

"If the reports I've heard are true, *you* killed Astaroth. You think you can restore some semblance of order in Hell?"

"Honestly, Great Dragon, I don't. I just hope to be the last major demon standing. The armies of Murmur, Jess, and Aim are weak. Astaroth's armies are leaderless. Nightmare is using his berserker scythe and failing to lead his armies. We'll be down to less than a thousand demons within a few weeks."

The Dragon shifted in his seat and winced. Gangrene started to suspect that he had been injured.

"If I may ask, Great Dragon, why are you still up here? Killing Abaddon doesn't seem like it should be a priority."

"What do you know of priorities? Your sole concern is to rule over a dying kingdom. I have my reputation to think of. No one escapes from the lowest circle of Hell. Not even the son of Michael."

"Reputations can easily survive on lies. I know Shadow plans on killing his father and there's a good chance he can. I know you've fought Abaddon already. We just say that *you* killed him instead of Shadow."

"How do you know that I've fought him?"

"The injury you're trying to hide. Unless Michael is running around on Earth somewhere, I imagine it came from Abaddon."

"Very perceptive. I'm not amused that you figured it out."

"Great Dragon, please return to Hell while there's still a Hell to be ruled over. We need your leadership."

"And what if Shadow fails to kill his father?"

"At the very least, Shadow will injure him. Send up assassins to finish the job. You can make this a win-win situation if you want to. Stop demons from killing each other off in Hell and then claim victory on Earth."

"If Shadow fails, I'm sending the Six up here with their armies to finish Abaddon off. I'm not risking my own army again until Armageddon."

"A wise decision, Great Dragon. We will do as you command."

"Then it is done. You are the new major demon of idolatry. Return to Hell with my armies."

Gangrene nodded and left.

CHAPTER 49

Sarah had been watching from the top branches of a tree three days ago when Shadow had brought Leech back from the dead. She knew that Leech's mind was messed up and had been debating what to do about it. She ultimately decided to pray and ask her grandfather to help them. She wasn't sure if he would and knew that he would try to find her, but she couldn't just leave them helpless. Even though she didn't want to admit, Sarah also knew that with the strength of a nephilim army trapped inside him, Leech might be the more logical candidate to take down Abaddon. As soon as Abaddon was dead, she could return to Shadow and apologize. Sarah bowed her head and began her prayer.

"Grandpa, I know you're not happy with the choices I've made and the creatures I've befriended, but Shadow needs your help. They found a way to bring Leech back, but his mind is scrambled and the nephilim are fighting for control. I know you can help him. Please come down here one last time for my sake and fix him. In the end, I think it could save humanity."

As soon as Sarah had finished her prayer, she grabbed the berserker staff and ran off into the night.

Gabriel entered the berserker camp and made his way towards Shadow's tent. When demons got in his way, he shoved them aside.

"I don't have time for this. I need to see Shadow. Now."

Gabriel entered the tent and drew his sword.

"Where is she? Where's Sarah?"

Shadow looked up from the book of spells he had been perusing, hoping to find something helpful for Leech.

"How the hell would I know? She stole the berserker staff and ran off."

"She prayed to me asking for help just a few minutes ago. I know she's around here somewhere."

"She'll be long gone by now, Gabriel. She doesn't want to be found. We've tried to find her for days now and can't even find a trace. If she prayed to you, I guarantee you she's no longer where she was when she did it. What did she need help with? She obviously isn't in any danger, because she doesn't want to be found right now."

"She wanted me to fix your friend. Something about his brain having issues and nephlim something or other. It's not really what I focused on."

Shadow got up from his seat and dropped the book.

"*Can* you help him?"

"I'm sure I could. I just don't see a reason to save a demon's life. I hated having to tolerate you for as long as I did."

"If you fix him, he'll kill Azazel."

"Why would he do that?"

"Azazel put him in this condition. He was trying to save his family and friends, so he had to take Azazel down. He nearly got Azazel the last time. If you bring him back, he won't miss this time. Azazel will go down for good."

"Didn't you promise me you would keep her safe? Aren't you concerned about the baby she's carrying? Your son or daughter?"

"I didn't do this. She ran away with the berserker staff so I wouldn't go berserk on Abaddon. Also… she wasn't pregnant when I told you that. She might be now though."

"I should just kill you and be done with all of this."

"We've played that game. It didn't solve anything. She's safe, Gabriel. She's trained as a berserker now."

"You let berserker demons train her? What's wrong with you?"

"Are you going to help Leech or not? You don't hold the cards anymore, Gabriel. You walked into a camp of berserker demons. Their leader, Adrenaline, has my back. I have two new nephilim recruits, Steam and Weapon. Lilith, Hypnos, and Thanatos are all here, too. I'm in control. I ask the questions."

Shadow briefly considered mentioning that Samael was with them too, but figured Gabriel might haul him back to Heaven. He wasn't exactly sure how Samael left Heaven and didn't want to complicate things.

"I'm tired of you, Shadow. I'm tired of your lies and I'm tired of deals that never end up working to my advantage. So I'll help you, but not simply because my granddaughter asked me to. You'll give something up this time so you can actually start learning what sacrifice is."

"I guess we can skip past the fact that I'm sacrificing more than any of the angels to put down the greatest threat Earth has ever seen. What do you want?"

Gabriel didn't hesitate.

"Michael's armor. It has sentimental value to the Heavens. It never should have left his possession. I want it back."

"This was a gift to me from Persephone, my grandmother."

"Maybe that's true. Maybe it isn't. With you, I never know. I honestly don't care at this point. You have my terms. I'm turning your question back on you. Am I going to help Leech or not? It's your call, Shadow."

Shadow gathered up his armor, placed it in a large sack, and handed it over to Gabriel.

"Do it. My friends mean more to me than shit like armor."

"I have to say, I didn't expect that. That's the first halfway decent thing you've ever said that I actually believe. If only you had kept your promise to protect my granddaughter with the same zeal... we wouldn't have to make trades like this."

"If you fail, I'll take the armor back and then I'll kill you. I'll only allow you to be here as long as you're useful. Fix Leech and the armor is all yours."

"Deal, but please remember that we both know you can't kill me."

Gabriel placed his hand on Leech's forehead and entered his mind.

CHAPTER 50

Adrenaline had received word from one of his spies that the Dragon and his armies were headed towards one of the passages that led back to Hell. Adrenaline immediately went to see Shadow and saw the Archangel Gabriel with his hand on Leech's forehead in some kind of trance. Adrenaline pointed at the odd scene and looked at Shadow, hoping for an answer.

"Long story. He's helping us bring Leech back. What do you want, Adrenaline?"

"The Dragon is headed back to Hell. I have reports that he hasn't been seen in a while. His armies are keeping him hidden. I'm guessing Abaddon injured him. It's the perfect time to strike and take him down for good."

"I can't go after him. Killing Abaddon has to be my priority."

"You gave me your word you would help us with the Dragon."

"That was never our deal. I told you he was my enemy. Our deal was that I would take care of Azazel. That's exactly what we're going to do once Leech is back. Then we move on to Abaddon."

"Maybe our agreement was not clear enough. It doesn't matter. I'm glad I trained you and I hope you rid the world of Azazel and Abaddon. I can't stay with you, though. My army will go after the Dragon. Would you consider sending someone with us?"

"Do you have someone specific in mind?"

"Muan. His transformation powers combined with the abilities of a berserker would make him a valuable warrior. I would offer him a middle demon position in my army."

"I'll discuss it with him. If he decides to go with you, he should be able to catch up fairly easily. Don't slow your pace on Maun's account. One more thing before you leave…"

Shadow went to the side of his bed and grabbed a sword. He handed it over to Adrenaline.

"Sarah left this when she ran off with the berserker staff. It's one of the two swords crafted by Azazel for Scapegoat. I know it's not the same as what you had… but still…"

Shadow handed the sword over to Adrenaline. Adrenaline took the sword and then held out his hand.

"Thanks, Shadow. I hope we see you again someday."

Adrenaline turned and left. He took his berserker army and went after the Dragon.

When Gabriel transported inside Leech's mind, he fell through the air and landed in swamp water. He grabbed at some reeds and lifted himself to his feet.

"Wow. I knew demons had filthy minds, but I had no idea it was going to be this bad."

Gabriel waded through the swamp waters until he heard what sounded like a fight and turned to head in that direction. He saw Leech fighting a large swamp monster made of vines, plants, and miscellaneous swamp garbage. Leech didn't seem to be making any progress; he continued to hack at vines without inflicting any damage. Gabriel ran at the swamp creature and drove his sword into the ground right in front of it. The monster divided into the nephilim that had formed it as it sailed backwards in the air. Gabriel removed the golden chain he had brought with him and threw one end of it to Leech.

"We're going to bind them with this and then throw them in the pit where they were keeping you a prisoner."

"Who the fuck are you?"

"Does it matter right now? You can either accept my help or lose to the swamp garbage beast over there."

Leech nodded.

"I'm in. How do we get back to the pit though? They brought me here to this swamp…"

"This is your mind, Leech. Focus on the pit and the area surrounding it. You can take us back."

Leech focused on the pit and the grassy area surrounding it. Leech and Gabriel were transported, with the nephilim, to the area. When they arrived, Leech got hit hard in the chest by one of the nephilim. Gabriel immediately began to wrap the nephilim in the chains while Leech recovered.

"I could use some help. Any time you feel like getting up. No rush. It's just a battle for control of your mind and body."

"You're a really intolerable… wait a second… you're…"

"Gabriel. Can you multi-task? Maybe connect the dots and bind the nephilim at the same time? Please?"

Leech got to his feet and started wrapping the nephilim in the chain as they attacked. He had to slash at a few with his axe, but they eventually had the entire nephilim army bound. Leech stuck his axe hilt in the ground and rested on the weapon, trying to catch his breath.

"Great. Now how do we get them in the pit?"

"We push. Make sure you're ready before we start because that's a lot of nephilim."

Leech took his time recovering and then let Gabriel know he was ready. The two of them slowly pushed the bound nephilim into the pit. When the nephilim landed at the bottom, Gabriel left Leech's mind and Leech opened his eyes.

Gabriel collected the sack containing Michael's armor and turned to leave. Shadow stuck Damnation in his face and shook his head.

"Not until I know he's back."

At the sound of Shadow's voice, Leech tilted his head up. He got off the table and ran to hug his friend.

"Shady! I knew you wouldn't let me stay dead!"

Shadow pulled back Damnation and addressed Gabriel.

"Take the armor and get the fuck out."

As Gabriel was leaving, Lilith brought Lucia into Shadow's tent.

"Shadow, she's teething. Do you have something for her to bite?"

When Lilith saw who Shadow was hugging, she ran to him and shoved Shadow out of the way. She started crying hysterically and Shadow took Lucia so she wouldn't accidently crush her between her body and Leech's. She kissed him, oblivious to everything else, and Shadow took the baby outside so they could have some time alone.

CHAPTER 51

The camp was a lot quieter once the berserker army had left to pursue the Dragon. Shadow asked Muan to go for a walk with him in the woods. Muan wasn't sure what to make of the request.

"Is there something you need before we find and kill Azazel?"

"No. There's just something I wanted to talk to you about. Adrenaline made you an offer before he left. I think you should take it."

"What was the offer?"

"A middle demon position in his army. He'd train you to be a berserker so you could combine your transformation powers with the fighting abilities and rage of a berserker. I've trained in their methods and they're a very powerful order."

"So after we kill Azazel and Abaddon…"

"No. They're going to fight the Dragon's armies. Adrenaline wants you to catch up with them and take the position now."

Muan looked confused.

"Did I do something to piss you off?"

"No. It's nothing like…"

"Then why are you sending me away?"

"It's better than anything I can offer right now. I don't have armies to command. All I can offer from here on out is the chance to die fighting creatures we're not even sure if we can kill."

"I don't care. I want to fight."

"Your loyalty is admirable, Muan, but let's be honest. You were a leader before all of this happened. You had your own armies and you were good at what you did. I don't think that should be thrown away out of loyalty. I think you should take Adrenaline's offer."

"And if I refuse?"

"I'm not demanding that you leave. It's your choice. I just think it's a lot better than being my personal tracker demon. You're more qualified than anything I can offer you right now. That's the reason I let Gangrene go and that's the reason I think you should go."

Muan sighed and looked at the ground.

"I hope it's not cowardly to admit this, but I'm not ready to die yet. There are still things I want to do. Things I hope to accomplish. If you seriously mean what you say, I think I'll accept Adrenaline's offer."

"I'm glad to hear that. It's probably best if you take off now. Lilith will throw a fit. I'm sure Leech will have something to say, too. I'll explain everything to them."

"When you get back, check your map. I marked something on there that'll help you out."

Shadow nodded. Muan turned into a crow and turned to leave.

"Just one more thing, Muan."

The crow turned back and listened.

"You were never a coward and you aren't one now. Pursuing your dreams is always harder than the escape that a quick death offers."

The crow appeared to nod before it flew into the air and glided into the sunset.

Shadow called a war council that night. He informed everyone that Muan had left and explained why. Lilith was angry, Leech was angry, everyone else seemed fairly indifferent. Shadow changed the topic.

"We need to split up again. I've tried to think of a different way to deal with this, but time is not on our side. The Dragon is leaving which means now is the time to strike. We need to deal with anyone who might interfere in my battle with Abaddon which means we need to deal with Azazel and Uriel. Thoughts?"

Leech responded before anyone else could.

"Azazel is mine. I'll take Lilith, Steam, and Thanatos. The rest of you can go after…"

Lilith cut him off.

"I don't think we should be splitting up again. All it ever does is cause problems. Why don't we all go kill Azazel and then all of us go deal with Uriel?"

Shadow shook his head.

"You still don't get it? If we let Abaddon destroy much more of the Earth, there will be nothing left to save. It's already going to take decades for humanity to get back to where they were after all the earthquakes, floods, tornadoes, and everything else he's been unleashing up here. The Dragon is out of the way now. So here's what we're going to do. Leech, Lilith, Steam, and Thanatos will go after Azazel. Samael, Weapon, and Hypnos will deal with Uriel. Make sure you take them out quietly. We can't have Uriel's armies following you back. I'll track down Abaddon. When Uriel and Azazel are out of the way, we all meet again and attack Abaddon together. I'll send word once I've found him and I'll track him until the rest of you arrive."

Weapon looked annoyed.

"I just got away from Uriel's army. You want us to go *back*? He'll kill us."

Samael shook his head.

"He won't. I can take him down this time. Leave Uriel to me."

Hypnos nodded.

"Yeah. Stop acting like a scared little girl, Weapon. You'll be fine."

Shadow looked around the room. Everyone seemed to at least be in agreement that his plan was a logical way to address everything. He moved on to the next step.

"We can't all teleport. There's a spell that can bring all of you to me after you finish your task. I had Jess write it down for me a while back and Steam thinks he can pull it off."

Steam nodded.

"That or all of your heads will explode. I think I got it though. We should be ok."

Everyone stared blankly at Steam. He smiled nervously.

"It was a joke. I've read Jess's incantations. I can pull it off."

Shadow placed a large black pot on the table and passed out knives to everyone present. Lilith looked excited.

"Finally! We're all going to become blood brothers!"

Shadow ignored her.

"We need a drop of everyone's blood for the teleportation spell. Lucia's already covered. She scraped her knee playing around yesterday and I got what I needed. Everyone else needs to cut a finger."

Lilith had already sliced her hand across the palm and was letting blood drip into the pot.

"Oh… well I guess I'll teleport really fast."

Everyone cut one of their fingers and let a drop of blood fall into the pot. Steam added some other ingredients from his backpack. He re-read the spell when he had finished.

"Alright. Shadow will be the transportation source. I need everyone else to say what they're going to do before they teleport to Shadow."

Leech's group said, "Kill Azazel" and Samael's group said, "Kill Uriel." The liquid in the pot started bubbling and turned a murky brown. Steam started handing out cups. Weapon protested.

"You've got to be kidding me. You want us to *drink* that shit?"

Leech had finally had enough.

"You're welcome to leave, Weapon. Thanatos can switch teams. We can do this without you."

Weapon didn't respond.

"No? Then shut the fuck up and drink."

Everyone drank a cup of the thick liquid and Lilith slowly helped Lucia drink some from her sippy cup. Shadow nodded his approval.

"Thanks, Steam. We'll split up tomorrow. Good luck."

CHAPTER 52

Muan caught up to the berserker army without any issues and accepted Adrenaline's offer. Adrenaline had Muan begin berserker training immediately. He caught on quickly and was soon learning to integrate his animal transformations into berserker rages. Adrenaline didn't have a large army, so he gave Muan control of half. His other middle demon, a berserker demoness named Nissa, was commander of the other half. The berserker demons in Muan's army respected him after they saw what he was capable of as a berserker demon.

After a few days of pursuit, the berserkers could see the Dragon's armies in the distance. Adrenaline invited Muan and Nissa into his tent to strategize.

"We have a couple of things to talk about tonight. First, we're working on making a new berserker staff. It isn't as powerful as the other two yet because we haven't used it as much. It hasn't absorbed enough rage or seen enough bloodshed. So it isn't actually a legitimate berserker staff yet. It'll get there eventually though and it enhances berserker powers slightly as it is. I'll be using it when we catch up to the Dragon."

Muan looked at the new berserker staff.

"Can I pick it up?"

Adrenaline nodded his consent. Muan picked up the staff and immediately felt the urge to hit both Adrenaline and Nissa in the face with it. He placed it back on the table before the urge overwhelmed him. Muan looked over at Nissa, but she shook her head.

"Nope. I've held one before. I know what it feels like. That's great that Adrenaline got a new weapon, but I don't need to touch it."

Muan sat back down and Adrenaline continued.

"Second, the Dragon disgraced our order in favor of those idiots in Nightmare's armies. They don't know the first thing about being berserker demons. They don't know our culture, our traditions, and the power they've been granted is misused. The goal of our attack is to demand to be reinstated into Hell's armies. We won't work for the Dragon directly anymore. I'll demand to be made a major demon. There's an opening from what I've heard. Astaroth was killed by Gangrene."

Muan grinned.

"Nice. Old Toxic Touch put down the snake bitch. Good to hear."

"If the Dragon denies my request, and it's likely that he will, I'll attack him directly. I'll go into a berserker rage and take him down for good. Nissa is in charge when I die."

Nissa looked pleased with the news and decided to rub it in.

"Don't feel too bad, little guy. I have way more experience fighting as a berserker and it's obvious that I should be in charge."

Muan laughed.

"Good for you, Nissa. I've worked for Shadow and commanded an army larger than all of Adrenaline's forces combined. I'm a better fighter and a better leader… but go ahead and feel good about yourself for being a berserker longer."

Muan started a slow golf clap. Nissa lunged at him, but Adrenaline cut her off and shoved her back.

"Enough. There's no need to insult and mock each other. This is going to be difficult enough as it is without us turning on each other. I won't have any more of that shit from the two of you. Understood?"

Nissa turned and left without another word. Muan stayed behind.

"You really want her leading the berserkers after you're gone? She's a hot-headed mess."

"It's an army of berserkers, Muan. They're all hot-headed messes. This is for the best. If our order is to be led into extinction, she's who I trust to get us there after I'm gone."

"So if the Dragon accepts you as a major demon, Nissa isn't necessarily your next in line then? Only if we're headed for extinction?"

"I think that's fair to say. The two of you are equal in my eyes if our order can live on. She has more experience if we need to rush into death."

Muan turned to leave, but paused before stepping outside.

"I'll keep that in mind and may even hold you to that."

A few days later, Gangrene received a report that a force of demons was rushing towards them. Gangrene immediately informed the Dragon, who emerged from his tent in demon-form as Lucifer. Gangrene could tell that the injury inflicted by Abaddon was nearly healed. Lucifer showed barely any sign of injury as he walked. He smiled when he saw who was approaching.

"It's Adrenaline and his outcast band of berserkers. So they fled to Earth when I disgraced their order and cast them out."

He turned to Gangrene.

"Be ready to destroy them. We have them ridiculously outnumbered."

Adrenaline stopped his army a short distance from Lucifer's armies.

"I will give you this one chance to accept us back. Not as one of your armies, but as an independent major demon with my own scythe and power. If this is unacceptable to you, I personally challenge you to a fight to the death."

Lucifer laughed. He held out his hands together and then pulled them apart. His armies opened a path straight to him.

"Attack then, berserker."

Adrenaline tightened his grip on the berserker staff and looked to Muan and then to Nissa. They both nodded. Then he charged. Lucifer didn't move. Adrenaline hit Lucifer several times in the face with the berserker staff. Lucifer smiled and took the hits for several minutes until a single drop of blood started to roll down his right nostril. He frowned, stepped back, and hit Adrenaline hard on the shoulder. He fell to one knee. When he got back up, Lucifer had changed form into a dragon and slashed with his right claw. At first, it looked like the claw had missed, because Adrenaline was still standing. Then, suddenly, his limbs and head fell from his torso and his body fell to the ground in six pieces. The berserker staff hit the ground and rolled a few inches from his open hand.

Muan looked at Nissa and could see tears rolling down her face. He knew that she was going to follow Adrenaline's final order, but he had to try to stop her anyways.

"That's Gangrene with the Dragon's armies. I can get him to talk to the Dragon. We can be spared. There's no need to throw our lives away."

"We aren't throwing them away, Muan. We're adding an exclamation point to Adrenaline's final words. That asshole deserves to die."

Muan turned into a cheetah, ran towards Adrenaline's corpse, and retrieved the berserker staff. Several demons in the Dragon's army tried to stop him, but none of them were able to. He ran back to his berserkers.

"Adrenaline told me that whoever held the berserker staff after he fell would be in charge of our order of berserkers. I hold it now. We will not rush to our deaths. I know the demon at the Dragon's side and I know he can be reasoned with. There is no need for pointless sacrifice."

Nissa looked at Muan like he was a piece of shit.

"You *liar*! Adrenaline left me in charge! Give me the staff."

She held out her hand. Muan shook his head. None of the berserkers looked ready to intervene.

"Take it from me if you think you can."

Nissa ran at him. Muan turned into a crow, caught the falling berserker staff in his beak and flew into the sky. He could already feel the effects of the staff flowing through him. Once he was at a height of about fifteen feet, he turned into a gorilla, aiming a fist at Nissa as he fell. When he landed, she was no longer there. He felt a strong kick to the back of his head and it pissed him off. The next kick was caught in his large gorilla palm and he lifted Nissa into the air. He grabbed one of her arms and one of her legs and let the berserker staff fall. He caught the staff on his foot. Then he pulled with all his strength and ripped Nissa in half. He kicked the berserker staff into the air, changed back into a demon, and caught it in his right hand.

"Anyone else have a problem with me being in charge?"

The berserkers fell to their knees and bowed to Muan.

CHAPTER 53

Samael, Weapon, and Hypnos hid on a rooftop and looked at the angels a block over. Weapon pointed at Cassiel.

"That's him. He has nephilim heads attached to his belt. I think he's one of Uriel's middle angels tasked with killing nephilim. If we kill him, Uriel will come."

Samael nodded.

"Good. I'll go in first and…"

Weapon grinned and shook his head.

"Nope. Here's how we play this. I'll fire off a rocket from over there…"

Weapon pointed at a rooftop closer to the angels.

"… and then the two of you come in from behind and take them out when they're chasing me."

Hypnos slapped Weapon hard on the back.

"I like that plan. Never thought I'd see you volunteer to be the bait."

"Well my plan has a rocket launcher in it. I haven't actually *hit* anything with my rocket launcher in a while. Samael? What do you think?"

"It sounds like a good plan. We'll wait in the bushes over there. I'll signal you when I want you to fire the rocket."

Weapon nodded and crawled down off the roof. He ran across the street and pulled a ladder out of his coat. He climbed the side of the house, put the ladder away, got his rocket launcher, and waited for Samael and Hypnos to get into position. Hypnos jumped head first into the bushes. Samael looked up at Weapon and nodded before hiding in the bushes himself. Weapon took careful aim and fired.

The rocket exploded in the middle of a large group of angels. Many of them were instantly incinerated and at least a dozen were seriously injured. The angels that weren't seriously injured or that were far enough away from the blast radius looked for the source. Weapon put his rocket launcher away, grabbed a couple of pistols from his jacket, and jumped down into the street. An angel quickly spotted him and pointed, alerting the rest of the angels. Weapon turned and ran, occasionally firing over his shoulder. The angels followed Weapon and Hypnos followed the angels, throwing daggers and putting them to sleep as fast as he could.

Cassiel didn't give chase. He looked around to see if any other nephilim were hiding in the area. As he turned towards the bushes, Samael jumped out and cut off his arms. He then kicked him in the midsection and Cassiel fell hard on the street. His wounds gushing blood, Cassiel looked up at his soon-to-be murderer.

"Samael. I never thought you'd show your cowardly face again."

Samael didn't speak. He brought his sword up with both hands, blade pointed squarely at Cassiel's chest. Before he could strike, a sword pierced his heart quickly and then withdrew. He fell forward and a strong arm caught him, turning him around and placing him on his back. He looked up and saw his killer, Uriel the Archangel.

"I told you the day you were cast out that I would find you and kill you, Samael. You've brought several abominations into this world and justice will only be served when I kill them. Don't worry, though. I *will* kill them. Hypnos, Thanatos, and Lilith. Still, justice won a small victory today with your death."

Uriel closed his eyes and made the sign of a cross. Samael spit at him.

"Fuck you and fuck Heaven. I regret nothing."

Uriel reached into Samael's open mouth, pulled out his tongue, and slowly cut it while Samael screamed. When his tongue was completely removed, Uriel threw it on the ground and stomped on it.

"No more speeches from you, blasphemer. If you refuse to die quietly, I won't give you the option."

Uriel saw Cassiel bleeding out on the ground.

"You can still save me, Uriel. Please…"

Uriel stabbed Cassiel's heart and he exhaled loudly, settling into death.

"I don't heal, Cassiel. I enforce the laws of justice. Thank you for your sacrifice. Your death will be noted in the records of Heaven."

Samael drew his sword and then threw it as far as he could with the last of his strength. He didn't want Uriel to take it as a prize. As he watched it sail through the air, he closed his eyes and died.

Weapon and Hypnos finished killing off the small band of angels that had run after them, including the angels Hypnos had put to sleep.

"We made good time, but I would have thought more of them would have followed you. We need to get back and make sure we clear out a lot more before Uriel shows up."

Weapon nodded.

"Let's go then."

It didn't take long for the nephilim to make it back. They ran back up the street and saw Uriel standing over the corpses of Cassiel and Samael. Weapon put his pistols back in his coat and grabbed a machine gun. Hypnos continued to stand there and stare at his father's body. Weapon grabbed his shoulder.

"I know it sucks, Hypnos, but we have to get out of here. We're outnumbered."

Hypnos turned his head and Weapon saw his pupilless eyes glowing white. He let go of Hypnos's shoulder and continued to slowly back away. Hypnos held out his hands and a harp formed. He positioned it correctly and began to play. The approaching angels started moving slower. Several of them started dragging their feet and a few dropped their weapons. Slowly, the entire army of Uriel laid down on the street and fell asleep. Uriel watched in horror. Hypnos's eyes turned red and he threw the harp on the ground. A smile crept its way up his face.

"You don't fuck with the nephilim. We are a nightmare that you never wake up from."

Hypnos held out his hands. Uriel could sense something creeping slowly towards him and he looked at his sleeping army. Blood. Blood slowly flowed out of angel eyes, angel nostrils, and angel ears. Hypnos put them to sleep and was now slowly killing them. When Uriel started to feel tired, he immediately drew his sword and teleported back to Heaven.

Weapon didn't dare touch Hypnos again. He put the machine gun back in his coat, pulled out a lawn chair, sat down, and waited. When Hypnos finally put his hands down and turned back around, his eyes had returned to normal. Weapon slowly clapped.

"Ho… ly… shit."

CHAPTER 54

Azazel had hidden himself very close to Abaddon, where earthquakes rattled the ground every few minutes, but he was still out of sight. Abaddon had grown even more terrifying and unpredictable and Azazel didn't want to interact with him anymore after what Leech had done to his Nephilim army. His injuries had mostly healed since his last encounter with Leech and he was strong enough to sense that nephilim were approaching. Instead of running, he waited to see who it was. If it turned out to be Shadow, he could teleport away. Anyone else was worth killing or recruiting.

Leech walked fearlessly towards him. Lilith, Steam, and Thanatos stayed a considerable distance back at Leech's request. Thanatos was having a hard time keeping Lucia happy, as the rumbling ground continually upset her. Steam summoned a levitating blanket of water for her to lay on and kept it a few feet off the ground so she wouldn't feel the tremors.

Leech stopped about ten feet from Azazel and drew his guns.

"It's time for Round 2, asshole."

"How are you still alive? I watched you explode…"

"Does it matter?"

"What brought you back?"

Leech pointed his guns at Azazel and then felt his arms slowly being lowered. He could feel something inside him object to attacking Azazel. Azazel grinned.

"So you took on the power of the nephilim you consumed. Pretty stupid since they worked for me. So why don't you turn around and start firing at your friends?"

Thanatos picked up Lucia from her levitating water blanket, handed her to Lilith, and got in front of them.

"Get out of here."

Lilith shook her head.

"Leech won't attack us. We'll be ok."

Leech turned and pointed his guns at Thanatos. Before he could fire, he threw them in the sand and drew his axe.

"Why don't you all excuse me for a while? I need to deal with some internal issues."

Leech drew a circle in the sand with his axe and a green circle appeared around him. He sat down, crossed his legs, and closed his eyes.

Thanatos looked menacingly at Azazel.

"Don't go running off. If we have to find you again, I'm not deferring to Leech next time. I'll kill you quickly and be done with it."

Azazel laughed.

"First of all, better nephilim than you have tried to kill me already and I'm still here. I keep their souls in a box in my workshop. Second, why would I run? This only plays out one of two ways. Either Leech comes out of his trance and I get a one-on-one fight or he comes out of his trance and turns on you. I'm fine with either outcome. They both sound entertaining."

Thanatos drove his axe into the ground and leaned on it.

"He's right. Both sound entertaining. The problem is the waiting. That sounds boring as hell."

Leech could feel himself being pulled into his subconscious and found that the imprisoned nephilim had gotten out of the pit somehow. They were working on breaking through the chains that bound them.

"Alright, guys. We need to come to some kind of agreement. Clearly keeping you all in a pit isn't working."

The nephilim continued to struggle, but one of them spoke.

"I am Sol, the nephilim of the sun. I could erupt in flames right now and free myself from these chains, but that would kill off the rest of my brothers and sisters. If you want to talk, show some goodwill. Free us. You have my word that we can discuss this without any of us attacking you."

Leech nodded. He took his axe and hacked at the chains until they broke. Some of the nephilim looked like they wanted to attack, but Sol shook his head at them.

"We keep our word. You all agreed that I would speak for all of us."

"And what if we no longer agree to that?"

"Then I'll help Leech kill you. This is his mind and we're never going to eliminate him entirely so we need to make some kind of deal."

The nephilim that had spoken backed away and Sol summoned a fiery chair to sit on. He gestured towards a rock. Leech grinned.

"So you get a fire chair and I'm supposed to sit on a rock?"

"You threw us in a pit."

"Fair point. Are you guys open to helping me kill Azazel?"

Sol stroked his chin and carefully chose his words before responding.

"Why would we do that? You're a demon. You fight for the demons. We're nephilim. We served Azazel and Abaddon in order to further the cause of nephilim."

"You've been misinformed. I don't fight for demons and I'm never going back to Hell. My best friend is a nephilim. The mother of my child is a nephilim. My daughter is a nephilim. With all of you assholes floating around in my head, I may as well be a nephilim, too… and in case you hadn't noticed, I came here with nephilim. Azazel doesn't fight for nephilim. He fights for himself. You heard what he said about storing nephilim souls in a box in his workshop."

"I knew Shadow is a nephilim… but you're claiming Lilith is as well?"

"She's the daughter of Samael and Vixen. Hypnos and Thanatos are her half-brothers."

"I'm still not sure if I believe you. Let's concede the point for now. If we help you kill Azazel, how does that benefit us?"

"I'm not sure that anything can *really* benefit all of you directly anymore. You're all kind of… non-existent. If I die, all of you are gone. You only exist as long as I do."

"Then why should we grant you all of our powers?"

"Because we can actually build something here on Earth. The demons have Hell. The angels have Heaven. Why not make Earth the realm of the nephilim? We can recruit, build up an army, and all of you would play a part in helping me lead it. I don't think you can hope for much more at this point."

"And we can roam freely in your mind, unchained? Not discarded in a pit like garbage? You'll listen to us when we need to speak to you?"

"Yes. We're bound as long as I wear the legion ring. We'll do what's best for the advancement of nephilim. I'm clearly invested in this. I want to see my daughter succeed."

Some of the nephilim looked skeptical, but Sol extended his hand.

"Alright then, Leech. We'll give this a shot. Don't think you can go back on this deal, though. You gave us your word."

Leech shook Sol's hand and immediately felt himself reentering his body on Earth. He retrieved his axe and guns before turning on Azazel. Lilith, Thanatos, and Steam watched with apprehension.

"The nephilim seem to like me better than you now. Ready to finish this?"

Azazel teleported in front of Leech and struck quickly with his sword. Leech could feel the blade touch his skin, but it didn't hurt. He looked at his arms and could see that they had turned into a hard, rock-like substance.

"Cool. Apparently one of the nephilim in my head can turn into a rock. My turn?"

Leech could feel his hand erupting in flames and he grabbed the arm that held Azazel's sword. Azazel dropped the sword and backed away. Before Leech could close the distance between them, Azazel teleported. Leech turned to look for him and saw him holding a knife to Lilith's throat. Leech drew his axe.

"Well that's an interesting turn of events that I wasn't expecting. I'd like to leave now and I think I'll take your pretty friend and daughter with me."

Thanatos grabbed Azazel's knife hand and twisted it back. There was a sickening crunch before Azazel dropped his knife. He fell to his knees and Thanatos motioned for everyone to get back. Leech charged and quickly drew a circle around Azazel. Within seconds, Azazel was enveloped in a green circle. Leech grinned.

"That's it for you. There's no clever way out of this."

Azazel laughed. He teleported outside the green circle and drew another sword from his belt.

"You're an idiot, Leech."

Leech grinned back at Azazel and nodded at his hand. Azazel's hand had converted into green energy and was slowly making its way towards Leech.

"No… there's no way you're…"

"That powerful? I'm a fucking legion of nephilim with demon powers. What the fuck did you think was going to happen when you teleported outside that circle? We'll finish this battle in my mind… a place where you can't teleport."

Azazel could slowly see his arm disappearing and converting into green energy that sailed through the air towards Leech's outstretched hand. Leech laughed.

"I'll meet you in my subconscious. There are some nephilim in there that want to see you again."

CHAPTER 55

Gangrene saw a small group of berserkers approaching. He grinned as he saw their leader, a small demon carrying a berserker staff. Some of the Dragon's demons looked ready to intervene, but Gangrene waved them off.

"Gangrene, we need to talk. In private."

Gangrene nodded and led the way to his tent.

"Not sure how you ended up in charge of a bunch of berserkers. I'm guessing a lot has changed since we last ran into each other."

"A lot of crazy shit has happened. Lilith and Shadow were able to bring Leech back."

Gangrene's eyes went wide.

"Shit. Are they coming back down to Hell? Are they…"

Muan raised both hands.

"It's ok. They're not interested in being major demons. They're crazy powerful and we just can't be around them anymore. It's time for both of us to move on. Shadow let me go. I was second in command to the idiot who just attacked the Dragon. Now I'm in charge of the berserkers. I want to come back to Hell. I don't want to be up here with nephilim anymore."

"And how do you think you're going to pull that off? The Dragon banished the berserkers to Earth."

"I have *some* leverage. I still have the necklace of Iktomi that Queen Persephone gave me. I have a berserker staff. I command the only legion of berserkers that actually knows the culture. The ones in Nightmare's army have no idea how to tap into the power properly. I just want an audience with him."

"He'll kill you, Muan. Probably eat you. You're small enough."

"Please, Gangrene. Just let me talk to him."

"That's stupid. That's putting me at risk. That's putting Raven at risk. He'll kill all of us. He doesn't want the berserkers back. Turn around and run away."

"If I can't convince him, I'll give you the berserker staff and we'll run. You get to present him with one of his lost relics. That should keep him from killing you."

Gangrene thought the offer over.

"Fine. Keep in mind right before you die that I tried to talk you out of this."

Muan grinned.

"Thanks. We'll wait outside the Dragon's camp until you come to get me."

Gangrene was able to convince the Dragon to hear Muan out. He brought Muan to the Dragon and threw him down on his knees.

"Speak, little demon. Gangrene said you have something to say that's worth my time."

"I want to become a major demon and lead the berserkers."

The Dragon looked angry. He changed form into Lucifer, drew his sword, and started advancing towards Muan.

"How is that any different than what the last berserker said?"

"I brought an offering with me to show the proper respect."

The Dragon stopped and grinned.

"What did you bring, little guy?"

"Great Dragon, I know that you banished this berserker order because they allowed Nightmare to take the berserker staff from your collection. We're in the process of making a new one and it's already incredibly powerful. I can continue to wield it myself and channel my own rage into it, or I can offer it to you now, as is."

"That's it? You started making a new berserker staff?"

"I also bring a gift from your wife, Persephone. One of her treasured artifacts that she entrusted to me."

Lucifer looked interested and sheathed his sword.

"Let's see it."

Muan pulled the necklace of Iktomi from his neck and handed it to Lucifer. He felt a little bad as he remembered the promise he made to Persephone when she gave him the necklace. He had mastered the power of transformation but was breaking his word and giving it to Lucifer instead of giving it back to Persephone. Muan dismissed his conscience. This was the only way to get what he wanted. Besides, he wasn't likely to ever see Persephone again. Lucifer looked the necklace over and then put it in his pocket.

"I accept your offering. I want the berserker staff right now, too. You will be the lowest of the Six and your order is not fully restored in my eyes, but I will allow you all to return to Hell under the leadership of the little guy."

Muan handed over the berserker staff. Lucifer turned back into the Dragon and pulled out one of his toenails. He turned back into Lucifer and called for a metal staff. He attached his toenail to the staff with heat from his hand and then handed the scythe over to Muan. Muan went to take it, but Lucifer didn't let go.

"If your order crosses me or fails me… ever again… I will wipe the memory of berserkers from Hell, Earth, and Heaven. Do you understand me?"

Muan nodded. Lucifer held the staff for another few seconds and then let go. He turned and started walking away.

"Back to Hell, everyone. I'm sick of being up here."

CHAPTER 56

Shadow checked the map one more time as he trudged through the snow at the top of the Earth. He was close and he could feel the Earth rumbling more and more with every passing second. Muan had found the spot where Abaddon had been sucking the life out of the Earth for the past several months and marked it on the map. Shadow planned to destroy his father before the others had time to complete their tasks and teleport to him. There was just one problem.

"I know you've been following me. Why don't you come out and give me the berserker staff? That would really make my job a lot easier."

Shadow's remarks were met with silence other than the continuous howling of the wind.

"Sarah... come on. I know it's sad, but I have to do this."

Shadow heard a voice, but he couldn't see where it was coming from.

"Why? Why do you have to kill him?"

"Because if I don't, he'll destroy the Earth for everyone. No more angels. No more demons. No more nephilim. Everyone else is either too stupid or too weak to deal with this... so I'm going to deal with it. If I live, I'm going to the Heavens to cut off Michael's head too. This is pretty much all his fault. He had so many chances to fix this, but he's too busy sitting on a gold fucking throne up there."

"I'm pregnant."

Shadow grinned and dismissively shook his head.

"You're not. You're saying that to try to convince me not to do this. It's not going to work. Please hand over the berserker staff. Please..."

"I'm not lying. I'm sure now that I'm pregnant. Why can't you just come stay with me? Don't abandon your son like your..."

"No. Don't even finish that thought. You're not pregnant. In fact... I'm starting to wonder..."

Shadow scanned his environment again and saw no one.

"...if you're even here. Fuck. I'm already starting to lose it."

Shadow realized that the noises that led him to believe that he was being followed could have easily been conjured by his own mind. Either that or Abaddon was playing mind games with him.

Shadow made his way to the top of a snowy embankment and saw his father as he looked down. Abaddon stood in a large area of scorched land and had two claws sunk into the Earth. He was pulling some kind of life force from the Earth itself. Shadow was intimidated at first. His father was as large and as powerful looking as Michael and the Dragon. The last time he had fought the Dragon, he was Legion with five other major demons with him. That wasn't an option now. Shadow exhaled loudly, pulled his angelic short blade from his belt, and shot a wave of blinding light into the area. Abaddon looked up, then removed his claws from the Earth and stood.

"Who the hell are you and why do you have my sword?"

"An interesting question. I used to think that you gave it to me. It turns out that was a bullshit memory my uncle gave me. You see, he felt guilty about betraying you and trained me to be a weapon. I was supposed to free you. I provided the distraction that gave you the opportunity to run. This sword…"

Shadow pointed his short blade at Abaddon.

"…was actually given to me by my grandmother, Persephone. It belonged to Michael before it was given to you."

"Why would Persephone give you my sword?"

"Because I'm your son."

Abaddon laughed.

"So I impregnated one of the demoness whores? Which one?"

"My mother's name is none of your business. I'm here to give you two options, Abaddon. Either you can stop sucking the soul out of the Earth and killing the inhabitants or I'll kill you."

Abaddon looked amused.

"If Cain wanted me put down, he should have come himself… or maybe Baal sent you. It doesn't really matter. I can sense power in you, but it's not enough. Throw down my sword, turn around, and walk away. This is your one chance to turn back, *son*."

Abaddon said the last word in a mocking tone. Shadow took Damnation in his right hand and Michael's short blade in his left.

"Cain and Baal are dead. You don't have a reason to…"

"A reason? I'm fucking insane. I've been tortured for longer than you've been alive. That's the only reason I need to do *anything* I want to. The moment has passed. It's time for you to die."

Shadow charged, knowing that there was a good chance that he wouldn't survive this fight.

CHAPTER 57

When Leech and Azazel entered Leech's mind, the nephilim immediately bound them both in chains and hit them hard until they were both on their knees. Leech looked to Sol and Sol started pacing.

"Recent developments have made us question which of you we should believe. Either one of you is powerful enough to take over this body. We just need to decide who that will be."

Leech tried to shake himself free.

"You promised me that…"

"Unfair bargaining position. We made that agreement under duress. What choice did we have? We're trapped in *your* head."

Azazel stood and was knocked back down.

"Leech killed all of you. Why is it even a question? Let me take over and dispose of the demon that murdered you."

"You see… we can't really trust you either, Azazel. You apparently killed dozens of nephilim and kept their souls in your workshop. We heard you admit as much to Leech. You're a kin-slayer just as much as Leech is a murderer."

Leech stopped struggling.

"So what do you want to do about this? I'll fight him again if that's what you want. I'd be happy to kill him."

Sol shook his head.

"No. We've already watched the two of you fight. We're not really interested in the outcome. We've heard your arguments regarding why we should side with you, Leech. Now it's time to hear from Azazel."

The nephilim turned to look at Azazel.

"It really comes down to whether you believe in Shadow or Abaddon. If Abaddon prevails, I should be your choice. If you think Shadow's strong enough to kill him, side with Leech. I think the victor of that fight should be easy to figure out."

"Any rebuttal, Leech? Keep it brief."

"Two points. First, if Abaddon wins, we will all fucking starve. He's killing off humans which means he's killing off our food source. Second, if Azazel is given control and Abaddon wins, he might just kill us anyways. He won't recognize Azazel in *my* body."

Several nephilim nodded as if what Leech was saying made sense. Sol turned to the nephilim.

"Let's make this quick. Majority rules. Who votes for Azazel?"

A number of nephilim hands went up. Leech guessed it was about half. Sol counted the votes and nodded.

"Alright and everyone for Leech."

The rest of the nephilim raised their hands, including Sol. Sol counted and grinned.

"Leech wins by three votes. Free Leech and throw Azazel in the pit."

The nephilim approached Azazel, but he melted through the chains and prepared to attack.

"You won't be throwing me in a pit. I'll take what I want by force. I don't take orders from weak nephilim that were killed by a demon runt. I…"

The nephilim all attacked Azazel at once, including those who had just voted for him. They punched and kicked him until he lost consciousness, rewrapped him in chains, and threw him in the pit. One of the larger nephilim found a large boulder and rolled it over the pit. Leech shook hands with Sol.

"Thanks. I did a quick count. I don't think I won by three. In fact…"

Sol grinned and spoke through his teeth.

"Shut up. Just go with it."

Leech left his mind and returned to his body.

"Azazel is dead."

Lilith handed Lucia back over to Thanatos and ran to Leech. She kissed him deeply. Steam started to speak, but Leech raised a finger signaling for him to wait. As he started to make out with Lilith, Steam started to wonder if he was going to get the chance to speak. Leech and Lilith finally pulled apart and Leech grinned as he caught his breath.

"So you're sure he's dead? He's not hanging around somewhere?"

"No. He's dead. He was technically dead shortly after he teleported out of that circle. In my mind, the nephilim beat him, chained him up, and threw him in a pit. Then they covered the pit with a boulder. I can't hear him in my subconscious and I don't think I have access to his powers. That's about as dead as he's ever going to be. Hopefully that spell you cast agrees and we teleport to Shadow."

Thanatos looked at Lucia.

"We're going to teleport now. Doesn't that sound like fun?"

Lucia clapped and nodded at her uncle.

CHAPTER 58

Shadow had landed some decent strikes with Damnation and his angel's blade, but Abaddon was inside his head. He started to anticipate Shadow's moves and didn't seem to be in any pain from the blows Shadow had landed. Shadow cloned himself dozens of times. Abaddon ignored the copies and continued to come at Shadow. Shadow summoned ice and shot it at his father. Abaddon was able to counter with the exact same move and the ice shattered between the two. Shadow tried to get in Abaddon's head and read his thoughts or make him hallucinate and he was swiftly rejected. Abaddon also seemed to have a lock on Shadow's teleportation. Shadow found that he could only move short distances and not beyond the snowy crater. His teleports covered less and less distance as his energy started to fade.

Shadow covered the snowy crater in mist, hoping that it would impair Abaddon's vision. He could see into the mist and knew that Abaddon was frantically searching for him. It was time. He couldn't delay what he had to do any longer. Shadow pulled out the small bag of berserker drugs and snorted its entire contents. He could feel the adrenaline and rage kicking in. It only took seconds before he transformed into a rage monster and rushed Abaddon.

Shadow summoned ice around both of his fists and swung relentlessly at Abaddon's face. He didn't stop to check his work. He just kept pounding. He couldn't hear the crunching of bones or the mushing of flesh. He saw everything tinted by a red glaze, until something struck him hard in the face. Shadow flipped over backwards and landed on his stomach. He was no longer a rage monster and could feel pain echoing through his head. There was a ringing in his ears. Abaddon's laugh drowned it out briefly.

Shadow looked up and saw that Abaddon's face was a twisted mess of bone fragments and hanging skin. Blood dripped from dozens of deep wounds. A green glow pulsed around his face and Shadow finally realized what was happening. Abaddon was healing.

"You didn't really think you could turn berserker and kill me, did you? I've been raping the Earth of its power for months while you slowly made your way up here. I sent the Dragon running back to Hell with a major injury. Who the hell do you think you are?"

Shadow could feel blood running out of both of his nostrils and curving its way down a cut on his forehead. He wiped it away before it reached his eyes. He propped himself back up with Damnation and stood defiantly.

"Who the hell do I think *I* am? Who the fuck are *you*? Everyone has sucky lives. Everyone has been wronged. Nothing is fair. Yes… you've been fucked worse than others… but that doesn't give you the right to come up here and kill everyone. Take it out on the Dragon. Go kill him. That's fine. I'll allow that… but I won't let you suck the Earth dry and end humanity and the race of nephilim. My name is Shadow and I am a god. I've nearly killed you once and I'll do it again. I'll keep doing it until you go down."

Abaddon closed the distance between them in seconds. He grabbed Shadow's arm and twisted it back until it was on the verge of breaking. Shadow dropped Damnation, but brought his short blade up hard and shoved it through Abaddon's shoulder. Abaddon cried out in pain and Shadow used the opportunity to break free from his grasp and teleport a short distance away.

Shadow tried to summon the rage he needed to turn into a rage monster again, but couldn't find it. His berserker drugs were gone. Damnation lay on the ground in front of Abaddon and the crazy nephilim had pulled Michael's short blade from his shoulder and was now wielding it. The wound was already starting to heal. Despite Shadow's speech, he knew he was outmatched. He summoned ice in one hand, fire in the other, and prepared to die. As he attacked with both the fire and the ice, Abaddon broke through both. He jumped into the air and Shadow knew he would bring the blade down right into his skull. Shadow closed his eyes and waited.

Seconds passed and Shadow heard Abaddon cry out in pain. Shadow opened his eyes and saw Thanatos standing in front of him, wielding Damnation. He helped Shadow to his feet and then ran off to attack Abaddon. Shadow fell again, but was caught by Leech before he hit the ground.

"How dare you start this party without us, Shady. Of all the stupid shit you've pulled, this takes the cake. Hypnos and Weapon aren't here, but the rest of us are. How do we kill him?"

"He's drained the Earth of power for months. We can't kill him."

Lilith walked up to Shadow and slapped him hard across the face. Leech looked shocked and was about to shove her back.

"No. We don't need the 'I'm beaten and tired' Shadow. We need the 'Do what I say and we can kill this guy' Shadow. You've always led us to victory. Wake the fuck up, Shadow. We're here. We're powerful. Tell us what to do."

Lilith was right. Giving up wasn't noble. It was the easy way out. Shadow got to his feet and shoved Leech away.

"Thanatos, toss me Damnation and start attacking with your axe."

Thanatos tossed Shadow's weapon back to him and started attacking with his axe. Steam looked at Shadow for directions.

"I need him distracted. Left side. You're going to conjure water and steam and shoot it at his eyes. Just the eyes. Don't aim it anywhere else because we're launching a fire attack from another angle. Understood?"

Steam nodded and ran off to do as Shadow instructed.

"Lilith, Lucia's going to play a role in this too. I know the two of you have been learning how to attack with fire. I don't know how you're going to get it through to your toddler, but both of you need to keep a steady stream of fire headed at his right arm. I don't want him capable of swinging at us. Get that short blade away from him. Make him drop it. Clear?"

Lilith nodded and ran off with Lucia. She spoke softly to the little demonness and then the two of them attacked Abaddon's arm with fire. Shadow turned to Leech.

"Get in close enough to drain touch him and then suck as much energy as you can. Don't let him kill you. He's going to think you're the killing blow, but you're just a distraction like everyone else. I need you to put your ego aside. Are you strong enough to do this?"

Leech's eyes started to glow green.

"We can do this, Shadow. Just promise you'll end it quickly."

Shadow nodded and Leech ran off to play his role. He took a couple of shots with his guns and then was able to dodge in without getting hit by Abaddon's random swinging fists. He grabbed the nephilim's shin and started siphoning off as much energy as he could. Abaddon cried out.

"It's not enough, Shadow. Your friends are all going to die."

Shadow leapt into the air and watched as Abaddon gathered up all of his friends in his monstrous fists. He started to crush them. Shadow took careful aim as he fell back to the Earth and came down with all of his power at Abaddon's head. He struck with Damnation over and over until he severed the nephilim's head from his body. Abaddon's lifeless form writhed on the ground until it finally stopped moving. His hands relaxed and everyone was able to break free. Lilith, Leech, and Steam looked hopefully optimistic, but Thanatos pointed above Abaddon's remains.

"It wasn't enough. His soul lives on and he's going to finish what he started."

Shadow saw a ghostly form of Abaddon slowly making his way back towards the center of the crater. He was about to start draining the Earth again. Shadow knew what he needed to do.

"Don't ever tell anyone that I'm a hero. I'm not. Humanity can go fuck itself for all I care. What I'm about to do is for Leech. It's for Lilith. It's for Sarah… and it's for…"

Shadow turned to Leech and handed over Damnation.

"Find Sarah. She's pregnant. I can't let my kid grow up without a father. Do me a favor? Be his dad for me. Will you do that, Leech?"

Leech let a tear roll down his face from each eye, but he wiped them away and nodded. Lilith started sobbing uncontrollably. She set Lucia on the ground and ran at Shadow.

"No! No!"

She clung to Shadow and wouldn't let him move. Leech had to pull her back kicking and screaming. Shadow turned to Thanatos and Steam and put a hand on their shoulders.

"Be proud to be nephilim. You did a great thing here today. Protect my friends when I'm gone."

They both nodded. Lilith continued to flail uncontrollably. Shadow signaled for Leech to let her go. She ran at him and he caught her by both shoulders and pressed her arms to her side so she wouldn't latch on to him again.

"It has to be this way, Lilith. Please just give me a proper goodbye."

Lilith calmed herself down and nodded. She hugged Shadow and kissed him on the cheek.

"Thank you, Shadow, for always watching out for me. I will never forget you. Never."

Shadow smiled at her and started making his way towards Abaddon's soul. He turned back one last time.

"Leech, I always wanted a brother. Thank you for being one to me."

Shadow took Michael's short blade in his right hand and cut open his own chest. His eyes glowed white before he stepped into Abaddon's soul and took it into his body. He cried out in agony and then teleported away.

AFTERWORD

Leech, Lilith, Thanatos, and Steam were able to meet up with Hypnos and Weapon within a few days of the death of Abaddon. Hypnos told them what happened to Samael. Leech was planning on recruiting and training an army of nephilim, but he told Hypnos and Thanatos they should go after Uriel and take revenge. Leech was surprised when Lilith didn't ask to go with them. She cried for several days when she found out about her father's death, but knew that it was more important to focus on being a mother to Lucia. She had no doubt her brothers would take care of Uriel. Steam and Weapon joined Leech, Lilith, and Lucia as they tracked down Sarah. They found her a year later.

Sarah listened without any emotion as Leech told her how Shadow had ultimately taken down Abaddon. He told her the whole story, including the promise he made to Shadow to look after his child. Sarah handed a small sleeping nephilim over to Leech.

"His name is Shade. He's Shadow's son. Raise him until I return with Shadow."

"Sarah… he's either dead or he's gone insane. Please don't…"

Sarah pointed the berserker staff at Leech.

"I still have hope. You said you'd take care of him. Keep your promise until I return. I'm going to find Shade's father and then we'll be a family."

Leech shook his head.

"You're making a mistake, Sarah. Don't…"

Sarah turned and ran away.

When the Dragon returned to Hell, Nightmare went insane from overexposure to the berserker powers in his scythe. When the Dragon sent part of his army to take Nightmare in, Nightmare drew Rage and no one was brave enough to attack him. He turned and fled. The demons did not pursue. They spread a lie that Nightmare was dead. The Dragon knew they were lying, since none of them brought Nightmare's scythe back, but he let the lie spread because it restored order.

The berserkers in Nightmare's army joined Muan's forces and were trained by actual berserkers. With order restored, demons began to make their way back to the now recovering humans on Earth. The

Dragon kept a much closer watch over the five new major demons and would no longer confine himself to the lowest circle of Hell.

Leech and Lilith took in Shade and raised him as their son. They also spent a considerable amount of time finding and recruiting nephilim. Leech had a permanent nephilim camp built on Earth and it became strong enough that angels and demons went out of their way not to pass by it. They kept an eye out for Shadow and there were occasional rumors that he had been spotted, but nothing was ever confirmed.

Thanks for reading Major Demons, the third book in my Angels and Demons series. Please consider leaving a review if you enjoyed it.

Team Demons shirts are now live on Amazon if you'd like to support the series. They come in several different colors and three epic designs. These are American Apparel shirts, so order a size or two larger than you normally would because they fit tight. Here are the links if you'd like to check them out:

http://bit.ly/SideWithShadow
http://bit.ly/TeamDemonsB
http://bit.ly/TeamDemonsW

MAILING LIST

My mailing list keeps you up to date on my fiction and non-fiction with new releases, exclusive offers, and free promos / giveaways. You can join my mailing list here: http://bit.ly/RJMMail

ABOUT THE AUTHOR

Randall Morris has a bachelor's degree in history from BYU and is currently pursuing a law degree at the University of Utah. He enjoys writing history articles, travel / photo books, and action / adventure fiction. He spent two years in the Philippines as a missionary and speaks fluent Tagalog. He has worked in the IT field for over seven years. His works are currently available as ebooks, paperbacks, and audio books. Morris has been a self-published author since early 2012.

Feel free to contact me:

Facebook: http://www.facebook.com/RandyMorrisAuthor

Twitter: @RandallJMorris

Blog: http://randyjmorris.blogspot.com/

Email: randallmorrisauthor@gmail.com

For more news on books from this author, updates, and free promos / giveaways subscribe to Randall Morris Author News here:

http://bit.ly/RJMMail

Adventure Fiction from Randall Morris

The Journals of Jacob and Hyde (Jehovah and Hades: Book 1)

U.S. http://amzn.to/13eos1j

U.K. http://amzn.to/19IMjZu

Jehovah and Hades (Jehovah and Hades: Book 2)

U.S. http://amzn.to/VyOAiV

U.K. http://amzn.to/H45Me9

Jehovah and Hades: Federal Case (Jehovah and Hades: Book 3)

U.S. http://amzn.to/URVxx2

U.K. http://amzn.to/1apnrES

Jehovah and Hades: Books 1-3

U.S. http://amzn.to/THcXwl

U.K. http://amzn.to/19IMRi5

Minor Demons (Angels and Demons: Book 1)

U.S. http://amzn.to/1cyKjCV

U.K. http://amzn.to/1dSttRO

Middle Demons (Angels and Demons: Book 2)

U.S. http://amzn.to/1AYgifW

U.K. http://amzn.to/1DJBRAj

Major Demons (Angels and Demons: Book 3)

U.S. http://bit.ly/MajorDemons

U.K. http://bit.ly/MajorDemonsUK

8440958R00130

Printed in Germany
by Amazon Distribution
GmbH, Leipzig